PETS ON PARADE

PETS ON PARADE

Malcolm D. Welshman

metro

Published by Metro Publishing Ltd,
3 Bramber Court, 2 Bramber Road,
London W14 9PB, England

www.johnblakepublishing.co.uk

www.facebook.com/Johnblakepub facebook
twitter.com/johnblakepub twitter

First published in paperback in 2012

ISBN: 978-1-84358-947-1

British Library Cataloguing-in-Publication Data:

A catalogue record for this book is available from the British Library.

Design by www.envydesign.co.uk

Printed and bound by CPI Group (UK) Ltd, Croydon, CR0 4YY

1 3 5 7 9 10 8 6 4 2

Papers used by Metro Publishing are natural, recyclable products made
from wood grown in sustainable forests. The manufacturing processes
conform to the environmental regulations of the country of origin.

Every attempt has been made to contact the relevant
copyright-holders, but some were unobtainable. We would be
grateful if the appropriate people could contact us.

PRAISE FOR *PETS IN A PICKLE*

'The author paints a vivid picture of many fascinating characters – human and animal – resulting in a most enjoyable and amusing read...The text gives the reader a most enjoyable insight into the unpredictable but fascinating life of the veterinary surgeon.'

Jim Wight, son of James Herriot

'It's fun and should bring a smile to your face.'

Sir Terry Wogan

'Your story is a corker.'

Richard Madeley

'I loved this book although I'll never be able to look at my vet in the same way again.'

Denise Robertson, Agony Aunt, ITV's This Morning

'It's a lighthearted "if you like animals, you'll like this, especially the two-footed variety" pageturner.'

Anna Raeburn, LBC Radio's 'Book of the Week'.

'There are a host of colourful characters behaving badly in this warm, funny novel.'

Woman's Weekly

'This book is laugh a minute material...I have not laughed so much reading a book for a very long time.'

Green (Living) Review

'Not surprisingly, this book has topped the Amazon bestsellers list and looks set to become an animal lovers' classic.'

Dogs in the News

'This book is sure to be enjoyed by all animal lovers and those who enjoy human comedy.'

CONTENTS

1
FINDING A HAPPY MEDIUM

When Madam Mountjoy walked into my consulting room that January morning with a black cat sitting benignly on her shoulder, and stated he was the reincarnation of an Inca emperor, I knew it was going to be one of those days.

Mind you, the morning had already got off to an uncertain start – and that was entirely my fault. It stemmed from the fact that I'd sent a Christmas email to our receptionist, not dreaming she was then going to brood about it all over the festive period, and still allow it to rankle now that we were into the New Year. Dear, oh dear. Where was your sense of humour, Beryl?

It had been an Internet card of a jolly Father Christmas standing on a red-tiled roof next to a chimney, going 'Ho, ho, ho'. Very seasonal, I thought. Very Christmassy. You clicked on the sack he was carrying over his shoulder and he suddenly became animated – he actually sprang over to the chimney pot. I expected him to pop down it. Wrong. He started to urinate down it instead. It tickled my juvenile sense of humour but it didn't tickle our receptionist's at Prospect House when I emailed it to her. I must admit I'd had an anxious moment when I clicked the 'Send' button, thinking perhaps Beryl might not see the funny side of it. Too right. She didn't.

It was apparent the moment I bounded into reception, full of good cheer, a smile on my face, ready to greet her with a chirpy 'Good morning'. That didn't cut any ice with her. Oh, no. Her frosty expression and the Arctic glare from her good eye – the other, as usual, just gave out its customary artificial glint of glass – were enough to freeze my bonhomie as if I'd just plunged through a walrus's blowhole.

My 'Good morning, Beryl … how are things?' instantly froze on my lips as I swiftly saw that 'things' were definitely not good.

Beryl pulled at the sleeve of the black cardigan draped, shawl-like, over her shoulders. It was an exaggerated gesture which spoke of a thousand grievances. But one was sufficient. 'Why don't you grow up, Paul? That email of yours wasn't funny.'

Uh oh. Seems my peeing Santa had a lot to answer for.

Beryl had turned back to the computer and was tapping away at the keyboard, her long, red nails flying across the keys. 'Which reminds me,' she went on, her face remaining impassive as she spoke, 'Mr Digby wants some more tablets. His Labrador's bladder is playing up again.'

I was tempted to say, 'Good job it wasn't his reindeer's …' but thought better of it. After all, I wasn't that much of a wit and, to judge from Beryl's icy look, she already considered me half of one.

Having re-established a fragile line of communication with Beryl by way of Mr Digby's bladder problems – an appointment to be made before further medication was prescribed – I breezed on down the corridor to do my usual ward round before starting morning consultations.

I met Mandy, our senior nurse, clip-clopping in her highly polished, black brogues up the corridor. As ever, I felt like jumping to one side and giving her a salute. She'd evoked that reaction in me ever since my initial run-in with her over the anaesthetic machine last June – when I was being interviewed for the post of assistant vet. A memory which actually still causes me to giggle ('Oh, do grow up, Paul,' my girlfriend would say), although, at the time, my squeaky giggling had been induced by the escape of nitrous oxide. As Mandy drew level, I tentatively raised my hand in a gesture of greeting while she sailed by accompanied by the crackle of her crisply starched uniform. A galleon at full stretch. Her prow plunging forward ... well, at least her ample bosom was. Her head barely turned as my 'Good morning' was acknowledged with a brisk nod and a curt 'Morning, Paul,' before her keel turned to starboard and she disappeared into the dispensary. Blimey. What had got into her bulwarks? So much for New Year festive feelings. Here, in Prospect House, they seemed to be festering fast.

Mind you, things hadn't been exactly a bed of roses back at Willow Wren first thing. My girlfriend, Lucy, the junior nurse at the practice, had had to get up ahead of me for the early shift and had been distinctly thorny.

'Don't know why you're so cheerful,' she muttered in response to my 'Morning, sweetheart,' as she pulled on her uniform, lights blazing, while I ducked back under the duvet and then listened to her downstairs crashing about getting herself some breakfast. Who's been peeing on your patch? I wondered. Not that Father Christmas again?

It was no better down in the ward.

'Hi,' I said as I walked along to where Lucy was scrubbing out a kennel. I was greeted with the suck of a squeegee mop, the slurp of it being shoved along the concrete floor, and a kick, accidental or otherwise, of the bucket of disinfectant. Right ... OK. There was something in the air – apart from the smell of dog dirt. Things that had to be said ... stuff to be sorted. But this was certainly not the right time or place, so I left Lucy to it.

There were only two in-patients to check. A pair of Golden Retrievers that, true to their name, had retrieved the carcass of a turkey while their owners had been out, and had then proceeded to demolish it jointly. The resulting haemorrhagic gastroenteritis had precipitated a frantic evacuation in every sense of the word. The owners had sought emergency help two nights back. The Retrievers had been hospitalised and, in the intervening period, their bowel functions had slowly returned to normal. Much to my relief. And to theirs, no doubt. Isn't it funny how the sight of perfectly formed crap can often provoke jubilation? Well, in me it can. Bit sad really. Anyway, the sight of theirs, waiting to be scooped up, did just that. The fact that Lucy would be doing the scooping up made it even more satisfactory. Now, now, Paul. Less of that.

I bent down and scratched the dogs' ears through the bars of the kennel door, telling them what a good job they'd done. They responded with a grizzle of pleasure and furious wags of their tails, no doubt eager to tell me it was none of my business. Just theirs.

'Well, at least someone's pleased to see me,' I said, loud enough for Lucy to hear. All I heard, in response, was a suck and a slurp. In a different situation, such as under a duvet, such sounds may have been far more welcome. But here, emanating from that dirty kennel, their erotic charge was a little dampened.

I walked back up to reception, determined not to buckle under the pervading gloom that seemed to have seeped into Prospect House that morning. Perhaps the sight of one of my bosses, Eric Sharpe, bouncing in would have helped to cheer everyone up. But that wasn't going to happen today. Wednesdays always saw Eric up on the golf course attempting to reduce his handicap. He was a small, balding vet who jounced around the hospital in a white coat far too big for him. But it covered a man of generous spirit who was always ready for a laugh and was usually able to lift everyone's mood. Beryl, though, her mind still flooded with the image of a urinating Santa, would have been a major challenge today.

'Don't think the heating can be working properly,' Beryl was saying. 'It's bloody freezing in here.' She was hunched forward on her swivel chair, pulling her cardigan up round her scrawny neck, looking very carrion crow-like.

Stone them, Beryl, I thought, she being the first crow I'd take a pot shot at. No, that was uncharitable. It seemed the mood in the place was beginning to affect me too. One thing I could be sure of – it wouldn't be affecting Eric's wife, Crystal, who was the other partner in the practice. She was out visiting one of her 'specials' as Beryl would put it – Lady Derwent, who always insisted that Dr Sharpe should be her Labradors' preferred vet.

'So,' I said, rubbing my hands together and mustering up as much enthusiasm as I could to face the glacier (Beryl). 'What have you got for me today?'

'The usual,' she muttered coldly, casting her good eye at me while the glass one did its customary robotic scan of the ceiling. It was a habit of hers that had unnerved me the minute I'd first set my own eyes on it last June.

'Right,' I said, rubbing my hands even more vigorously, before parting them to clench my fists.

Beryl continued to give me the eye – her good one – and, observing my hand movements, said, 'Told you it was cold in here, didn't I?'

I pictured my hands rapidly flying over the computer to settle round her neck, but restrained myself with a 'Let's get on with it then.'

Beryl was quite right about the 'usual'. There was a string of standard consultations: three booster injections in a row. Very routine stuff. Jab – jab – jab. Hang on a minute. I pulled myself up, reminding myself that it might be routine for me but certainly not for the dogs involved, as it wasn't every day they got hauled into the surgery to be confronted by Paul Mitchell (BVSc, MRCVS), qualified last year. Prospect House my first job. Been here just over six months. Still a relatively new boy but a wee bit jaded by all the routine stuff.

'Now, Dandy, there's a good lad,' I muttered as I raised the scruff of the Cairn on the consulting table and slipped the needle under the skin of his neck. He didn't so much as whimper or flinch. 'What a good boy,' I added, trying to sound encouraging, as I rubbed his scruff once the booster vaccination had been given.

'Now what can I do for Bertie?' I asked, as I tackled the next case, still attempting to muster some enthusiasm. Goodness, what on earth was happening to me? My spirits definitely seemed to be flagging.

'Bertie's anal glands are giving him gyp again,' said his owner, giving me a quizzical look. 'Needs them emptying.' Yippee. Just the fillip I needed!

6

I suppose I must have been about halfway through the morning's list when the atmosphere suddenly changed in quite a dramatic fashion.

It was the appearance of Madam Mountjoy that did it. I saw from the details on the computer screen in the consulting room that she was a new client and was bringing in a cat named Antac. Good start. Made a change from all the Flossies, Cuddles, Blackies and Sooties. Cripes, this cynicism had really set in.

So in wafted Madam Mountjoy with her Antac. I use the word 'wafted' deliberately as this woman seemed to float into the consulting room and hover in front of the consulting table as if inches off the ground. Not that she had anything particularly angelic about her, and there was certainly nothing fairy-like. True, she was swathed in layers of calico in the form of a white kaftan which could have lent her a sylph-like appearance had she not been so fat that no amount of loose clothing could have concealed the mountains of flesh heaving beneath it. She resembled a large wedding cake whose tiered layers had collapsed and folded in on one another. Her hair was silver-grey, and haloed her face in a wild tangle to stream down over her shoulders. That face had an element of the moon about it. Full, white and cratered with acne scars. From her ear lobes dangled silver broomsticks, a silver pentangle hung between her breasts, while her wrists tinkled with the myriad of silver bangles that enclosed them. If all that wasn't striking enough, she had the most disconcerting eyes. Huge, slanting eyes with troubling grey irises, surrounded by thick, black layers of mascara which could have out-kohled Cleopatra.

The look she gave me seemed to bore into me, as if wishing to strip me naked and expose my soul. Wow. This was suddenly intensely unnerving. Still, I had been moaning about how mundane the morning had been so far so I shouldn't have been complaining if it was about to change, should I?

With difficulty, I averted my eyes from hers and turned my attention to her cat.

'So this is Antac?' I enquired as an opening gambit.

Even her cat had an air of the unreal about him. Not for him transportation in a routine cat basket. Nor, indeed, was he attached to a collar and lead like some cats presented to me in surgery. No, Antac was on Madam Mountjoy's left shoulder, unrestrained, looking every bit an Egyptian pharaoh's deity. Gleaming black fur ... piercing yellow eyes ... sitting bolt upright, motionless.

'He's not Egyptian,' said Madam Mountjoy, as if she'd been reading my mind. Spooky. That's when I learnt he was a reincarnation of an Inca emperor. The statement was made without her batting an eyelid, a feat which would have been difficult to achieve anyway due to the heavy encrustations of mascara that gummed up her lids.

'Right ... yes ... well ... So, what's the problem with Antac?'

'He needs his toenails cutting.'

'Toenails?'

'OK. Claws then.' Madam Mountjoy shrugged and raised her eyebrows. 'They keep digging into my shoulder. It's upsetting my Akasha.'

'Akasha?'

'It's the world's energy source. It's how I fuel my magic.'

'No need for British Gas then,' I was tempted to say, but resisted, as I suspected this lady considered herself some sort of witch or mystic and the last thing I needed was for her to suddenly magic up a wand from beneath her kaftan and turn me into a frog. Not that I thought of myself as a prince, charming as I might appear to be. Instead, I gave her a wan smile and explained that it would be best if the toenail ... er ... claw trimming was done on the table.

'Did you hear that, Antac?' said Madam Mountjoy, swivelling her head rapidly round to face the cat. For an instant, I was reminded of that possessed girl in *The Exorcist* and wondered if Madam Mountjoy was about to throw up. Instead, she spewed out the words, 'You're being summoned onto the table.'

I had picked up the nail clippers and was casually waving them in front of her, in cool dude mode. My heart sank as I heard her address the cat in that way. 'Well, it would be easier all round,' I said, my voice a touch whiny.

'Antac quite understands, even though we're not speaking in his native tongue,' said Madam Mountjoy, sharply.

That unnerving feeling returned.

As she spoke, the cat sprang down onto the consulting table, sniffed the surface, his tail a ramrod, and then sat, his tail sweeping round to curl over his front paws.

'He commands that you now proceed,' said Madam Mountjoy.

'I might need to restrain him,' I warned, my voice still wavering a little.

Madam Mountjoy waved a dismissive hand. 'He's had to endure far greater ordeals in his past life, I can tell you.'

Not wishing her to embark on a tale of his heroics, I lifted Antac's front left paw, squeezed it gently to unsheathe the claws and clipped each one back a fraction. To my amazement, the cat sat there impassively, with scarcely a twitch of his whiskers, and continued to do so as I tackled the claws on his other paws.

Once I'd finished, Antac got to his feet, turned and leapt back onto Madam Mountjoy's shoulder, where he settled himself back into his former stance.

'Ah, that feels much better,' sighed Madam Mountjoy, rotating her shoulder, causing Antac to sway a bit although he managed to keep his balance. 'Yes. I can now tune in more clearly, with no interference.'

Long wave or medium wave? I wondered. Now, now, Paul, don't tempt fate.

Madam Mountjoy suddenly took a deep breath and crossed her bangled arms over her breasts. They shook ... the bangles, that is. She closed those kohl-lined eyes of hers, the lashes whipping together, and began to emit a sing-songy sort of hum rather like a kettle starting to whistle. Oh Lord, was she falling into a trance? That could spell trouble, especially as she hadn't paid for her consultation yet.

Then, in a falsetto whisper, she spoke. 'The aura in here is very unpleasant.' The silver broomsticks in her ears swivelled from side to side and her mouth dropped open, her tongue darting out to expose a silver stud embedded in its tip. 'Very unpleasant. Very off-putting,' she added, her tongue rattling back behind her teeth.

Hark who's talking, I thought, rattled myself by her peculiar turn. Mind you, I had to admit there was quite an atmosphere in the consulting room. Quite pongy, in fact. But I put that down to the nervous Alsatian who'd earlier defaecated on the spot where Madam Mountjoy was now standing.

She fanned her long black nails in front of her face and her eyelids snapped open again. 'It's very strong,' she added. 'You should let me cast a spell. Cleanse the place.'

I didn't know about casting spells or not. If anything, she

could have put in a spell of cleaning, but I couldn't see her knuckling down with her broomstick to give the place a clean sweep. Of course, I kept mum for fear of frog-induced repercussions.

It was at that point that Antac gave a loud miaow. I must admit, it made me jump a bit as he'd been so quiet up to then. Madam Mountjoy seemed unperturbed. She turned to him and bent her head down so that her ear was almost touching his nose. 'What's that, Antac?' she asked. There was another, more muted miaow.

Madam Mountjoy straightened up and stared at me with those laser-like grey eyes of hers. Very unnerving. 'Antac informs me that many feline spirits have departed from here. Posses of them are at this very moment circling above us. You need to be exorcised.'

Posses of pussies, eh? I bridled. What a nerve. OK, I might not be the most competent of vets and I admit the occasional cat had slipped beyond its ninth life through my fingers. But posses of them? Come on. I wasn't that bad. This old crone was out of her head.

Suddenly realising Madam Mountjoy was getting inside mine, I hastily terminated the consultation and accompanied her through to reception, where, having paid her bill, she tapped Antac knowingly on the head, looked at me and uttered in a sombre voice, 'You have been warned,' before swirling out of the front door, broomsticks whirling, bangles clanging.

'Crikey,' declared Beryl, giving her departing figure the eye – her good one – 'she's enough to put the wind up anyone's sails. Which reminds me, Mrs Jenkins wants some more of those charcoal granules for her Cleo's flatulence.'

I thought I'd seen the last of Madam Mountjoy, but if I'd had the ability to see into the future – as she apparently could – I would have realised that wasn't going to be the case.

It must have been about two weeks later, time enough for Beryl to have pushed the urinating Father Christmas to the back of her mind – at least I assumed she had, judging from her better mood – when she mentioned Madam Mountjoy. Beryl was standing in front of the electric heater in the office, the sleeves of her woolly, black cardigan hanging down her sides as usual – why she never put her arms in the sleeves, I'll never know – rubbing her hands together having just returned, 'freezing' as she put it, from her morning cigarette, smoked by the open back door leading to the exercise run in the garden. Although smoking in Prospect House was strictly taboo and enforced rigorously by both partners, Crystal and Eric, a concession to Beryl's addiction of the past 50 years had been made whereby she was allowed her daily quota of fags, to be smoked either out in the exercise yard or, if the weather was too inclement, on the back doorstep with the door open wide enough for her to exhale the smoke through the gap.

'Yes, I remember her,' I said at her mention of Madam Mountjoy's name. 'Seems I was under threat from the spirits of cats I'd bumped off. Or some such nonsense.'

'Well, she's been in touch,' whispered Beryl, bringing her hand up to cover the side of her mouth. Always the dramatist, is Beryl.

'Really?'

'Yes, really.'

I smirked.

'It's not funny, Paul,' she hissed, her glass eye fixed on me.

I swallowed hard. 'No, of course not.'

'She's contacted me from the other side.' Beryl gave an exaggerated wink of her good eye while the glass one swivelled wildly heavenwards.

'You mean ...' I faltered, pointing upwards. 'She's passed on?'

'No, no,' said Beryl, tutting, still with her hand cupped over her mouth. 'She's been in touch from the other side of town. Teville Gate.' Beryl must have seen my bewilderment, more induced by her glass eye swinging down to glare at my crotch rather than from learning that Madam Mountjoy lived over in Teville Gate, since she went on in an exasperated tone of voice. 'She's worried about Antac.' Beryl glanced over both her shoulders and then over mine before continuing. 'Apparently, he's been in the wars.'

'The Aztecs have got him, have they?'

'Shhh ... it's no joke. Madam Mountjoy thinks he's been possessed.'

I began to feel another smirk coming on.

'It's serious, Paul,' she reprimanded.

I bit my lower lip. 'Yes, of course, you're right,' I said, suppressing the bubble of laughter welling up in my throat. 'You'd better get her to come in.' I failed to stop the bubble of laughter from bursting out. 'And let me see what's got into him,' I spluttered. 'A Roman centurion? Or maybe a Benedictine monk?'

Beryl's false eye stopped rotating and lined itself up with her good one to show her disapproval of my frivolous mood (that juvenile sense of humour again). She fixed me with a cold stare that brought me up straight. 'I offered her an appointment but she turned it down. Apparently, that time she came in ... she got spooked.'

'Really?'

'So she says. That's why she insists you visit.'

'Over at Teville Gate?'

Beryl nodded. 'And it has to be you.' Her voice dropped an octave. 'Apparently, you are a kindred spirit with whom she can bond.' Beryl nodded sagely. 'So ...' She let her voice trail off. Ooo-er. Seemed I was in for a bit of hocus-pocus. Very tricky.

Madam Mountjoy's place of spiritual bondage over at Teville Gate turned out to be at the end of a terrace, a corner shop called 'The Olde Wiccan Shoppe'. It was a wet, dark, late January afternoon when I parked a few doors down from the shop and, turning the collar of my raincoat up, beat a rapid path to her shop door. Above it, there was a skull with glowing eyes and a skeletal finger beckoning me in. Creepy.

I half expected the shop to be full of witches on the spend, loading their wicker baskets with bags of frozen fingers and spare ribs, bundles of frogs' legs and jars of newt jelly. But the place was empty. Yet it still felt claustrophobic on account of the dim lighting, the overpowering smell of incense, and being stuffed from floor to ceiling with shelves – on one side loaded down with wands, dowsing crystals, lucky flying witches and miniature cast-iron cauldrons; on the other side, shelves groaned under the weight of books of all shapes and sizes, catalogued by subject matter. *The Idiot's Guide to Casting Spells* and *The Good Witch's Guide to Wicked Ways* were two titles that caught my eye. The latter book was on the counter, open at a chapter on potent ways to get your man, and looked very well thumbed. I began to feel distinctly uneasy; this was not helped when I spotted a small occasional table over in one corner, on which was a bowl containing what looked like locks of hair, alongside a burning candle, a mantra of love inscribed on an embroidered card and, behind these items, a gold photo frame containing ... I had to move closer and stoop down to make sure ... yes, it was ... a head-and-shoulders picture of me.

At that point, I thought it wise to beat a hasty retreat, but, as I turned to leave, a figure glided out from behind a rack of elves, pixies and plastic fauns at the back and moved rapidly across to block my exit.

'Ah, Mr Mitchell,' exclaimed Madam Mountjoy, in a low, seductive voice, 'I've been expecting you.'

To do what? I wondered, thinking of the love spell on the table.

'Do come through to the kitchen, please.' She curved a black-nailed forefinger at me and beckoned.

Oh dear, what was she brewing up? A heady love potion that she'd force me to swallow on pain of death? Something concocted to turn me into a horny demon?

'Would you like a cup of tea?' she asked.

'Er, no thanks.'

'Something stronger perhaps?'

'No. Not if you don't mind. I'm on duty.'

'Shame. Another time, maybe?' Madam Mountjoy threw her arm across her chest, her hand enfolding her right breast. 'I don't know what gets into me sometimes.'

Me neither, I thought. Although I could guess what she was after. But I wasn't going to stoke her fire. Demon or no demon.

'Never mind.'

'Sorry?' I said, startled.

She gave a wry smile, and the merest flicker of her kohled eyelashes. 'It's Antac you've come to see.'

'Well, yes, that's why I'm here.'

15

'Indeed. So do come through.'

I expected to enter a witch's den. Not necessarily a cauldron hanging over a pile of burning logs, but certainly something akin to the image of Madam Mountjoy I'd conjured up. But her kitchen was modern. There was a gas range – black, naturally – a microwave, and in one corner stood not a broomstick but a Dyson. There was a shelf on which was stacked a line of glass-stoppered jars. Spaghetti, rice and sugar, I recognised. I wasn't so sure about the jar containing the dried, shrivelled carcasses of frogs. Well, that's what the leathery, brown lumps looked like to me, but then my mind had gone into overdrive ever since spotting the love spell in the shop. The kitchen was filled with a sweet, rather sickly smell. More hocus-pocus in the making, I thought, glancing across at the range on which a black, covered pan was quietly bubbling, emitting the occasional hiss of steam. Probably a stew of newt, snails and puppy dogs' tails.

'Just a load of rhubarb,' said Madam Mountjoy, giving me a wistful look. I swear she was reading my mind.

Today, as on the previous occasion when I'd met her, Madam Mountjoy was wearing a voluminous white kaftan, cut low at the neck, the hem trailing across the kitchen floor as she swept to the middle, turned and faced me. She put her palms together as if to pray, an action that caused her silver bangles to cascade down her forearms. Her black-lined eyes snapped shut while the lashes continued to flicker, a movement that was echoed in the rest of her body. It was all of a twitch, as if there were internal weights being shunted and pulled about, and, although concealed by the kaftan, it gave rise to an uneasy feeling that the body beneath those layers was preparing itself to be fired into orbit. It just needed a deep thrust to

16

ignite it. Well, I certainly wasn't going to light her touchpaper. The mental image coincided with her opening her eyes abruptly and staring at me, her face full of disappointment.

'Just trying to summon up Antac,' she explained, a little peeved. She stretched her closed palms above her head and tried again. 'Antac … Antac … Where are you?' She arched her head back to gaze up at the ceiling. 'Antac, come down and show yourself.'

For a split second, I had a vision of the cat materialising from thin air, careering down from heaven, paws splayed, to land at Madam Mountjoy's feet. Clearly, it wasn't a vision shared by her, as with an exasperated click of her tongue stud against her teeth, she glided over to the fridge, pulled out a half-empty tin of tuna and, with a spoon from an adjacent drawer, rattled it inside the tin. That did the trick. Antac suddenly appeared in a flash. He padded round the edge of the units until he reached the fridge, where he turned, arched his back, tail up, and sprayed against the door, a steady stream of urine shooting up the side.

'Just look at that,' seethed Madam Mountjoy. 'It's so out of character. I reckon he's been cursed. Possessed by another person.'

A peeing Santa briefly flitted through my mind, and I silently rebuked myself for being juvenile. Yet again.

Madam Mountjoy went on to explain that they had been having a battle recently with a certain Sybil Clutterbuck. 'They' being the Order of the Golden Dawn, a coven of white witches over in Chawton. It seemed this Sybil had been the High Priestess up until last month when, due to the discovery that she'd been fiddling her expenses – a new broom paid for out of club funds – they had cast runes to

17

have her replaced. Only she had refused to step down. Apparently, club rules stated that casting runes for new priestesses could only be carried out on the fourth night following a new moon. In her case, the runes had been cast on the fifth night, so, according to Sybil, they were invalid. As Madam Mountjoy had been the one to forward the motion to have Sybil removed in the first place, it was she whom Sybil blamed.

'And this is the result,' said Madam Mountjoy, pointing at her cat.

I couldn't quite see the connection between an embittered witch and a spraying cat. In fact, to be honest, I couldn't see it at all. A fact that Madam Mountjoy saw all too well, as she went on: 'Antac's been acting strange ever since. I've tried all sorts of things. Lunar scheduling ... herbal remedies ... and I am just going through some ancient mantras from my dictionary of spells. It's all Sybil's fault. She's put a spell on him, you see.'

At last, I did see. Sort of. I certainly could see the dangers of becoming embroiled in some sort of witch warfare. Drawn broomsticks at dawn. Cudgels in the coven. It was all getting a bit nonsensical. Everyone getting in a flap. The word 'flap' coincided with me glancing round the kitchen and observing that the back door had a cat flap in it.

'Is that new, by any chance?' I asked.

'Well, actually, yes,' replied Madam Mountjoy, nodding – an action which caused the silver broomsticks in her earlobes to swing violently.

'And have you had any unwanted visitors?' I wasn't thinking spirit-wise – more flesh and blood. 'You know ... local cats.'

'Now you come to mention it, I have seen a couple slip in. I soon shoo them out though.'

'Well, there's your answer then.' I went on to elaborate. I felt pretty sure that Antac had been unnerved by the encroachment of strange cats on his territory. Nothing to do with being put under a spell by some demented old crone. The response to the invasion of his space was to mark out his territory by spraying.

Having explained this to Madam Mountjoy, I then went through a plan of action to counter the behavioural pattern, with tips on how to clean the sprayed areas and prevent reoccurrence of spraying in those spots. When I'd finished, the look of relief that spread across Madam Mountjoy's face suggested a whole cauldron of pee had been voided. Her lips puckered into a smile. Her blackened eyelashes fluttered in wild elation.

'Oh, thank you, Mr Mitchell, thank you so much,' she gushed, advancing towards me, her kaftan billowing open against her breasts, her lucky charms fully displayed. 'You've raised my spirits enormously. Is there something I can do to raise yours? Massage your aura maybe?'

'Er, no, I don't think so,' I spluttered, and beat a hasty retreat.

When I got back to Prospect House, Beryl was agog to learn what had gone on. Her 'You don't say … goodness … did she really?' peppered my account as her good eye stood out like an organ stop while the glass one rotated a full circle at every juicy detail.

'You'll have to watch out for her in the future,' she warned, when I'd finished. 'She obviously fancies you.'

'Who does?' We both turned, startled, as Lucy, striding into reception, asked the question in a rather brittle voice.

'Oh, hi,' I said, feeling guilty for no real reason, other than the fact that, for the past few weeks, I'd been treading rather carefully, with Lucy's mood swings making her liable to flare up at the slightest thing. I didn't dare to try lighting her touchpaper for fear she'd go off like a rocket.

'One of Paul's clients,' said Beryl. 'She's taken a shine to him.'

Beryl, Beryl, Beryl ... that's not helping, I thought.

'Good for her,' snorted Lucy, throwing me a glance that conjured up a barrage of barbed arrows winging my way, each with my name on it, destined to score a direct hit. 'I'm working the late shift tonight,' she added gruffly, addressing me. 'So I'll stay over upstairs. Just make sure the animals are fed.'

The animals she was referring to were the menagerie of waifs and strays we had accumulated over the past six months we'd been living together in the practice cottage over the Downs in Ashton. Among them, Nelson the deaf little terrier; Queenie, and two other cats; and, of course, Gertie, the goose given to me to fatten up for Christmas, but who had become a family pet instead. I wasn't so sure 'family' was the appropriate word to use in the current circumstances, with Lucy and me circling round each other on emotional tenterhooks. How long that was going to continue was anyone's guess. Maybe I needed the likes of Madam Mountjoy to read our tea leaves. Or palms. Or whatever.

'She's in a bit of a mood, isn't she?' said Beryl, watching Lucy flounce out. 'Wonder what's got into her?'

I wondered, too. It certainly hadn't been me for quite a while.

2
BERYL'S
BEAU JANGLE

'**D**o you think you'll get one?' queried Beryl, ten days into February, scratching the prominent mole she had under her chin.

One what? I wondered. A punch on the jaw from Lucy? Things were no better with her. Still bumpy. Whatever was bugging her had yet to be exorcised. Madam Mountjoy's intervention was still a possibility.

Beryl studied her scarlet talons briefly and then looked up at me. 'I was thinking of a St Valentine's Day card. You know … from that medium.'

'Oh, come off it, Beryl. You're just winding me up.'

'Well, you never know. You're certainly not going to get one from Lucy, that's for sure.' Beryl finished scrutinising her nails and proceeded to fish in her handbag for her packet of cigarettes, ready for her back-door smoke. We were in the office at the time, having our coffee break. It was a small room, five steps down from the reception area, and had a window that overlooked the parking area in front of Prospect House. That was an advantage for Beryl, since, whenever she took a break, she could keep an eye – her one eye – on any cars coming in and, by leaving the office door open, keep an ear open for any clients who might have sneaked in unseen via the path along the side of the property; a path which gave access from the Green, a remnant of what had been the village green before Westcott-on-Sea expanded as a retirement town in the mid-Fifties.

I knew she was right about Lucy, although I was reluctant to admit it; and I was certainly not prepared to discuss it in any detail. 'What about you then?' I asked, determined to change the subject.

'Me?'

'Yes, you. I'm sure there's bound to be a secret admirer amongst all our clients.'

Despite the thick layer of powder clinging to Beryl's cheeks, I could see them begin to redden, a flush creeping up from her scrawny neck. '*Now* who's doing the winding up?' she muttered, her lips disappearing in her mouth as she absent-mindedly fingered her mole again. Then she added, 'I have had my share in the past, you know.'

I didn't know and was curious to find out. All I did know was that she had once been married, and there was a daughter in California and a son somewhere in Australia. But Beryl wasn't to be drawn. The only thing on her mind at that moment was the cigarette she was desperate to draw on; and with a little inflected 'Mmm' to suggest there was more to her than met the eye – her good one – she quickly disappeared through to the back door to have her smoke.

My comment about secret admirers hadn't been entirely tongue-in-cheek as, when I mentioned the possibility, I did have one particular client in mind – Mr Entwhistle.

I had met the gentleman one lunch break during the hot

spell of June the previous year, just after I'd started as an assistant clinician. The heat inside Prospect House had been stifling, despite windows and doors flung open everywhere – that itself was a curse as it meant the pungent smell of rotting seaweed down on the beach wafted in, even though the beach was over a mile away. That apart, I was still thankful to get out, and I headed down past Prospect House, through the tunnel of rhododendrons that had once been part of the house's Victorian gardens and now served as a hidey-hole for young courting couples.

I crossed the Green to the shops lining the far side, a small complex catering for the cul-de-sacs of bungalows that had spread out like a web from the Green over the past few decades. Although bounded on three of its sides by busy arterial roads that headed down into the centre of Westcott and its main attractions, the pebbly beach and pier, the Green was still a popular recreational area; and on that June scorcher, there were youngsters playing tennis on the courts provided by the Council, while office workers dotted the brown-scorched grass, grabbing themselves a bit of tanning time. The office girls stretched out in their halter tops and short skirts made their end of the Green particularly desirable for elderly gentlemen dreaming of days gone by when they had the physiques to expose themselves with similar candour; and so, at lunchtimes in the summer, the park benches there were always packed.

Apart from the display of youthful flesh, the only other feature of the Green to stir up any excitement was the magnificent oak that stood at the apex of the Green, adjacent to, but over the road from, Prospect House. There'd been heated debates in the local newspaper and a campaign group set up to save the tree as the Council had deemed it unsafe. In the event, it had recently been struck by lightning and split in two, necessitating its complete removal. The demise of that tree brought Cyril the squirrel into our lives, a fascinating episode in my early days at Prospect House and one which helped to form a strong bond between Lucy and me. Heavens – how different things had become between us. We'd need to make a Herculean effort and foster a herd of baby elephants to establish the same degree of rapport now.

My main objective that lunchtime, besides escaping from Prospect House, was to grab a baguette and some buns for tea from the little bakery I'd discovered soon after starting work at Prospect House. With my penchant for sweet things, especially when presented as sticky iced buns, or custard doughnuts – maybe Madam Mountjoy could enlighten me as to whether I'd been an elephant in a previous life – I soon became a regular customer at 'Bert's Bakery' as it was called.

So, with a bag of Bert's buns to one side of me on a green park bench (at the less crowded end of the Green, overlooking an unimaginative border of sparsely planted rows of sickly, red geraniums and stunted, orange marigolds, acres of bare soil between each weedy plant, evidence of council cutbacks, it would seem), I was tucking into a ham and cheese baguette with Bert's own mayonnaise dressing, when a Border collie appeared from behind the bench, sidled up to me, slowly sank on his haunches and rested his black-and-white head on my right knee, eyes fixed on my baguette.

'Oh really, Ben. Do behave yourself,' said a voice, and a gentleman stepped onto the tarmac path to one side of the bench. I judged him to be in his early sixties, somewhat on the short side, with a spritely step. He had cropped, snowy-white hair with a fluffy-looking texture, only slightly receding at the temples, blue, sentimental eyes and a sweet but weak mouth, nipped in at the corners. His clothes suggested 'dapper', from the open-necked, crisp white shirt through the light-blue blazer to the fawn trousers with razor creases in them. White-and-blue spotless deck shoes completed the picture of a neat, well-groomed, gentlemanly chap.

'I'm so sorry,' he said. He stopped a few feet from me and clicked his fingers at the collie, who instantly responded by slinking over to him, where, at the double click of his owner's fingers, he sat down. 'Good boy, Ben,' the man murmured, reaching down to pat the collie's head. 'He's a devil when it comes to titbits,' he went on, looking across at me. 'Especially if it involves doughnuts.'

The collie now had his eyes fixed on my bag of buns, his tongue lolling out. I moved them quickly to the other side of my lap.

'Would you mind?' The man gestured to the empty space I'd created.

'No, of course not.'

The gentleman sat down, the collie coming round to sniff where the bag had been, before settling himself between us.

I felt obliged to comment on the dog. Well, I was a vet, wasn't I? 'You've got him well trained,' I remarked.

'Well, apart from his scrounging,' replied the gentleman. 'That's always been a problem ever since he was a puppy.' As feared, once I'd mentioned the dog, I was subjected to his full history. But it allowed me to eat my baguette without interruption. I was told Ben was nearly 13 years old. He, Ernie Entwhistle, had owned the collie since he was a 12-week-old puppy. Never done sheepdog trials, although he had been to agility classes and won many trophies over the years. Been fit as a fiddle up until the last year or so, when he'd begun to stiffen up. Problems in his back apparently. 'I take him over there,' said Mr Entwhistle, turning to wave the fingers of his left hand in the direction of Prospect House. 'They've always looked after him.'

At that point, I thought it best to mention I was a vet there.

Mr Entwhistle nodded. 'In that case, you'll know Ben's vet, Dr Sharpe. A very kind lady. Very kind indeed.' The gentleman's eyes suddenly lit up. 'Perhaps I shouldn't say it, you being her colleague and all that, but ...' He hesitated and then suddenly blurted out, 'She's a bit of all right is that Dr Sharpe!' He cleared his throat. Had he sported a handlebar moustache, I could have pictured him twiddling it at that precise moment with a harrumph of embarrassment.

Mind you, I was no better. Me, who, when having set eyes on Crystal at my interview, was immediately besotted by this Julie Andrews lookalike with her coppery curls, intense, steel-blue eyes, the dimpled apple cheeks. Oh boy ... I have to confess, I'd climbed every mountain with her in my dreams for more nights than I cared to admit in my first few months at Prospect House. Fortunately, the peak of my passion had now passed and, although I still had the occasional Maria moment, the sound of music to my ears was now much more the murmurs of love between Lucy and me. Well, that is until a couple of weeks back, when the do-re-me from our relationship suddenly went fa ... a long, long way to run.

Mr Entwhistle also informed me that he thought the receptionist a very sympathetic character.

'You mean the lady with the black hair?' I tactfully chose not to mention her glass eye.

He nodded. 'Beryl Wagstaff. The one with the glass eye.'
Ah, well.

'She's been with the practice for many years,' I said.
'Probably well over 12.'

'At least that,' he said wistfully. 'She remembers Ben as
a puppy. He's always pleased to see her. Gives her a friendly
lick. Such a nice lady.'

To judge from Mr Entwhistle's enthusiastic tone of
voice, I suspected he'd not be averse to giving Beryl a
friendly lick as well.

Several weeks after that meeting, we met again, only
this time over the consulting table in Prospect House.
Mr Entwhistle was the epitome of good manners. First,
he confessed to what I already knew, that he normally
saw the lady vet. But Dr Sharpe had been fully booked
the day he wanted to have Ben checked over. Beryl had
offered him an appointment with me, saying – and I
blushed at this point – I was a 'very kind and caring
young vet'. Mr Entwhistle had remembered me from our
meeting on the Green and thought Ben had taken to me
straight away. I could have interjected at that stage,
and reminded him I did have a bag of buns by my side
which might have had a strong influence on Ben's
obvious attraction to me. Whatever, the upshot was that
Ben had shuffled slowly into my consulting room and,
with a click of Ernie's fingers, had sat down, waiting to
be examined.

I'd already scanned through the collie's notes, reading
that the weakness in his hindquarters had been developing
over the past ten months, and that arthritis of the spine was
suspected. As yet, no X-rays had been taken. Courses of
anti-inflammatory pills had been prescribed with back-up
painkillers to be used as and when required.

I crouched down level with the collie. Mr Entwhistle gave two clicks of his fingers and Ben raised his front left leg for shake-a-paw. I duly shook the outstretched paw and said, 'Hello, Ben.'

'So, how've things been?' I asked, looking up at Mr Entwhistle.

'Well, he's certainly beginning to slow up a bit more,' he admitted. 'But then if we're talking about arthritis, I suppose that's to be expected.'

'But the tablets help?'

Mr Entwhistle nodded. 'Keep him comfortable.'

'Let's get you standing,' I said, turning my attention to the collie. I gently placed my hand under his tummy and levered him into a standing position before edging round to his backquarters, instructing Mr Entwhistle to stand by the side of the dog's head, holding on to his collar. 'This might hurt,' I warned.

I began to knead Ben's spine between my thumbs, starting mid-way down his back and gradually working towards his tail, pressing down gently every centimetre or so. Three-quarters of the way down, my gentle pressure elicited a moan from him and he abruptly sat down. 'Think we've located the spot,' I said, reassuring the dog by telling him what a good boy he was. 'I suspect we've got some spondylitis here,' I went on. 'But unless we take an X-ray, we won't really know the extent of the problem.'

Mr Entwhistle nodded. 'That's what Dr Sharpe said the last time I came in.'

'So?'

'OK. Best if you get it done then.'

I suddenly sussed the reason for Mr Entwhistle's reluctance. 'We won't have to anaesthetise Ben, you know.'

'You won't?'

I shook my head. 'He's so well behaved that my guess is he'll lie still without having to give him one.'

I instantly saw the look of relief that flooded Mr Entwhistle's face. 'But Dr Sharpe had said ...' His voice trailed off, uncertain whether to continue.

I guessed what he was going to say but, being the gentleman he was, he didn't want to question Dr Sharpe's judgement – that Ben would have to have an anaesthetic before he could be X-rayed.

I explained that I just intended to take a lateral X-ray of the spine, which meant Ben would only have to lie on his side. Should I have wanted to do a more thorough screening involving X-rays taken from different angles, then that, of course, would necessitate anaesthetising him. So, with those reassurances, Mr Entwhistle signed the consent form to have Ben admitted for X-ray. I overheard Beryl reassuring him yet again out in reception, telling him Ben was in safe hands and that I knew what I was doing. Gosh, what an ally she was proving to be.

Not so Mandy. She of the imperial nature, demanding and commanding, that made working with her so fraught on many occasions. That August morning, last year, proved to be one of them.

I was scribbling Ben's details in the ops book, having put him in the remaining empty kennel down in the ward, when Mandy came bustling into the prep room.

'What's this?' she said querulously, peering over my elbow at the book. 'Not another op surely? We're fully booked as it is.'

I explained it was just a routine, quick, spinal X-ray that was required.

'Will still need an anaesthetic,' she said sharply.

I told her the collie was such a well-behaved dog that I

thought we could get away without having to knock him out. 'And anyway, I only want a lateral shot,' I concluded.

Goodness. If looks could kill … Mandy's doe eyes widened, her lips tightened; in fact, her whole body seemed to tighten under her starched, green uniform as if I'd inserted an electric probe into a particularly sensitive area. As, at that stage, I had only been at Prospect House for two months, and still conscious of being the new boy, I'd bitten my tongue whenever I felt Mandy was overstepping her mark. And here she was, about to do it again.

'It's not the way we do things here,' she snapped. 'Crystal always insists on a general anaesthetic for these sorts of cases.' Mandy paused, and ran her hands down her white pinafore as if suddenly sensing she was stepping out of line.

I raised my eyebrows but remained silent, just tapping the biro I still had in my hand against the edge of the work surface.

'That way we can get the best X-rays,' she tailed off lamely.

I gave one final, sharp tap of the biro and replaced it firmly on top of the open page of the ops book; and then gave Mandy the sweetest smile I could muster before saying, 'Don't you worry … I'll get Lucy to give me a hand.' My pulse racing, I swung sharply on my heels and managed to reach the corridor outside before 'You cow!' exploded from my lips.

As anticipated, it was a simple task to take the required X-ray of Ben's spine. He just lay stretched out on the table with the X-ray plate under him and didn't move while Lucy clicked the button of the machine from behind the safety of a screen. When I showed Mr Entwhistle the films, I was able to point out the bony growths that had developed between the lower vertebrae of the spine. They showed as bridges of bone that were impinging on the nerves supplying Ben's hind-legs, and were clearly the cause of his pain and the difficulty in moving.

'Bit like sciatica then,' said Mr Entwhistle.

'Very similar, yes,' I replied.

That had been the previous summer. During the early part of the winter, Mr Entwhistle had come in for repeat prescriptions; on those occasions, I often caught him having a chinwag with Beryl. Ben, it seemed, was relatively stable but did have his off days when he was reluctant to move around much.

'We know how he feels, don't we, Ernie?' said Beryl to me on one occasion, laying a sympathetic hand on Mr Entwhistle's arm as she handed him Ben's tablets. 'With all this damp weather, we both tend to seize up a bit.' She looked across at me. 'But we keep going.'

Mr Entwhistle chuckled. 'Well, we do our best. And you know what they say – if you don't use it, you'll lose it.' He turned to Beryl. 'And you, my dear, have certainly not lost it.'

Beryl's powder-packed cheeks began to glow and she emitted a girlish giggle while the wings of her heavily lacquered, coal-black hair flapped like a raven's, the solitary hair on her mole twitched and the white of her glass eye shone like a scoured lavatory tile. I was damned if I could see in her what Mr Entwhistle evidently saw; but then whatever takes your fancy, Ernie ... mole and all.

Hence my allusion to a St Valentine's Day card from Mr Entwhistle when Beryl and I were discussing the matter that February morning. But before Cupid's dart had a chance to wing its way over, the Hand of Fate gave us a mighty big slap.

Beryl came charging down to the office the day after that discussion, just as I was finishing my coffee break, her face ashen, her bony hands shaking. 'Ernie ... er ... Mr Entwhistle's just phoned. Ben's collapsed.'

'You'd better get him to bring him in.'

'I've told him to,' she replied, all of a jitter. Her agitation remained evident in the way she kept darting from her computer at the reception desk to the front door, opening it to peer out whenever she heard the sound of a car on the gravel.

'Ah, he's arrived,' she said, when at last she spotted a dark-blue Fiesta pulling up. 'I'll go and give him a hand,' and before I could say, 'Let one of the nurses help him,' she'd dashed out to appear minutes later with a dejected-looking Ben being carried in her and Mr Entwhistle's arms. There was much gasping and wheezing as the two of them struggled down the corridor and into my consulting room before they finally managed to lower Ben to the floor where he lay awkwardly, panting rapidly, his hind-legs splayed out behind him.

Beryl hovered a minute, staring down at the collie, her hands to her mouth, before my 'Thanks, Beryl' dismissed her with a click of the consulting room door.

Mr Entwhistle stood, catching his breath a moment before saying, 'Ben got out of his box this morning and then collapsed. He hasn't been able to stand since.' A tear coursed down his face. 'I hate to see him looking so distressed.'

I knelt down and Ben raised his head, his eyes full of fear.

'There, there, old fella,' I murmured, stroking him. He responded with a lick of his lips and a whimper before he started to pant heavily again, his head sinking down again. I wanted to see if I could get Ben to stand. So I levered Ben onto his sternum and then Mr Entwhistle supported the dog's shoulders while I slipped my arms under Ben's tummy and hoisted him up. He stood with me still supporting him, the muscles of his back legs trembling violently; but as soon as I began to loosen my grip, his legs just slid away from him. All power had been lost. Pinching his toes and the use of a needle to prick the skin of his hindquarters demonstrated that all feeling had been lost as well. There was no reaction. No whimper. No turning of the head to indicate he'd felt anything. Ben was paralysed.

Mr Entwhistle sensed what I was thinking and in a muted voice said, 'I think Ben's time has come.' He began to sob.

'Well, we could try some stronger anti-inflammatories and see if there's any response over 24 hours.' I didn't sound convincing and Mr Entwhistle wasn't convinced.

'What would you do if he was your dog?' he said.

'Well ...' I hesitated.

'I don't like to see Ben suffering like this,' interrupted Mr Entwhistle, choking as he said it.

'No. I agree.'

There was nothing more to be said. An understanding had been reached. A decision made. Mr Entwhistle asked if he could stay with Ben, and when Mandy came in to help hoist Ben onto the consulting table where his front leg was shaved and the vein raised, he buried his face in Ben's neck. I inserted the needle and swiftly injected the lethal dose of barbiturate. As Ben's trusting, brown eyes slid away from me and sunk down, a solitary tear coursed down Mr Entwhistle's cheek and, with a quiver of his lower lip, he whispered in Ben's ear, 'Bye, bye, my old mate. Bye, bye.'

I, too, had a lump in my throat, being witness to the end of a long and loyal relationship. Even Mandy, the queen bee of Prospect House and never one to show her emotions, had eyes glistening with tears. As for Beryl … well, she just threw her arms round Mr Entwhistle, and the two of them stood hugging each other in the middle of reception, not a word spoken.

Two days later, I saw Beryl opening a card which had been left for her in reception. A St Valentine's Day card to accompany the bouquet of red roses she now had displayed next to her computer.

'I wonder who it's from,' she said, giving me a sly wink. As if I didn't know.

3

BYRE
GONE DAYS

Did Lucy get a St Valentine's Day card from me? No, I'm afraid she didn't.

I felt a bit mean for not getting her one. I'm normally a bit of a romantic at heart, so a box of chocolates or a bunch of flowers wouldn't have gone amiss. Or at least a card as a token of my affection. But that was the trouble – the affection, or rather the lack of it, which now seemed to be the case most of the time. Lucy was so terribly moody; and each day I woke up wondering whether it was going to be another of 'those days', one of monosyllabic replies to my questions, accompanied by a long face which seemed to get longer as the day wore on until I felt her jaw would end up scraping along the ground. Her mood affected me and I began to feel a little resentful at having to put up with it all. So, no Valentine's card. Tough titties.

'Don't think that was a good idea,' said Beryl, having just returned from her morning puff at the back door and now spooning three sugars into her black coffee. She'd shown me the card she'd received from Mr Entwhistle – a very romantic, red-edged affair, with red bows and red roses encased in a red, velvet heart. I didn't have the heart to tell her I thought it rather over the top, especially as, inside, he'd glued a snapshot of himself centred on another velvet heart, like he was some sort of heart-throb. Yuck!

I could imagine the reaction I'd have had from Lucy if I had done the same. But then I didn't consider myself a heart-throb. OK, I liked to think I wasn't too bad looking. I did have rather a sharp nose – 'aquiline', my Mum would say, while she caressed her own prominent snout (thanks, Mum) – and I did have one slightly protruding front tooth. And yes, I suppose my ears were rather on the large size – 'You take after Prince Charles,' my Dad always said (thanks, Dad) – so I always made sure my hair overlapped them. But at least I *had* hair, a good head of it, which I usually kept cropped short, although I sported a fringe as I had an unusually high forehead – a sign of intelligence, Mum was always quick to say (thanks again, Mum). Currently, my brown hair had blond highlights to match the gold stud in each earlobe. I thought this gave me a touch of the David Beckhams. Lucy had been less than sympathetic when I returned from the hairdresser's with my new style. 'David Beckham?' she'd snorted. 'The nearest you get to him is dribbling in bed.' (Thanks, Lucy, love you too.) I think she was referring to my habit of snoring on my side, with my mouth wide open and saliva seeping out onto the pillow. Not the nicest of habits when trying to score.

'I guess things between you and Lucy are still a bit ...' Beryl was saying, trailing off, unable to find the right words. I could have supplied plenty: 'iffy' ... 'difficult' ... 'off and on'? Definitely more off than on.

Even Eric had noticed. He'd come bouncing into the

office earlier on, ruddy cheeked, bald head glowing, muffled in a winter jacket and bright orange scarf, complaining how cold it was outside while Beryl shuffled past, her hands pulling the sleeves of her black cardigan across her chest, saying it wasn't much better indoors.

'Full of the joys of spring, I see,' he said to her receding back as she climbed the steps to reception. 'Mind you, you're not much better,' he went on, looking at me. 'Talk about winter blues. You seem really down in the dumps these days. So does Lucy.' He held up his hands. 'Not that I want to interfere, but for the sake of the practice … you know, we do need to get on with each other. Control our emotions, even if we feel like throttling someone.'

'Eric.' Beryl's voice rang out. 'I hope you're not going to be too long.'

He raised his eyebrows and pointed a finger towards reception. 'Good example up there,' he continued in a whisper. 'It can be quite difficult at times, but you learn to cope.' He gave a nervous grin.

'Eric! I've booked you several visits this morning.'

'So if there are any issues you'd like to talk over …'

'Eric!'

'We could have a jar over at the Woolpack one lunchtime.'

'*ERIC*!'

'Coming, Beryl.' With a final grimace at me, Eric sprang away.

It was kind of Eric to lend a sympathetic ear. But that was him all over. He might have given the impression of being a bumbling, rather inept sort of chap, and, indeed, he did nothing to play down that image, always flapping round the place in a white coat that was several sizes too big for him. He was also usually tieless, and the brown cords he invariably wore were creased and slightly shiny at the knees. It was as if he was making a statement – take me or leave me. A lot of clients left him, preferring the clipped, professional image of his wife, always smartly turned out, even when it was an emergency in the middle of the night.

'Crystal keeps a set of clothes specifically for those times,' he once confided in me, his tongue a little loosened from the couple of pints consumed over at the Woolpack that lunchtime.

Those liquid lunches, although not excessive, were strongly disapproved of by Beryl. It wasn't the drinking as such – she wasn't averse to the occasional port and lemon; and, in fact, the bottle I'd bought for last year's 'What Were You Wearing When the Ship Went Down?' party went down very well with Beryl. At the end of the evening, she was seen weaving round Willow Wren, with a glass containing at least eight slices of lemon from constant replenishments, proclaiming herself free for a Jolly Roger. No – it was more the beery fumes exhaled by Eric on his return, coupled with an even more ruddy complexion than normal, so that cheeks, nose and bald head glowed a bright amber, like one of those roadside beacons warning you of impending danger.

The danger in this case was the watching eye and waspish tongue of Beryl, who would pounce as soon as Eric breezed into reception. There'd be an exaggerated sniff, a fan of the scarlet talons in front of the face, and a direct reference to Eric's slightly inebriated state in the form of a withering comment, usually a standard one, along the lines of, 'God, Eric, you could anaesthetise a Great Dane in one breath.' Although the breed and size of dog could vary according to the intensity of Beryl's outrage at the time.

Eric took to stuffing a couple of peppermints in his mouth

before confronting Beryl should he have been over at the pub. Of course, it didn't fool her. The trouble was, whenever I thought I might have a touch of halitosis – possibly through having had one of Bert's garlic bread baguettes – and had been sucking a mint myself, I, too, became the target of one of Beryl's eye-drilling scans. Most unnerving.

I could hear the dialogue up in reception between Eric and Beryl getting louder and more heated by the minute; intrigued, I tiptoed up the stairs to lean in at the door behind Beryl. Eric was facing her, the other side of the counter, looking at the visits book while Beryl was tapping the computer screen with one of her scarlet nails. If Eric had been red on arrival, he was now slowly turning puce.

'I can't see how I can fit all of these in,' he exclaimed, his hand slamming down on the page that listed the visits Beryl had set up for him that morning.

'Well, if you'd got cracking sooner,' replied Beryl, 'I'm sure it wouldn't have been a problem.'

Eric was peering at the list. 'You've got me down to visit Miss Millichip's sows.'

'9.30 … yes.'

'To do what? It doesn't say here.'

'The usual.'

'Which is?' Eric's voice was getting more exasperated by the second.

'They need their trotters trimming. You do it routinely every six months.'

'But you've got me booked over at the Stockwells at the same time. I can't possibly be in two places at once, can I?' Beads of sweat had broken out on Eric's forehead as he visibly tried to control himself. 'Can I?' he repeated, in a controlled snarl.

'Don't you use that tone of voice with me,' snapped

Beryl. I could see the wings of her coal-black hair springing up, all of a quiver.

'Well, you shouldn't have double-booked.' Spittle had appeared at the corners of Eric's mouth.

'I can't help it if the Stockwells called in requesting a visit as soon as possible. You'll just have to do the Millichip trimming later on.'

'Beryl,' seethed Eric, 'it's not for you to tell me what to do.' His hands were gripping the edges of the counter, his knuckles white, and he was swaying backwards and forwards, his eyes wild, glaring at her.

Now what had he just been telling me about how important it was for everyone to get on? Hee-hee ... count to ten, Eric. Self-control.

'So how are we all this morning?' The words were clipped, clearly enunciated in a mid-shires accent, and were uttered by Crystal Sharpe as she swept into reception from the car park and swirled to a halt next to her husband. 'Sorting out the visits, are we?' she said, smiling sweetly round at everyone, her Cupid's lips parting to show an even row of glossy, white teeth. 'No problems, I hope.' She gave Eric the full-on, penetrating stare of her steel-blue eyes before switching her attention to the visits book. She ran a well-manicured, unvarnished nail along the top of the page and, within seconds, had sorted out the morning's workload, without a murmur of protest from anyone.

Eric was to trim the trotters, she would see the few clients booked in for me and I would visit the Stockwells and see to the calving. I would? I gulped. Of course I would. I would do anything for Crystal. Besides, as she said, I'd been to the Stockwells before when they had that cow stuck in the quarry and they'd been impressed by how helpful I'd been then. So I was to hurry along and see what

I could do to help them this time. 'I take it you've no problem with that, Paul?' she had said.

Bewitched, bewildered and rather bedazzled, I shook my head and obediently trotted out to my car, checking I had all the necessary calving ropes, gown and instruments ready to get to grips with a potentially difficult calving. And, more importantly, as I drove out of the car park, I realised I needed to get in the right frame of mind to tackle the Stockwells.

Madge and Rosie Stockwell were twin sisters, originating from Yorkshire, who had moved down to Sussex over 30 years earlier to take on Hawkshill Farm, secreted away in the side of the Downs between Ashton and Chawcombe; and here they'd remained ever since, in what could only be described as a time capsule. Little had been done to keep pace with modern advances in farming, and they had ticked along with a motley collection of sheep, the flock now reduced in size, as was the herd of Jerseys which now numbered only 12. I had been called out last summer to attend to Myrtle, one of their Jerseys, who had gone down with milk fever. Boy, that had been an experience; their slow, unperturbed way of going about things had driven me nuts, especially as we'd had an emergency on our hands, but as they'd said on my arrival, 'Doesn't pay to be in a hurry. Now't gained if vet breaks leg ...' while they watched me rush across their yard and almost do precisely that when I slipped in a cow pat.

Once on the dual carriageway, I headed north over the Downs and dropped down into Ashton where the practice house, Willow Wren, was situated. Taking the road west towards Chawcombe, it was a mile or so before the narrow lane on the left wound back up the northern slopes of the Downs and took me to Hawkshill Farm. Although it had

41

been many months since my last visit, I still remembered the Stockwells' instructions regarding the gate: 'Second one on the right and make sure to close it after you.' The gate was still there in much the same condition as before. Bleached oak, five bars reduced to four, and that fourth one just as loose, although an attempt had been made to prevent it from dropping out of its bracket by some strands of orange bailer twine tied round it and secured to the upright. It was all rather rickety and, as I prised open the latch, the gate dropped on its hinges and I had to lift it and drag it back across the gravel track.

The farm, tucked down in a hollow, was obscured by a thick veil of mist this morning, so I wasn't able to see the details that I'd found so attractive on my previous visit: the undulating pitch of the clay-tiled roof; the flint walls set in courses of red brick; the tiny lattice windows painted white; the oak-panelled front door, weathered grey. And all of this complemented by the landscape beyond – a patchwork of fields, hedgerows and the spire of Chawcombe church in the distance.

But not today. Today, the background was a blur of grey as banks of low cloud rolled down and obscured everything in droplets of icy mist. Last time, as I drove down the winding track and into the brick-paved yard at the side of the house, I'd been struck by the lack of TV aerial, satellite dish or white PVC conservatory to mar the sense of the farm being locked in a time capsule. So fanciful was the impression of rustic charm due to the oak tithe barn with its exposed beams, linking the knapped flint stables to the house, that I'd half expected a Hardyesque figure to emerge to greet me – Tess, Bathsheba, or Susan Henchard perhaps – certainly not the gnome-like creature that had shuffled into view – Madge Stockwell.

Today was no exception, save that two, rather than one, gnome-like figures emerged through the mist in the yard like phantom goblins from *The Lord of the Rings* rather than Julie Christie lookalikes from *Far from the Madding Crowd*. Madge and Rosie Stockwell – identical twins, dressed identically in brown tweed trousers, stuffed into black wellies and, I suspected, identical green, army-style pullovers, although this time it had to be a guess as their upper halves were obscured by brown, rubber capes, buttoned tightly at the neck, stretching down to calf level, with side vents for their arms which were currently tucked inside. The overall impression was of two over-inflated buoys, an impression given more credence by the fact that they were standing in a yard ankle-deep in water.

As I got out of the car, the two sisters splashed towards me.

Never knowing who was Madge and who was Rosie, each having a tomato soup complexion, hooked nose and mousy, pudding basin-styled hair, I addressed them as one. 'Morning, ladies. See you've had quite a bit of rain here.' I pointed at the flooded yard.

Both sisters shook their heads simultaneously. 'It's not rain,' said one caped figure.

'Vet thinks it is,' said the other.

'But it's not, Madge.'

'I know it's not. It's the leak in that outside tap,' replied Madge.

'It's an outside tap that's leaking,' explained the sister who I'd now worked out was Rosie.

'It needs to be fixed,' said Madge. 'We'll get round to it in time.'

'We will, Madge. In time,' said Rosie, nodding her head slowly.

I felt a nervous tic start to throb in my temple at the mention of time. I was being reminded of how time meant nothing to the Stockwells. As Beryl had warned me before my first meeting, it was no use hurrying them as they lived in a world of their own. Everything had to be done at their pace.

But, like the time I'd rushed out to treat their Jersey with milk fever, time was still precious; and this time there was a calving cow requiring attention. I assumed she was going to be in the tithe barn and said as much to the sisters as I opened the boot of my car and started to collect up my calving equipment.

'Vet thinks Deidre's in barn,' said Madge, turning to Rosie.

'But she's not,' said Rosie, shaking her head, dislodging a drop of water from the end of her nose.

'I know she's not. She's out in Fox Meadow.'

'That's right, Madge. Fox Meadow. Deidre's out in Fox Meadow,' went on Rosie, looking at me.

'That's where you'll find her,' explained Madge, also staring at me.

'Fox Meadow,' said Rosie in case I required extra confirmation.

The tic in my temple was now throbbing at full throttle. 'Look, ladies,' I said quickly and a little too curtly, 'we haven't got all day. Your Deidre needs looking at as soon as possible. Just take me to Fox Meadow, OK?'

'Rush. Rush. Always in a rush,' murmured the Stockwells in unison.

'Shall I show him?' said Rosie, turning to Madge. Or was it Madge turning to Rosie?

'You can if you like. Or I'll go.'

'Don't mind.'

'Or we could both go.'

44

'Probably best if we both went.'

'OK.'

'We'll both go,' they chorused, their ruddy cheeks glowing.

I started to grind my teeth. 'Well let's get going then,' I seethed, hastily donning my boots and waterproofs as the mist turned to a steady drizzle, while handing calving ropes and the rest of the kit to the twins.

As we splashed across the first meadow, water seeped up my sleeves and crept down my collar and mud worked its way up and over the edge of each boot.

'Is it much further?' I gasped as the gate to a second meadow was opened.

'Vet's asking is it much further,' said one twin, squelching to a halt.

'Heard him,' said the other with a squish, closing the gate behind us.

'Well?' I asked, squashed between them.

'We're here,' they said as one. 'This is Fox Meadow.'

The meadow consisted of a small field bounded by overgrown hawthorn hedges – the irregular tops an undulating line of brown spikes in need of cutting back; the grass was poached round the perimeter with patches of mud and puddles leading to a large, corrugated-roofed field shelter, inside of which huddled a group of about ten or so Jerseys, some of which were desultorily snatching mouthfuls of hay from a pile heaped in one corner.

'Deidre's over there,' said one of the twins – Madge, I think. She pointed to the far side of the field where, through the drifting sheet of drizzle, I could just discern the outline of a cow, only her flanks visible, the rest of her below the level of the grass. 'She's gone down in the ditch,' added Madge.

'Dear old Deidre,' said Rosie.

Between them, the twins explained that earlier they'd noticed Deidre had separated herself from the rest of the herd, showing signs of unease, standing alone, tail flicking, gazing into the distance, emitting the occasional soft moo.

'Thought then she might be due to calve, didn't I, Madge?' said Rosie.

'You did, Rosie.'

'I did, Madge.'

'And you were right.'

'I was.'

So they went back to get a head collar and rope to bring her in but on their return had found she had gone down the side of the ditch that flanked the field, normally dry and grass-filled, but now soggy and water-filled – as I discovered when we got to Deidre and found her hindquarters partially submerged.

'Couldn't get her to budge,' commented one twin.

'No, we couldn't,' said the other.

'But we did try,' said the first.

I asked about contractions and was told some had been seen earlier but they had since eased off. There had been no sign of a water bag bursting, although in these wet conditions that could easily have been missed. I felt in a real dilemma here. Deidre certainly looked as if she was about to calve. An internal examination could establish whether the calf was engaged in the cervix and correctly positioned; but there was no way that was going to be achievable with Deidre's back end half under water. As if reading my thoughts, the heifer gave a grunt, contracted her abdominal muscles and thrust both hind-legs down through the lank grass of the bank, an action which pushed her rump back level with the field so she was now splayed diagonally across the ditch.

'OK, let's go for it,' I exclaimed, and, taking a deep breath, tore off my jacket and sodden shirt and gritted my teeth as I pulled on the red calving apron one twin held out to me, gasping as the freezing rubber slapped across my chest. Lubricating my arm with the oil the other twin gave me, I cautiously levered myself down onto the slippery bank and, while Madge – or was it Rosie? – held Deidre's tail back, and the other twin, having secured a head collar, was kneeling down, gripping it tightly under Deidre's chin, I slowly slipped my arm inside the cow, feeling the warmth of the animal's birth canal instantly enfold me as clouds of steam eddied out.

With my arm buried up to the elbow, I eventually managed to touch the calf's head and felt it tweak back as I pinched its nose. At least the calf was still alive.

But to judge the calf's head in relation to the size of the heifer's pelvis, I had a sinking feeling that we weren't going to have a normal birth. I just felt that head was too big to pass through. Which meant only one option for a safe delivery. A Caesarean.

I stood up, rapidly re-dressed and told the twins. They sploshed round from either end of the prone cow, only stopping when their hooked noses were almost touching.

'Did you hear what vet said, Madge?'

'I did, Rosie. A Caesarean.'

'That's what he said, yes.'

'I know. So what do you think?'

'Best let vet do it.'

'That's what I think's best,' said Madge. Or was it Rosie? The problem now was how to get Deidre back to the farm, since there was no way I could contemplate carrying out a Caesarean under such dire field conditions unless absolutely forced to. Even if we did manage to haul her back, there was still the problem of who was going to help me. I really didn't feel it fair to put the onus on the Stockwell twins to assist.

The first problem resolved itself when Deidre gave an almighty bellow and heaved herself up into a sitting position, at which point Madge and Rosie suddenly sprang into action and bent down, pushing at Deidre's rump, the slope of the bank helping them to roll Deidre sideways until her back legs folded in under her. She gave another loud snort and then shakily rose to stand on all four feet.

Problem two was resolved by a mobile call to Prospect House, where Beryl informed me she'd organise someone to come out and help straight away; that created a new problem of its own, though, when after waiting a few minutes while she went and conferred, I was told Lucy was on her way. 'Hope you don't mind ...' were Beryl's parting words.

No, actually I didn't mind. Although Lucy was only a trainee nurse, she'd already shown her aptitude for the work involved, with an understanding, patient manner when dealing with creatures of all shapes and sizes, a natural empathy not clouded by sentimentality and that niggling 'love for animals' so often expressed by people and which so often obscured and undermined the professionalism required by veterinary nurses to ensure that some of the less glamorous aspects of the work were carried out. That aptitude had been clearly demonstrated the time I had to deal with the Richardsons' difficult foaling – their darling Clementine with her breech birth. Lucy's support and reassurance as to my capability to deal with the crisis that night had been instrumental in us hitching up. Maybe Deidre's problem would be the catalyst required to bring us back together again. We'd have to see.

The Stockwells and I had managed to push and cajole Deidre across Fox Meadow and the adjacent field, slipping and sliding into the yard just as Lucy drove down the gravel track.

'You remembered to close gate,' said one of the twins as Lucy climbed out of her somewhat battered old Fiesta, a present from her Mum when she reached her 18th a year back.

She nodded and then looked at me before saying, 'I've brought out the sterilised emergency op pack and some additional artery forceps. Hope that will be sufficient.' She dropped her gaze as she finished, and opened the rear car door to gather up the equipment, taking it across the yard to the tithe barn as instructed by the twins, quickly tiptoeing to avoid too much water getting into her shoes.

'These young 'uns ... always in a hurry, Rosie,' said Madge.

'Rush, rush, rush. Always in a rush,' I heard her twin mutter as I, too, scooted ahead into the barn while Deidre was slowly coaxed in by the sisters. 'There, there, take your time,' they were saying as the heifer nervously shuffled onto the straw covering the cobbled barn floor. At least we were now all under cover and I did have somewhere to operate. Not ideal, though, I thought, gazing up at the cobweb-festooned timbers that arched above us; from the central span of one hung a dust-covered bulb which, although lit, scarcely penetrated the shadows of that cavernous interior.

I began to shiver, feeling the muscles in my arms and legs

tremble. Was it my wet clothing or nerves at the thought of what I was about to do?

'Here, put these on,' murmured Lucy, handing me a pack containing a T-shirt and operating gown. 'Wasn't sure if you'd want them. But at least they're dry.'

'Thanks.' I removed my jacket and stripped off my wet shirt. Having put on the ops clothes, I felt much better, although still apprehensive at what lay ahead. One of the twins had tied Deidre to a large iron ring embedded in the flint wall. The heifer was now standing there, next to an old wooden manger, its frame pitted with woodworm, with her head down, her dark eyes dull, partially obscured by her long, black lashes, and her hooves sifting backwards and forwards in the straw. She was clearly distressed. The sooner I operated the better.

'Could we please have a couple of straw bales over here …' I gesticulated at the stack at the far end of the barn. 'As quick as you like.'

Madge and Rosie didn't do 'quick'. In the time it had taken them to amble down and bring back a bale each to make a makeshift operating table, I'd drawn up the dose of local anaesthetic required to give an epidural, had pumped Deidre's tail to locate the right spot between the lumbar vertebrae and had given the injection. Some difference to that time last year when I'd given Clementine a similar spinal injection to stop her straining. Then I'd been all fingers and thumbs.

The operation site now had to be prepared.

'I did bring the clippers,' said Lucy, holding them up. 'And they're fully charged. I checked before leaving.'

Good girl. More brownie points.

'You can do it,' I said, outlining the area on Deidre's right flank that required shaving. 'And perhaps one of you would like to get me some hot water,' I continued, turning to the Stockwells who had lined themselves up by the straw bales.

'Vet wants some hot water, Madge.'

'I heard him, Rosie.'

'Shall I get it?'

'You can if you like. Or I can go.'

'Whatever.'

'You go then.'

'OK, Madge. I will. But it might not be that hot. Boiler's not on.'

'Vet will just have to make do.'

'He will, Madge, he will.'

By the time Rosie had returned with a bucket of water, Lucy had finished shaving Deidre's right flank and had scrubbed it with antiseptic and wiped it down with surgical spirit; and I had injected more local anaesthetic in the skin parallel to the spine to deaden the nerves that ran out to the area where I was going to make my incision.

I scrubbed my hands with antiseptic, rinsing them in the water provided by Rosie, which, as she had predicted, was tepid, and dried them on some sterilised paper towels from a pack Lucy had opened. I extracted a large green drape from a similar pack and spread it across the straw bales and then Lucy opened the third sterile pack, containing the instruments, and tipped them out. Scalpel, artery and rack-toothed forceps, needle holder, scissors, catgut and nylon, swabs and a gauze pad with a variety of different-sized needles threaded through it tumbled onto my makeshift operating table.

'OK ... ready?' I said, poised with scalpel in hand like a conductor about to wave his baton.

'I'm ready,' said a twin. 'Are you, Madge?'

'Yes, Rosie, I am.'

'We're ready, vet,' said Rosie.

A brief smile of reassurance flicked across Lucy's face. 'You'll be fine, Paul,' she whispered.

I dropped my wrist and the blade plunged deep into Deidre's hide to slice down the flank and reveal the underlying bed of glistening white connective tissue criss-crossed with small, pulsating arteries and the dark red striations of the muscles, some of which twitched involuntarily.

As I sliced deeper, the first of several small arteries was cut. A fine jet of blood sprayed into the air and splattered down my gown, stopped only by a pair of artery forceps clamped to the spurting, severed vessel. I cautiously cut deeper until – with a quiet puff of the vacuum being broken – the abdominal cavity was entered. Enlarging the aperture, I revealed parts of the digestive tract – the grey, glistening, rounded end of the rumen, a sea of small bowel, the dark curve of a kidney – but my main focus was on the massive wall of womb directly in front of me.

It bulged and rippled as the calf inside twisted about.

I took a deep breath, realising it was going to be a mammoth task to get the gravid uterus in line with the incision I'd made and then, holding it still, cut through the uterine wall and extricate the calf. And so it proved. Even with both my arms immersed in Deidre's abdomen and enfolded round the womb, I could barely lift it to the edge of the wound.

'Lucy, I think you'd better scrub up and give me a hand here,' I gasped.

She swiftly did as instructed while I grimly held on to the womb, pushing it out towards me as best I could.

'Now see where those feet are poking up?' I nodded at

the tent of grey uterine wall I was supporting, level with the gap in the abdominal wall. 'Put a scalpel through that.'

Lucy reached between my arms and cut where I had indicated. A tiny hind-leg immediately popped out.

'Rope it quick.'

That done, I took the scalpel from Lucy and enlarged the uterine incision to winkle out the other hind-leg, which she roped as well. The two of us then hauled on the ropes and the steaming body of the calf slithered out of the womb, up and over the edge of the abdominal incision, to collapse in a pile of mucus and membranes in the straw.

'Rosie, Madge, see to the calf,' I urged and was pleasantly surprised to see them move with the speed of – not exactly lightning – but with sufficient alacrity to ensure they'd pulled the calf up by its hind-legs and had swung it to and fro to get its airways cleared, and had then been rewarded by a splutter and a cough.

'It's a boy,' said one.

'So I see, Rosie,' said the other. 'A boy.'

'That's what I said, Madge.'

'I know.'

'It's a bull calf,' they chorused at me.

I wasn't really paying attention as there was a pressing need to get the uterine incision stitched and over-stitched as it was rapidly contracting down now the calf had been removed. Within minutes, it would be a tenth of its size. Lucy held up the cut edges while I sewed, and then assisted as I closed the abdominal wall, drawing the layers of muscle and connective tissue together and running sutures through them. Finally, the skin was pulled across and stitched in place, leaving a long, pink line down Deidre's flank.

One of the two Stockwells had been rubbing the calf's

coat with a handful of straw while the other waited until I'd finished suturing and dusting the wound with antiseptic powder, and then released Deidre's halter from the iron ring. The heifer immediately swung round and started to lick and nuzzle her new offspring.

Lucy, with quiet efficiency, packed up all the instruments, clothes and ropes, taking them across the yard to the back of her car.

'Vet and his young 'un will be needing wash,' declared a twin.

'Indeed they will, Madge,' said Rosie, getting to her feet and stepping back from the calf.

'Over in kitchen, then,' said Madge.

Lucy and I cleaned ourselves up with the soap and tepid water provided and, having declined the offer of a cup of coffee – for fear it would take hours to make – we made our way back into the yard accompanied by the Stockwells. Before leaving, we decided to check on the calf.

The sight of a newborn creature starting on its life's journey never ceases to amaze me, whether a hatched chick flapping its bare wings for the first time, a little froglet swimming or a baby crying with unfocused eyes, waiting to latch on to its mother's milk. Deidre's calf was no exception. He seemed to be all legs, gangly, long-limbed, uncoordinated, as he attempted to stand, his rump up in the air, aquiver, only for him to topple forward onto his side. Undeterred, he tried again, heaving himself up, staggering like a boxer coming round from a knock-out blow. This time, despite lurching backwards and forwards and twisting to one side, he remained standing, all four limbs splayed out; and as if to proclaim his achievement, he emitted a gurgly 'Naaarh' while Deidre curled her tongue round his head with a reassuring 'Naaarh' of her own.

'Dear old Deidre,' murmured one twin, looking over the half-door of the barn.

'She is a dear, yes,' said the other, gazing in as well. 'Best if we left her to it.'

'I think it's best, Madge,' said the first, nodding.

'That's what I said, Rosie.'

'I heard you.'

'It's fine by you then?'

'I think it's best, Madge.'

'You've already said that.'

'Just agreeing with you.'

'You think the same then.'

'I do, Madge.'

'We think it's best,' they chorused, swinging round, as one, to look at me. 'What do you think?'

Oh dear. Best to say our goodbyes, and we did so with the customary addition of 'Contact us if you have any worries.'

Hopefully, the Stockwells wouldn't have any worries. I couldn't say the same about myself. I drove ahead up the gravel track from the farm and stopped at one side to open the gate and allow Lucy through in her Fiesta. Was I opening the gate to a new future together or, to judge from the lack of acknowledgement as she drove away, just closing the gate firmly on our relationship, in much the same way as I slammed the Stockwells' gate shut, once I'd driven through it? Hmm … only time would tell.

4
COTTAGE SPY

I'd first bumped into Lucy last June, on the day I went for an interview at Prospect House – 'bumped' in the literal sense of the word.

I'd breezed in that day, surprisingly undaunted by the prospect of the interview, although I was aware that one of the Principals of the practice, Dr Crystal Sharpe, had quite a reputation in the veterinary world as a leading figure in hospital management – in fact, she had been instrumental in turning Prospect House into the country's first small animal hospital some 26 years earlier; and I already knew from papers she'd had published in the *Veterinary Record* that she had a keen interest in orthopaedics and was on several high-profile committees dealing with issues of animal welfare.

Bounding through the front door, I almost tripped over the young nurse. She was behind it, stooped over a mop, wiping the floor.

'Whoops, sorry,' I exclaimed, careering to one side, narrowly missing her. I was aware of hazel eyes, blonde wispy hair, a lock of which had fallen loose across her forehead, and an elfin-like, freckled face which was to jump about in my imagination during the weeks to come.

It was the Richardsons' foaling that brought us together – difficult, fussy clients of Crystal's. Lucy had helped out that night, as unflappable and efficient as she was with the Stockwells. After the foaling, we'd driven back over the Downs as dawn had broken, the eastern sky a ribbon of pink. I'd stopped to look across undulating fields slowly being brushed with yellow by the rising sun and, on the coast, the sea had begun to sparkle like a necklace of diamonds being gradually drawn from its black velvet box. We'd sat in companionable silence, absorbing the view until I reached over and tentatively laid my hand on hers. It wasn't retracted. How different this latest encounter at the Stockwells had been – a blanket of fog ... a cold, depressing outlook ... the slamming of a gate about to fall apart. It didn't bode well.

Yet, in the previous six months, we'd got along fine. There had been ups and downs, but nothing that couldn't be sorted. And during that time, we were very lucky to have the practice cottage, Willow Wren – over the Downs at Ashton – at our disposal. It was the end of a terrace of three 19th-century labourers' cottages – the other two now converted into one – and had been built by the village pond with its fringe of willows, hence the name. The pond disappeared in the 1970s to be replaced by bland, lookalike, three-bedroom properties which now surrounded the cottage to the east and south, although an original high, flint wall granted a degree of privacy for its long, narrow back garden.

At the front of the property was a tiny square of lawn which you could look out onto from the lounge and the bedroom above it; beyond, through a coppice of spindly silver birches and three towering beech trees, in which there was a large rookery, you could just make out St Mary's Church, the incumbent of which, Reverend James, was to become a colourful character in our lives.

The cottage itself was whitewashed with a red-tiled roof sloping down to a more recently added kitchen. The two ground-floor rooms had been knocked into one, the original oak beams of the ceilings, still with their chamfered edges, exposed, and the large fireplace, concealed for years behind 1950s and then 1970s-styled fire surrounds, had been uncovered and restored with a new honey-coloured oak bressumer and a facing of old bricks. The kitchen door led onto a small, south-facing patio, a great suntrap sheltered by the wooden panels of next door's fence. Here we were to enjoy many alfresco meals, but also some moody ones, as our relationship bucked and swayed.

There was a small, raised brick edging to the patio, beyond which a narrow lawn stretched down parallel to the wall, the border between the two a mass of cottage garden-style bulbs, shrubs and plants. It was a delight to get on the Internet and track down the names of the different species and I anticipated the arrival of spring when some of the shrubs would burst into bloom. Little did I realise that, when that time came, my anguished thoughts would be elsewhere, pushing the yellow of forsythia, the sweet smelling pink of daphnia and the striking red of japonica to the furthest recesses of my mind.

What delighted Lucy the most when she first moved in with me – apart from the limitless sex on offer – was the discovery of a row of small aviaries running down the length of the flint wall, partially buried beneath a jungle of rambling roses and brambles.

'What a find!' she exclaimed enthusiastically. 'It's just what I want ...' a phrase I heard on several occasions in our bedroom, as well.

Within days, she'd trained in the roses and hacked back the brambles; she then set to on restoring the flights, converting them into accommodation for her collection of budgerigars, one rabbit and two guinea pigs.

To this small menagerie was later added Gertie, our Embden goose, given to me to fatten up for Christmas, but becoming a pet when she alerted us to an impending burglary.

Then there were three cats, headed by Queenie, a long-haired, white-and-grey Persian, who reigned over the others, hence her title; and an elderly, sweet-natured, but deaf, Jack Russell called Nelson – the black patch over his left eye accounting for his name, despite Lord Nelson having been blinded in his right eye. His previous owner, an elderly lady who had gone into a residential home, obviously hadn't been that strong on her history. Perhaps she would have been safer calling him Patch.

Lucy and I had been in Willow Wren just over two months, delighting in its garden and delighting in each other, when Joan and Doug Spencer, our neighbours next door in Mill Cottage, informed us they were selling up.

'We want to be nearer our daughter over in Gloucestershire,' Joan explained. 'And what with the two grandchildren growing up so fast, we felt it best to make the move now.'

'Wonder who we'll get as new neighbours?' pondered Lucy, peeping out of the front window as the 'For Sale' board went up next door.

The Spencers had kept themselves very much to themselves and were extremely tolerant of all that went on in our cottage, especially as the partition wall was thin and none too soundproof … as I discovered one weekend when I was attempting to do a patch-up job in the bathroom. The timber-framed dividing wall had plaster infill, layered on laths of wood, and one small section of plaster just above floor level had dropped out. I was on hands and knees, prising out the loose edges, when a strip of exposed wood splintered, and plaster on the Spencers' side fell away, leaving a gaping hole.

'Bloody hell,' I muttered. I'm not sure what it is about peepholes but the very name conjures up an eye voyeuristically peering through, spying on whoever might be on the other side. And I confess I was guilty of being one of those Peeping Toms. I was squinting through the hole just as Joan came into her bathroom, pulled down her knickers and squatted on the loo, inches away from my face. Whoops.

Doug was very understanding about my botched attempt at DIY. 'That's the problem with old houses,' he said cheerfully, as he set to and repaired their damaged side of the partition wall with me watching – from his side not mine. 'You never know what you're going to find.'

I agreed wholeheartedly, as I tried to banish the image of his wife with her knickers round her ankles.

It was only a matter of a week or so before their cottage was sold and a speedy completion meant the Spencers moved out in late August.

'I think you'll like the new owner,' said Joan, coming round to say her goodbyes, as the removals van shunted its way out of the hard standing adjacent to their cottage and, with much grating of gears, pushed down through the tunnel of silver birch trees and out past Willow Wren. 'She's a widow whose son lives over in Chawcombe. He's the vicar of St Augustine's.'

'Oh, you mean Charles Venables,' I exclaimed.

'You know him?'

I did. Well, sort of. Only last month, I'd been coerced into judging the pets at St Augustine's annual church fête – a last-minute replacement for their usual vet who had gone suspiciously AWOL. I could see why he had done so, once the judging got under way. It was a chaotic, shambolic affair and, in the end, suffering from the plethora of demanding, threatening owners and the seemingly endless number of fat, slobbering black Labradors that were presented to me, I decided the winner would be a lad with a well-behaved Labrador, not realising I'd chosen the Reverend Charles' own dog. All very embarrassing.

Once the Spencers had departed, we awaited, with interest, the arrival of Mrs Venables. Not that we were being nosey, mind you. Just a little curious. I wouldn't want anyone to think we suffered from what I call 'net curtain twitch'. But Lucy and I were both standing to one side of the upstairs bedroom window – the best vantage point – mugs of coffee in our hands, when the removals men arrived and started unloading the lady's belongings from the back of their van, which they'd conveniently reversed up really close, enabling us to peer straight down into it. Excellent.

'Hey, look,' exclaimed Lucy, using a finger to move the curtain slightly back to get a better view, 'she's got a piano.' It was a small upright, nothing grand. 'Wonder if she plays?'

'No doubt we'll hear if she does,' I replied, thinking of the lack of sound-proofing.

'That's a nice dining table. Looks Victorian,' she said, as the removals men manoeuvred an elegant, oval table with pedestal legs down the ramp. 'And that chaise. Very classy,' she added. 'Although I don't like the red brocade. Bit old-fashioned. Still, she's certainly got some tasteful pieces.'

'Honestly, Lucy,' I said, pulling her away from the window. 'Don't be so nosey.' But I couldn't resist one last look and spotted a removals man carrying in a large aspidistra in an ornate, green-and-purple china pot. Nice.

When, the next day, Mrs Venables came round to introduce herself, she was very much as I'd expected a lady who owned a piano and an aspidistra to be. Mind you, we'd already sussed her, watching her the day before, trotting in and out to the removals van, giving orders in a crisp, no-nonsense tone of voice, very much in control – not that we could actually hear what she was saying, try as we might – the outer walls of the cottage were solid and over a foot deep, and we thought it a little too obvious to open the window. We weren't that nosey. Besides, later, we could always put our ears to the partition wall.

'Hello, I'm your new neighbour,' she said when I opened the front door. 'Eleanor Venables. Thought I'd pop round to make myself known.' She held out her hand and we exchanged a very firm handshake. I judged Eleanor to be in her early sixties. She had a round moon face, a little wrinkled round the eyes, echoed by a deep line running down from each corner of her mouth, which had the effect of divorcing her chin from the rest of her features and gave the impression of a ventriloquist's dummy being manipulated from behind – the chin jolted up and down when she spoke. The impression was maintained by brown eyes, flecked with grey, which swivelled past my shoulder as she took in the contents of our tiny hallway and then zeroed in to fix on me. But this lady was no dummy. You could tell from the cut of the heather tweed jacket and skirt she was wearing and the finely embroidered white blouse that Eleanor had taste. And the thick sweep of platinum-grey hair, tied back in a perfect chignon, gave her a slightly imperial image, which, coupled with the fragrance of lily of the valley – a perfume my mother adored – made for an attractive if slightly formidable lady – one who I envisaged could make an ideal president of the local Women's Institute, and run it with charm and decorum while ensuring everything got done exactly the way she wanted.

Her way, at that precise moment, was to be asked in, and, having introduced myself, I felt obliged to invite her to step inside. 'I'm afraid it's a bit of a mess,' I apologised as Eleanor surged past me and swept into our living room.

'But charming all the same,' she replied. 'I do so like your fireplace. I have a similar one, although mine has the original brickwork.' She walked over to the fireplace and ran her hand down the brick veneer. 'That could always be taken off I suppose.' She reached up and patted the oak bressumer. 'Mine's original. But at least this one's in keeping.'

I felt the tic in my temple begin to start up. Ever so slightly, but there nevertheless.

'Still,' she said, turning to me, 'we must feel privileged to live in something that's part of our national heritage. Don't you think?' She arched her grey eyebrows imperiously.

I couldn't argue with that; and didn't dare.

The sound of the back door opening was a welcome distraction. Lucy's voice called out from the kitchen. 'Paul, Bugsie's got the bloody squits again. I told you we should have cut down on his greens.'

'Er, Lucy,' I shouted, 'our new neighbour's just popped round to see us.' I smiled weakly at Eleanor.

'Oh shit, sorry.' It was Lucy again. 'Just get my boots off. Won't be a sec.'

Eleanor's chin worked up and down. 'So tell me, Paul, how long have you and, er – Lucy, is it? – lived here?'

'Just on three months,' interrupted Lucy, emerging from the kitchen in stockinged feet. 'Hello, I'm Lucy.'

Eleanor stretched out her hand.

'Better not,' said Lucy, 'just been mucking out Bugsie's hutch.'

Eleanor's hand was rapidly withdrawn.

'Would you like a cup of coffee?'

'Er, maybe another time. When you're not so busy.'

And not so dirty, I'm sure she was thinking.

'Oh, we're always busy, aren't we, Paul?' said Lucy, pushing a strand of hair from her eye. 'That's the way it is when you have animals.' As if on cue, Nelson snuffled through from where he'd been snoozing in the kitchen and stopped a metre or so from Eleanor.

The terrier looked up at her with rheumy eyes and emitted a high-pitched woof.

Startled, Eleanor took a step back.

'Don't worry,' I reassured. 'Nelson's perfectly harmless. A real softie. But he's getting on and is a bit deaf.' I bent down and tickled Nelson's ears. He gave another little woof vaguely in the direction of Eleanor and then, having decided he'd done his duty by alerting us to the presence of a stranger in the cottage, he ambled back to his box in the kitchen.

'Have you any pets?' I asked her, thinking that she wasn't really the type to have a pet; besides, I hadn't seen any sign of one yesterday. So I was surprised when she told us that, yes, she did have a pet – a tortoiseshell cat called Tammy. As she mentioned the cat's name, her face lit up.

'She is very independent,' Eleanor said. 'But then aren't all cats?' She uttered a tinkling laugh.

Uhmm … I could foresee problems arising when Queenie and co. met the new cat on their territory.

'You can say that again,' said Lucy, heartily. 'My Queenie can be an absolute bugger.'

Eleanor's face dropped. Her chin snapped up and down. 'Well, I'm sure we'll all get along,' she said, a little hesitantly, her confidence ebbing slightly. 'Meanwhile, I mustn't keep you. I've got lots to do as you can imagine.'

'Do you need anything,' asked Lucy, wiping her hands down the sides of her jeans. 'Milk, sugar?'

Eleanor shook her head firmly. 'Oh no, dear. I brought everything with me. I always like to be well prepared.'

I'm sure you do, Eleanor, I thought. I'm sure you do. But it turned out she wasn't prepared for what occurred in the ensuing months.

5

LET US PREY

It started with a decapitated mouse.

'Tammy, how could you?'

I didn't have to put my ear to the partition wall to hear our neighbour's cry of anguish. Although muffled, it was pretty clear that Tammy had done something to annoy Eleanor. Later that Saturday afternoon, I discovered the cause of her vexation when, as I was doing a spot of weeding in the long border running down the back of our garden, I saw the top of Eleanor's grey head over the panelled fencing that divided our two properties. She was muttering to herself, her tone of voice plainly reprimanding.

I was in a good mood, relishing my weekend off, taking advantage of the glorious, late summer sunshine to work through any hassles at the practice – and there had been a few – by venting them on some serious gardening; in particular, cutting back the edge of the lawn where it had encroached on the border and endeavouring to ensure I kept a straight line down from the cottage. It really was a pleasure to be working with such rich, dark, loamy soil, and I could imagine the owners or tenants working the same patch down the centuries. My unearthing, last week, of some shards of clay pipes just reinforced that feeling.

So seeing Eleanor walking down her garden prompted me to put a temporary halt to my spadework and, resting one foot on the heel of the spade, I called out cheerfully, 'Hi there, Eleanor. Grand afternoon, isn't it?'

The grey head stopped, approached the fence and Eleanor's moon face rose over it. It wasn't exactly radiant. 'It would be if it wasn't for the likes of this ...' A yellow, rubber-gloved hand appeared, holding between finger and thumb the tail of a headless mouse whose body swung beneath it. 'Tammy brought this in and deposited it on my hearth rug.' There was a visible twitch of disgust from the moon face. 'I was just going to bury it.' Her other hand appeared, equally sheathed in a yellow rubber glove in similar mint condition, but this one was holding a pristine trowel which caught the sun and flashed at me.

I rammed my spade in the edge of the border and walked over, stepping onto a small pile of bricks which I'd neatly stacked there, remnants of the edging to the patio I'd constructed earlier in the summer – with Crystal's blessing, of course, as it wasn't my property. Why stack them there, halfway down the garden, alongside the boundary fence? Well, no obvious reason, although it did make it easier to get a better view of my neighbour's garden when no one was about. It was an attractive garden, twice the size of ours, being formerly two plots before the pair of cottages had been combined; the Spencers had obviously spent a lot of time redesigning it with the incorporation of a screened-off vegetable plot and a secluded patio – which became significantly less secluded if I stood on my pile of bricks. Right at the bottom of the plot, in one corner, they'd created a tiny wild patch, consisting of a pond flanked by a clump of reeds, with a couple of water lilies on its surface and a bank of native plants – pink campion, bergamot and meadowsweet amongst them – which were allowed to grow unhindered. It was to this spot that Eleanor was heading.

I was in the mood for a bit of a chinwag but Eleanor, waving the decapitated mouse at me, said, 'I'd rather get rid of this first, if you don't mind.'

I watched as she resolutely continued with her rodent disposal strategy, her tall, angular figure clad that afternoon in all the classic colours one would choose for such treks into the wilderness ... even though it was only a patch of overgrown garden: spotless, green corduroy trousers; matching green waistcoat over a light-green linen, short-sleeved shirt; and soft, green rubber wellies, complete with buckles at their tops. The only accessories that clashed with her country image were the pristine yellow gloves – and, of course, the headless mouse.

Once the carcass had been disposed of by burial beneath a holly bush, Eleanor negotiated the circular slabs set round the edge of the pond; she did it with arms stretched out, gloves held up in front of her, and studied each stone circle before placing a boot precisely in its centre. She dithered a moment when the stones stopped at the edge of the lawn and then, having decided the dry turf was unlikely to foul her wellingtons, she crossed over to continue her chat with me.

'I do wish Tammy would stop bringing in these offerings,' she said, with a little shudder, waving her now slightly soiled trowel in the air. 'Such a beastly habit.'

But, as with all habits, it was to be repeated. And only a few days later.

Lucy and I had just got home from Prospect House, having been on the early rota so that we finished at 5.00pm, which meant we had a few hours before it got dark to unwind; on such occasions we would often have a mug of tea on our little patio and soak in a bit of late afternoon sunshine. That day was no exception. There were a few straggling, pink roses still in flower over the kitchen door and, lying on my lounger, eyes half closed, I could hear the drone of several bees as they dragged themselves from bloom to bloom. From beyond the front of Willow Wren came the noisy cawing of the rooks returning to their nests in the beeches adjacent to Reverend James' garden; but their cacophony was sufficiently muted by the intervening cottage walls so as not to be intrusive. The same couldn't be said for the Reverend – he was driven to distraction by the daily onslaught, which he often blamed for his disjointed sermons, having been disturbed in the writing of them by the rooks. I'd often seen him from our front window, pacing up and down the rectory garden, with his notes in hand, waving them at the nests above him. Perhaps seeking divine intervention? But I guessed not. Unlike St Francis of Assisi, whose compassion for animals had elevated him to being their patron saint, James did not emulate this, judging by his incessant fist waving and the stream of invectives that poured out from his garden.

Feeling exhausted after another strenuous day at the surgery, with the sun still sufficiently warm on my face to lull me into semi-slumber, I began to nod off, vaguely aware that Lucy, on the lounger next to me, had also fallen asleep – there was soft, sibilant snoring coming from her direction.

Then came the scream … a high-pitched, wavering scream.

'Bloody hell! What on earth was that?' I exclaimed, jolted from my reverie with such a start that I found myself sitting bolt upright, staring wildly round me.

Lucy's eyes fluttered open. 'What?' she said, yawning.

'That scream. Didn't you hear it?' Further explanation was

unnecessary, as from the other side of the fence adjacent to our kitchen came the distraught voice of Eleanor Venables.

'Why, you horrible little cat. How disgusting!'

'Uh-oh ... something's up,' I whispered to Lucy, giving her a lopsided grin. They say curiosity kills the cat, but I was prepared to take that risk and leapt from my lounger and sprang onto the pile of bricks I'd stacked next to the kitchen in case I ever needed to peep over the fence. Well, you never know when you might have to look in on a neighbour. Like now.

'Why, Eleanor, whatever's the matter?' I exclaimed, heaving into sight to look down at her, my eyes like organ stops, gagging to find out what was going on.

Although Eleanor had sounded distressed, the sight of me ogling her ensured her customary composure was rapidly restored. She was standing just inside the kitchen door and pointed to the step. 'It's Tammy again. Just look.' On the step were the mangled remains of the back end of an animal; grey fur, two legs, and a bloody trail of guts spilling from the severed abdominal cavity.

'What is it?' asked Eleanor, putting a hand to her mouth.

'Looks like a rabbit to me.'

From my side of the fence, there was a gasp from Lucy. 'It's not our Bugsie is it?'

'No, no,' I said, turning round to reassure her. Our rabbit had distinctive black-and-white markings, whereas the half of rabbit lying at Eleanor's feet was plain grey ... apart from the splashes of red.

I did the gallant thing and went round to shovel up the mortal remains and then, later, having dissected out the bones, gave them to Nelson for his tea. Waste not, want not. And certainly Nelson appreciated them. He licked his bowl clean, pushing it noisily round the tiled floor of the kitchen, and then waddled into the sitting room, wagging his stumpy tail, and gave a loud burp.

He wouldn't have cared for the next trophy Tammy brought in.

I was first alerted by the frantic ringing of our front-door bell. Well, not so much a ringing, since water had got into the workings and it now sounded more like a frog being garrotted. Whatever, summoned by the persistent croak, croak, croak, I found a very agitated Eleanor Venables standing on the iron grille in front of our door, her brown brogues lifting alternately as if she were marching on the spot – thereby tapping out a metallic, rhythmic beat from the grille beneath them. Add to this Eleanor's strident tones, and one could sense a military campaign in the making. And I guessed, correctly, that I was going to be the advance guard.

'Oh, Paul, thank goodness you're in,' she said, her hands clutching the lapels of her jacket, several strands of her normally well-coiffured hair blowing across her face. 'You just won't believe what Tammy's brought in now.' Eleanor stopped shifting on the spot and shivered. 'It's all too much. You'll have to get it out for me.'

'Sorry, I don't quite understand.'

'It's wriggled into my drawers. You'll have to get it out for me.'

For a brief moment I thought something had become lodged in her underwear, hence the agitation and marching on the spot, but I quickly dismissed that as a product of my overactive and puerile imagination. Nevertheless, I felt myself blush at the thought. Eleanor, perceptive as always, even in her current predicament, was quick to read my thoughts as she went on to state quite sharply, 'I meant "under" not "in" my drawers, Paul. My *chest* of drawers.'

'Sorry, sorry,' I murmured. 'For a moment I thought ...'

'Yes, yes,' interrupted Eleanor, dismissively, while colouring a little. 'But, whatever, I'd appreciate your help in getting it out for me.'

The 'it' in question turned out to be a young grass snake which Eleanor had spotted Tammy carrying upstairs, its front and back ends thrashing about from both sides of the cat's mouth. Eleanor had chased after the cat in time to see her drop it on one of her slippers, from whence the snake rapidly slithered under her furniture.

'Can you see it?' she queried, as I lay stretched out on her carpet, peering into the darkness under her drawers.

'No. Can't see a thing. Maybe it's crawled elsewhere.' It was a statement which prompted Eleanor to leap onto her bed with a 'Oh my God ...' and a '... you must find it for me.'

There were several likely bolt-holes in Eleanor's bedroom. The dressing table – a nice Edwardian piece with inlaid wood round its edge and a fluted, oval mirror – could be dismissed as it had fine, tapered legs supporting it well clear of the floor. The matching wardrobe, with glass infill doors, was another matter. A snake could have easily slithered behind it in the gap I could see between the wardrobe and the skirting board. Then, there was the bed. A rather splendid, heavy, wide structure with a high headboard carved with wreaths of flowers, echoed by the base with similar ornate carvings; and between them a rich, quilted cover – a patchwork of golds and reds – complemented by four large, tapestry cushions. A snake could have got lost in all of that, although, while I knew that grass snakes can climb, I didn't think this youngster would have done so; and besides, if I'd suggested that as a possibility, Eleanor would have hit the roof – well, the ceiling at least, there not being much headroom between that and her bed. No, better to leave her cowering among her cushions and explore the more obvious area under the bed. And that's where I found the snake, coiled up next to the socket for her bedside lamp. Imagine her reaching down to turn off her light and touching the snake. What a shock that would have been. Especially if it had wriggled and thrashed the way it did when I grabbed it.

Having pulled it out, I got to my feet and reassured Eleanor that I'd release the snake well away from her cottage.

'You might not have to,' said Eleanor, climbing down off her bed to cautiously look at the snake from a safe distance. 'Looks dead to me.'

The young snake had indeed gone limp in my hand, and its head had twisted round and its jaws had dropped open. I knew that feigning death was a defensive mechanism in grass snakes to deter would-be predators and explained this to Eleanor.

'So the snake's still alive?' she said, her chin clicking furiously up and down.

'Yes.'

Eleanor leapt back on the bed.

I suggested putting the grass snake down in her patch of wild garden, next to her pond, as they liked damp areas, but she was adamant that, if I did, she'd never, ever venture down there again. So I found myself traipsing round the side of Willow Wren and down the footpath alongside our back wall, to an area just beyond the end of the garden which was boggy with a few clumps of reeds and a row of three huge willow trees, all that remained of the village pond that had once been there. The snake continued to lie limply in my hand, but I was now aware of the other defensive mechanism used by grass snakes – the secretion of a foul-smelling liquid. The snake had squirted the fluid out before trying its death act, and it had oozed over my fingers so they now reeked like fish fingers that had been putrefying in the sun for several days. Boy, did they pong.

Having curled the inert snake up under some reeds, I returned to Willow Wren and was immediately ejected by Lucy as being unbearably offensive due to my rancid hands. I then spent the next five minutes or so scrubbing my fingers and nails under the outside tap with the soap and scrubbing brush Lucy had flung out of the window.

A few months later, I was to be deemed 'offensive' by her again, although then it was not due to whiffy fingers – more, as she saw it, to my malodorous mood. Hmm …. she could talk! But that was the trouble – she didn't. She kept things bottled up. I felt sure it was only going to be a matter of time before all those pent-up emotions would explode. But when?

It was early March, that time when spring is beginning to show itself. The crocuses were out, the daffodils were beginning to nod their yellow heads and there was a stirring of nature, birds more strident in their singing, bustling through the hedgerows, nest building. Tammy, too, had become more alert, as if, after a temporary hibernation, she'd awoken to sally forth and claim her first trophy of the fledgling year.

Eleanor Venables brought it round in a shoebox. 'What do you think it is?' she asked as I lifted the lid and gently pulled back the tissues Eleanor had placed over it. She'd mentioned on the phone, before coming round, that Tammy had brought in a bird which was in a state of shock and would I please have a look at it. So I was expecting a stressed blue tit, robin, maybe a wren, but certainly not what the removal of the tissues revealed.

'Good Lord,' I exclaimed, carefully lifting out the bird.

75

There was no mistaking the grey plumage, the distinctive yellow crest and yellow cheeks with their splash of orange on either side. 'It's a cockatiel.'

'How on earth could Tammy have got hold of that?' queried Eleanor.

I shrugged. 'Escaped pet, maybe?' Either that or Tammy had stalked into someone's house and pounced; but that seemed highly unlikely. 'Whatever, the bird's pretty shocked.' I carefully stretched out each wing to check if either was broken. They were fine. I ran a finger up through the bird's feathers, both on its back and underneath. No signs of puncture wounds from Tammy's teeth. In fact, the cockatiel seemed remarkably unscathed; but it was breathing rapidly, its beak wide open, and was staring, unblinking.

'Best thing is to keep it in this box, in a warm place, and give it a chance to recover,' I said, replacing the bird and putting the lid back on. 'Let's see how it is in a couple of hours.'

I didn't need to be told by Eleanor that the cockatiel had recovered. It was all too clear from the screeching that suddenly started up later that day and which the partition wall did nothing to muffle. And over the next few days, it started to become a source of irritation to both Lucy and me. It wasn't so bad in the evenings when we got home from work as it was getting dark by then, and we assumed the cockatiel had settled down to sleep for the night since it was quiet next door. But with dawn breaking earlier as the days progressed, our wake-up call from the bird's wretched screeching slipped back each morning.

'For Pete's sake, tell her to keep the bird covered up,' Lucy moaned one morning as the cockatiel's shrill squawk drilled through the wall at 5.45am and woke us both up.

But even with an old curtain draped over the cage I'd lent Eleanor from the hospital, it made no difference. I guess the cockatiel heard the birds outside begin to twitter and thought he'd contribute in his own Aussie way. No problem had he been in the Outback. He could have shrieked to his heart's content. But next door in Ashton was a different kettle of fish.

And talking of fish, I was reminded of the fishy fingers I'd had to endure last September when I rescued Eleanor Venables from the coils of that young grass snake. Although I didn't begrudge having done it and wasn't expecting any favours in return, I did feel a bit niggled that she wasn't now being a little more sympathetic to our grievances over the cockatiel's screeching. Besides, I thought all the squawking would be irritating for her, too. Not a bit of it, as she explained when I went round to confront her over the matter.

'What's a little chirrup here and there,' she said, 'when it's meant Tammy's stopped bringing home all those poor little creatures?'

It seemed the cockatiel had become a distraction for Tammy.

'She's forever stalking under Wilfred's cage,' admitted Eleanor. 'So I do have to be a bit careful. But better that than having snakes and the like in the house.'

Wilfred, eh? Hmm. It seemed Eleanor was becoming quite attached to the bird. I dug my ex-fishy fingers into my palms and tried another tack, reminding her that maybe this 'Wilfred' was someone's pet and that he was being missed. That was a mistake.

I got a severe look of reprimand from Eleanor; her grey-flecked eyes narrowed, a furrow appeared between them, as her jaw momentarily clamped shut only to flick open and for her to say curtly, 'I did put a card in the corner stores. But there's been no response.' Slapped wrist, Paul.

So it looked as if Lucy and I would have to put up with Wilfred's vocals, they being in stark contrast to ours – ours being negligible; Lucy and I were still in non-communicative mode. We resorted to using the spare earplugs left over from the days when we had our own noisy cockatoo – Liza – whom eventually, driven to distraction by her shrieks and squawks, we managed to re-home. Ironically, it was with Eleanor Venables' son, the rector of St Augustine's over in Chawcombe – he and his wife were potty about parrots and had four of their own before Liza's arrival. Sad to say, though, I only used the earplugs at night to ensure I wasn't woken up too early. The feeling I got when I pushed them into my ear canals – one of disconnecting from the world – was a feeling that I was reluctant to part with in the mornings when I had to unplug myself and reconnect with the real world and the sharing of it with Lucy. I think she felt the same, although we didn't have the time, or – more likely – didn't have the inclination, to discuss it and work through our problems. But had I had Madam Mountjoy's ability to see into the future and realise what was going to happen only weeks away, then I might have felt differently.

In the event, I could have discarded those earplugs regardless of what was going to happen between me and Lucy, since one Sunday morning there was silence from next door. Not one squawk. Not the slightest chirrup. For a moment, I thought maybe I'd dislodged a lump of wax in my ear, leaving it smeared across my eardrum and causing temporary deafness; but no, I could hear Lucy slamming about downstairs in the kitchen all too clearly.

I finished shaving and went down.

'Quiet next door, isn't it?' I said. 'Wonder if anything's happened to Wilfred.'

I got a sullen look and a shrug for my efforts. 'There's some breakfast in the bottom oven,' said Lucy. 'I'm going out to feed the animals.'

After a rather charred couple of rashers of bacon and a slice of toast and marmalade, washed down with my standard mug of green tea, I nipped out to get the Sunday papers from down the road at the corner stores and returned to find Eleanor Venables standing at the little gate that led into our back garden, discussing something with Lucy. The way Eleanor was leaning over the gate, her hands gripping the ironwork, her jaw working up and down furiously, I sensed we had another crisis to deal with.

'Ah, Paul, just the man,' she said, turning from Lucy as I approached, papers tucked under one arm. 'It's Wilfred. He's gone missing.'

My immediate reaction was to shout 'Yippee' and punch the air with my free arm, thinking perhaps we'd no longer have to put up with the cockatoo's screeching; but realising that would appear unseemly in a supposedly kind and caring vet, plus the sight of Eleanor's moon face etched with distress – not to mention Lucy's glare – I decided a more sympathetic approach was required. So I masked any elation by putting on a face which I hoped showed sufficient concern and said in a voice which I hoped echoed that concern, 'Oh, I'm sorry to hear that …' a statement which had Lucy narrowing her eyes and pursing her lips contemptuously.

'Yes,' said Eleanor. 'I came down this morning and found the cage door open. You can imagine how I felt.' She clasped a hand to her bosom. 'My first thoughts were that Tammy had got him as there were no signs of him anywhere.' For a moment Eleanor's jaw stopped clicking

79

up and down, and then began again. 'But I don't think she has. She's stalking round the cottage, sniffing in all the corners as if she's trying to find him. So I think we should try as well.'

'Sorry?' I said, perplexed.

Lucy interjected. 'Eleanor's asking if you'd go round the village with her. See if you can track down Wilfred. I've told her you wouldn't mind.' A thin smile played across her lips. Thanks, Lucy.

'I'm so sorry to disturb your Sunday, Paul,' said Eleanor. 'But it would be very helpful. Besides, a lady on her own ... you never know.' Eleanor thrust her hands into her quilted jacket and pushed her elbows into her sides. It seemed she was wary of who she might bump into in the undergrowth of Ashton, other than a cockatiel. But I didn't think she had anything to be frightened of. The occasional gaggle of youths hung out with their BMXs on the recreation ground next to the sports hall and there was the old girl who daily would sit over on one of the council benches to feed the squirrels. Still, Lucy had already committed me to escorting Eleanor round, so I really didn't have any choice in the matter. As to what we'd do if we did find Wilfred, I hadn't a clue. Seems Eleanor had a plan, though.

'I thought if I popped back and got Wilfred's cage and some bird seed, we might persuade him in. Should we spot him, of course. What do you think?'

I thought it an extremely silly idea but, before I could say anything, Lucy remarked, 'Worth a go. Unless Paul has any other bright ideas?' She gave me a look that spoke of undisguised ill-feeling. What could I say? It was already a done deal.

So Eleanor excused herself and hurried back to her cottage, returning with the bird cage and a large packet of seed. The cage was large and she found it difficult to carry; every so often it dipped down and dragged along the ground.

Lucy seized the opportunity to say, 'Let Paul take that.' I'm damn sure there was a smirk on her face as she suggested it.

So, five minutes later, I found myself struggling round the muddy perimeter of the recreation field, trying to keep the cage clear of the ground, as I slid, slopped, squelched and got soaked from the wet shrubs I was struggling through, while Eleanor kept her well-manicured self on the safety of the tarmac path. Hell's bells. What were we going to do if we spotted Wilfred? Was Eleanor going to call out to him, 'Come along, Wilfred. You've been a naughty boy. It's time you came home now,' and get me to put the cage down and then expect him to fly over and hop in once I had opened it, having scattered some seed in front of it and backed away on tiptoe? Fat chance.

And, of course, I was proved right. Not that we ever caught a glimpse of Wilfred. No. Not a dicky bird. In fact, very few birds. One wren trilled in alarm from the safety of a thicket of holly and a robin hopped out onto a branch and peered down at me before deciding to beat a hasty retreat. As I trailed round, I was subjected to the sniggers of some youths in baggy jeans, looped round their thighs, exposing the elastic of their designer underwear, who slouched by; they had whooped and jeered, nudging one another and pointing the finger – second one, upright, palm facing inwards – at me. Even Reverend James pointed a finger – first one, also upright, wagging – at us from behind the safety of the rectory's front window.

We thought he was indicating the possible whereabouts of Wilfred. Either that or he meant the bird had passed away and was heading heavenwards. He opened the window and leaned out to explain. As usual with James Matthews, the explanation was long and circumlocutory, spoken in his customary braying, droning voice, which, every Sunday, proved a challenge to his meagre congregation as they attempted to stave off impending somnolence, to which only the jarring interjections of the rooks outside prevented them from succumbing.

He said, 'I was latterly perusing the notes for the sermon I intend to deliver this evening when on looking out of this window from which I'm now leaning, I happened to espy a bird which, to my recollection, is not one of our native species and surmised that this bird, being, by my deduction, to have originated from more exotic climes and therefore being in flight across the rectory garden, must have escaped from the confines of someone's abode. And thus seeing you with a cage equipped to house such a bird I suspected you were seeking something comparable to that, if, indeed, not the bird that passed me by.' The vicar took a deep breath. 'Would I be correct?'

In the time he'd taken to inform us he had probably spotted Wilfred, Eleanor and I·had drawn level with his garden. This abutted the rec, separated from it by a flint wall – a wall not high enough to stop passing walkers from getting a good view in if they stood on tiptoe – a fact I soon discovered when taking Nelson for his constitutional – and it was certainly not high enough to discourage local youngsters from chucking over their empty tins of Coke and lager, crisp packets and other silver-foiled items disposed of after sex below the sleeping rooks of a Saturday night. 'God moves in mysterious ways,' Reverend James once murmured as I stopped to pass the time of day as he was collecting various artefacts discarded by local youths during the previous weekend's activities – which on this occasion included a pair of briefs, a sock and a bra. 'Just only wish he'd move them elsewhere.' For once, he was quite succinct as he dropped the discarded garments in a bin bag. Not so today. Reverend James called us round to the side gate which linked the rectory to the church and then hurried out of the house, his cassock billowing about him, to give us a detailed description of the bird he'd 'espied'.

'It was of a size which precluded it being of the tit family and, besides which, it had the colouring which would not have fitted a member of that family, it being grey for the most part, although being in flight and at some distance from the window out of which I was looking, meant that any other coloration of the bird's plumage may have escaped my attention even though I do have a particularly good ability to enable observation of things at a considerable distance without the need to resort to glasses ... although I do have a pair of binoculars which I would have brought to my assistance had there been time to retrieve them from the hall stand where I keep them before the bird had left the garden.' He stopped. A deep intake of breath followed.

'When was that?' I asked.

The Reverend scratched his chin. 'Let me see now. I'd just finished morning service and had come back over for coffee which Marjorie usually has ready for me around 11.15am. I had partaken of several sips when the bird in question flew into view.'

'About half an hour ago then?'

The vicar nodded. 'That would seem a good approximation of the time lapse between then and now.' He clasped his hands together and tilted his head to one side, his lips curling back over a mouthful of teeth like a horse about to neigh. 'Do I surmise the bird may be of your ownership?' He unclasped his hands and pointed to the cage I had dropped by my side.

'It's mine actually,' intervened Eleanor, crisply. 'Wilfred, a cockatiel.'

I turned from Reverend James to Eleanor. 'I'm not sure if you two have met,' I said. That was a mistake.

Reverend James nodded his head vigorously. 'Oh yes, yes. Indeed, we have had the pleasure of making ourselves acquainted when the good lady first moved into Mill Cottage and I made it my duty to call in on her. Is that not so, my dear?'

Eleanor's chin dropped sharply as her mouth opened, but before she had a chance to say anything he went on: 'At that first meeting it was with great pleasure that I discovered through conversation' – no doubt one-sided, I thought – 'that Eleanor, here, already has connections in this part of the world inasmuch as her son, who it transpires is of the same faith as me and went to the same college as me, is the vicar of our neighbouring parish of Chawcombe.' Reverend James beamed benevolently at Eleanor. 'Words failed me, didn't they, my dear?'

They did? My God.

Eleanor reached out and patted his arm. 'Not quite, James. Not quite,' she said, managing, at last, to get a word in.

Having established without a shadow of a doubt that they did know one another, I picked up the cage and pointedly rattled it. 'Well, at least we know Wilfred's alive,' I said. 'Let's just hope he turns up safely somewhere.'

'We can only pray,' murmured Reverend James.

Wilfred did turn up again, although not strictly as prayed for since it was in the jaws of a cat – Tammy's jaws to be precise.

I was alerted by the screeching that erupted from next door the following Thursday afternoon – my half day off. I was giving the back lawn a light cut – the first of the season – when it started. Initially, I thought it was Eleanor having one of her turns, Tammy having started trophy hunting again. I was sort of right and wrong. Right in that Tammy had started to bring things in again; wrong in attributing the screech to Eleanor. It was Wilfred, brought home by Tammy that morning in a somewhat dazed state, but now almost fully recovered as this first screech of the day suggested.

I stood on my pile of bricks by the kitchen while Eleanor filled me in on all the details from the door of her kitchen.

'Little short of a miracle, don't you think?' said the moon-faced woman, beaming from ear to ear. 'Our prayers have been answered.'

'Indeed, yes,' I said, forcing a smile. Reverend James had a lot to answer for, I thought, as Wilfred emitted another piercing shriek from inside the cottage.

It didn't quite end there either. As spring slipped into summer, Tammy's hunting skills were ably demonstrated by the variety of creatures she brought home, usually to be deposited on Eleanor's mat just inside the kitchen door. I was told of some and was witness – from my observation point on top of the bricks – to others. There was the frog that hopped in circles round the kitchen floor; Eleanor collected it up by sliding the slimy green creature into a plastic storage box using the lid and presented it to me, wondering if it was injured. I had little knowledge of amphibians, apart from the few owned by Mr Hargreaves who once came into surgery with a tree frog that, on being X-rayed, showed it had suffered a fractured tibia – it had healed of its own accord. Eleanor's frog seemed fine so was released into her pond. Surprisingly, it was done without a drop of squeamishness from her.

I blew caution to the wind and remarked on her *sangfroid* and the fact that she now never scolded Tammy when she ran in with her offerings.

'Well,' she said, 'it's because Tammy was so wonderful in bringing back Wilfred all in one piece. Completely unscathed. I still can't believe it.' She shook her head, causing her grey chignon to sway slightly. 'So I can't possibly reprimand her now when she returns with her little tokens of affection. It would be so unfair on her.'

Fair enough. It was no real concern of mine as long as I wasn't going to be requested to extract some wriggling reptile from her drawers again. So I was rather surprised, the following Sunday, to hear the raised voice of Eleanor, reprimanding her cat, saying, 'That's really wicked of you, Tammy. Paul will be absolutely furious.'

Me? Furious? Intrigued, I was up on my pile of bricks in a flash. And I have to confess, I could feel a bit of a smirk on my face as I looked over, thinking I was about to see another of Tammy's trophies. And indeed there was another trophy. Eleanor was holding it.

'I'm so sorry,' she said, lifting up the chewed lump of flesh, a guilty look on her face. 'I've a horrible feeling this could be yours.'

She was right. My smirk rapidly vanished as I recognised the lump of mutilated flesh Tammy had sneaked home with – it was the side of pork I'd been defrosting in the kitchen, ready to roast for lunch.

The swine!

6

SUPER-MANNED BUT NEARLY BANNED

When I told Beryl about the mangled joint on the Monday morning, she listened, her head forward, shoulders hunched, her powdered face immobile, the bottom lip of her scarlet mouth hanging open. 'Really? Well, I never!' she remarked when I'd finished; and then, still staring at me lopsidedly, the powder on her face cracked as her lips creased back and she started to snigger, her shoulders began to heave, her eyes – both of them– began to water until, with a loud snort, she started to cackle with laughter, swaying back and forth on her office stool like a demented crow.

'OK ... OK, Beryl,' I huffed. 'It wasn't that funny,' thinking perhaps a little more sympathy should have been forthcoming at the demise of my Sunday lunch. While Beryl reached up the sleeve of her black cardigan to pull out one of her inexhaustible supplies of tissues and dab at the remaining tears still trickling down her face, I turned to look at her computer screen and peered at the list of appointments booked in for me through to 10.30am; the rest of the morning then being left clear for the routine spays, castrates and dentals – most of which would have been admitted already, their owners having signed the consent forms, Mandy or Lucy checking the animals hadn't had food or water overnight, before carrying cat baskets or dragging reluctant dogs down to the kennels. 'Got quite a full morning, I see.'

'The usual Monday morning panic stations,' sniffed Beryl, blowing her nose, her giggling now under control, her face having reverted to its usual deadpan expression. 'By the way, your mention of Mrs Venables and her cockatiel reminds me I've got one booked in for you to see this evening. At least now you'll know what you're looking at.' She said it without a trace of irony. That was the thing with Beryl – she often came out with comments which you could argue were withering or sarcastic but, when spoken with that deadpan face of hers, they left you wondering whether she realised what she was saying. My guess was that she knew precisely what she was saying, as once, when I was having my tea break with her, she admitted that she was a plain speaker and, as a result, would occasionally 'get peoples' backs up'.

Having felt niggled by her reaction to my tale about Tammy, I refused to be drawn any more, and merely gave a tolerant smile. Referring back to the appointments list, I saw a name which I deliberately picked up on. 'I see Mr Entwhistle's coming in this evening,' I remarked casually, and, as suspected, the mention of his name made Beryl's face instantly light up again.

'Yes,' she said, barely able to suppress the enthusiasm in her voice. 'He said on the phone that he's got a new puppy. Wants to bring her in for her vaccinations. Crystal was getting rather booked up so I offered him an appointment with you. He seemed happy enough with that.'

Thanks a bunch, Beryl. Another tolerant smile ... only to have that smile immediately wiped off my face when she continued, 'There's a lady coming in soon with a sick Schnauzer which sounds quite poorly. I thought it could be serious, so I've had to double-book you.'

Beryl didn't elaborate. But I knew that if she considered it serious, it probably was. Beryl had been working at Prospect House for many years now and was experienced enough to sift out any priority cases over the phone; and, indeed, I reckoned she could have diagnosed what was wrong with many of them before they were seen. So I awaited the arrival of the Schnauzer with some trepidation.

Meanwhile, as I was about to leave reception and get ready to start the appointments list, there was a scuffling and skittering of paws on the vinyl behind me as a dog was reluctantly dragged in by a harassed-looking man in his mid-thirties. The man was powerfully built, tall, wearing a brown tweed suit with waistcoat, white shirt and tie, sporting a dark brown trilby and round, brown, framed glasses giving his face an owl-like expression. He looked familiar, although at first I couldn't place him. Then in a flash – a sort of Superman flash – it came to me. A Clark Kent lookalike – him off the *Superman* movies – although the dog he was dragging in was far removed from Krypto, the Superdog of the comic strip. The hound shared the same colouring – white – and had an equally long tail and big ears; but whereas Krypto was a large dog, this one was tiny – a titchy terrier whose large ears and long tail were wildly out of proportion to his small, elongated body, supported by stumpy little legs that barely kept his undercarriage from scraping along the ground. Definitely some Dachshund in his breeding, I thought. A weedy little specimen. So, no Krypto.

However, he was wearing a red jacket which, with a stretch of the imagination, you could have thought of as a cape, although I couldn't see him using it to fly into action. As it turned out, he didn't need anything to fly into action. I found that out to my cost later.

The Clark Kent lookalike had to yank on the dog's lead to drag the terrier across to the reception desk, the dog having now promptly sat down firmly on his haunches, back legs splayed out either side of him, his red cape (jacket) spread out on the floor behind him.

'Oh for heaven's sake, Archie, behave yourself,' said the man, his voice full of exasperation, as he slid the dog forward to draw level with the desk and confront Beryl. The peeved look on her face suggested that she in no way considered herself Lois waiting for Superman to fly in and sweep her into his arms – not that Beryl could possibly have been swept up by anything other than a broomstick, which she'd have fitted admirably with her black clothes, evil eye and long red nails.

'Sorry if I'm a bit late,' said the man, addressing her. 'Got held up in traffic.'

Beryl's normal response to latecomers, whether for admission for ops or for appointments, was an audible click of her tongue against her teeth and a rather tart, 'Well, I'm sure we can still fit you in.'

Her response to this man was no exception.

The little pooch had started to shake and was panting heavily, saliva pouring out of his jowls. The man bent down and scooped him up under his arm.

'Calm down, Archie,' reassured the man, 'no one's going to hurt you.' The man glanced at Beryl and smiled wanly. 'Anyone would think the end of the world was nigh,' he went on. Whoosh. Was he about to turn into the caped crusader, I wondered? The dog shook his head and a string of saliva arched up and over the desktop to splatter down on Beryl's keyboard.

'Archie, for heaven's sake, you're embarrassing me,' said the man, as Beryl pursed her lips, took a tissue from the horde up her sleeve and, with an exaggerated swipe, mopped up the offending dribble and dropped the sodden tissue in her wastepaper basket. 'You must be Mr Henderson,' she said brusquely, checking her computer screen. 'Archie's coming in for a dental. Am I right?'

Mr Henderson nodded. 'Dr Sharpe warned me a few teeth might have to come out.'

Ah, there we go, I thought. One of Crystal's clients. If it had been a ruptured knee ligament or some complicated internal surgery she would have had it booked in to do herself. But rotten teeth. Well, Paul could deal with those. I gritted my own teeth and slipped out ready to start my appointments, having seen two people, both with cat baskets, come in through the front door and who were now queuing behind Superman (Mr Henderson), waiting to be transported to another world (my consulting room).

I was running ten minutes late by the time the double-booked appointment Beryl had mentioned turned up. The poorly Schnauzer I was presented with was of the miniature variety, salt and pepper, with clipped beard and short upright tail. They're normally alert, sharp little dogs, full of vim and vigour. Not so this female. You didn't have to be a vet to see we had a very ill dog here. Her owner, a Mrs Little, did little to hide her feelings as she carried the dog in and lowered her onto the consulting table.

'Thank you for seeing me at such short notice,' she said, her eyes glistening with tears, the mascara round them smudged. 'Bo-Bo's not at all well.' The Schnauzer just lay there, on her sternum, head down between her extended front paws, eyes glazed, unfocused, pupils dilated.

Since starting at Prospect House, I'd gradually perfected a standard approach to my consultations, usually beginning with a 'Good morning/afternoon/evening ...' depending on the time of day, directed at the owners with a 'Come in' as they entered the room, carrying pets in baskets or cages or – in the case of dogs – in arms, or beside or between legs, or sometimes disappearing rapidly down the corridor, being pulled towards the exit.

Having overcome that initial hurdle, I would follow it up with a friendly 'Hello, Tibbles ... Cindy ... Fluffy ... Rex ... Sabre ...' My cheerful 'How are you feeling today?' I had to curtail and use more selectively. It was OK if it were a dog or cat coming in for its annual booster, bright-eyed and bushy-tailed. But for a pet that came in dull-eyed and droopy-tailed, such a phrase was not appropriate as the animal was obviously feeling bloody rotten and would have said as much. For a short spell, I did try 'What can I do for you?' But I stopped that after my encounter with Francesca Cavendish, an out-of-work actress, who had swept into the consulting room with Oscar, a Maltese, wrapped in her pashmina. My 'What can I do for you?' was countered by a 'Darling boy, it's not what you can do for me but what you can do for my darling Oscar.' I then tried 'So what seems to be the problem?' only for Miss Cavendish to retort 'That's for you to find out, sweetie.' After a few months in practice, I acquired a short list of phrases from which I would select one to fit the circumstances of a particular consultation.

My initial observation of Mrs Little's Bo-Bo made me want to utter 'Bloody hell, she's sick!' But that wasn't on my list so I had to resort to an 'Oh dear, we seem to have a poorly little dog here.' Not quite so dramatic but the sentiment expressed was just as heartfelt. I started to ask the standard questions as I examined Bo-Bo.

'How long's she been like this?'

Mrs Little hesitated before she spoke. 'Er, just the last 24 hours.'

I suspected it was longer. Those tears wetting Mrs Little's cheek could have been induced by guilt. Especially when she went on, 'My husband thought it might be a tummy upset. She does get them from time to time.'

'So she's got diarrhoea then?'

'Well, no. But she has been sick several times. And she's off her food.' Mrs Little bent over the Schnauzer and stroked her head. 'I've tried her with all her favourites – tuna ... fresh chicken. But she's not interested.' Mrs Little shook her head and gave a little sob.

By now, I'd checked Bo-Bo's temperature – slightly below normal. Checked her eyelids – congested. Felt her pulse – erratic and sluggish. All suggestive of a toxic dog. My list of differential diagnoses began to narrow. The next two questions would narrow it further and probably allow me to reach a definitive diagnosis.

'Is she drinking more than normal?'

Mrs Little nodded. 'Why yes, heaps more than normal. Could it be her kidneys then?'

I ignored her question and posed the second of mine. If the answer was going to be 'No' I had a pretty shrewd idea of what was going on. 'Is she spayed?'

'No. My husband was against the idea. He was hoping to have some puppies from her. But we never did.'

Classic condition. Yes! I suddenly reprimanded myself. No cause for jubilation here just because I reckoned I'd diagnosed Bo-Bo's problem. A careful feel of her abdomen would give me further evidence that I was on the right track. Or, more appropriately, on her tract. Having gently rolled the Schnauzer on her side without a murmur of protest from her, I had used my fingers each side of her tummy to knead her distended abdomen and, in doing so, felt a large, soft mass yield beneath them. Yes, I was definitely on the right track – her uterus was grossly enlarged and no doubt full of pus. Bo-Bo was suffering from pyometritis – an infection of the womb. Sometimes in such cases, if the cervix remains open, the infection drains out and you see a sticky vulval discharge. But if the cervix remains closed, the infection, unable to escape, builds up in the womb, causing it to grossly dilate, and consequently leads to toxaemia and collapse. Precisely what we were seeing in Bo-Bo. I explained all of this to Mrs Little and ended by saying: 'We need to operate and remove her infected womb. But I do have to warn you, she's in a very toxic state so it's not like a normal hysterectomy. The risks here are much higher.'

Tears welled up once more in Mrs Little's eyes – this time there was no doubting their sincerity. 'You mean she might die?' She leaned over and kissed Bo-Bo's head. 'Oh my poor sweet,' she whispered. In response, there was the merest wag of the Schnauzer's tail.

'We'll, of course, do our best,' I said with more conviction than I felt. That line wasn't in my list but I could hardly say 'You shouldn't have left it so long before coming in.' But I surmised that this had been developing for quite a few days and not just suddenly overnight as had been suggested by Mrs Little. Still, now was not the time for recriminations. I had a feeling those would be wrought on a certain Mr Little when she got home.

I took the decision to admit Bo-Bo straight away and

lifted the inert little dog off the table and carried her down to the ward while instructing Mrs Little to go back out to reception where Beryl would get her to sign the necessary consent forms.

As I passed the alcove door to reception, Beryl swivelled round in her chair and said, 'Thought it might be a pyo.'

'It is,' I replied and hurried on. Here again, Beryl's uncanny instincts had proved right, although she'd had the good grace not to prejudge the problem earlier on.

I saw Mandy step out of the preparation room as I came down the corridor, and she stood there watching as I approached with the dog in my arms, her face set in what, over the months, I'd come to think of as 'Mandy mode'. Under normal circumstances, she had a pleasant enough face, rounded, a little chubby maybe, but Rubenesque, pink cheeks, snub nose, unblemished skin framed by a no-nonsense auburn bob – she had none of this frizzy or straggly long hair which constantly escapes the confines of hair clips or grips to dangle down over operating sites, threatening their sterility, as witnessed on several lady vets in past TV programmes, forcing me to utter the words, 'Get a grip.' I can still hear my previous girlfriend, Sarah, moan every time I said it. When things were going Mandy's way, her face would be all sweetness and light; she could be the apple of your eye. But when things weren't going her way – ouch! I'm not sure what fruit you could compare her to – a lemon perhaps? Sour grapes? Whatever, her look was guaranteed to give you the pip. And one way in which to get that sucking-on-lemons look was to upset her ops list for the morning. Something I was just about to do.

I suspected she knew that since her expression changed from rosy-appled to bitter-lemoned in the time it took me to get down that corridor; in fact, when I drew level with her, such was the look of her pinched-in lips and the narrowness of her eyes, she could have just finished sucking on a whole basketful of lemons.

'It's a pyo,' I said, rather weakly. Where was my manly voice when I needed it?

'Right,' said Mandy, briskly. 'We'll get that sorted once we've finished the morning's ops.'

I knew that, on the rare occasions when additional ops came in from morning appointments, they would be tagged onto the end of the list, often meaning they wouldn't get done until the afternoon, especially if they involved re-sterilising some of the instrument packs. It wasn't usually a problem. But I felt uneasy about leaving Bo-Bo those few extra hours, hours in which her toxicity would only get worse, making the operation even more risky. No – I wanted to get her spayed as soon as I finished seeing my few remaining clients and ahead of the routine spays and castrates and – I suddenly remembered – Superman's dog's dental. Well, that could certainly wait until the afternoon, and even be postponed if necessary.

'No,' I said, my voice much more manly. 'We'll do her ahead of the list.'

'But ...' faltered Mandy, going bright red.

'I'll be right down when I've seen my last client,' I growled deeply, interrupting her as I handed over the Schnauzer. Gosh, I sounded positively Neolithic. I adjusted my loincloth (lab coat), swung my cudgel (stethoscope) over my shoulder and pounded back up to my cave (consulting room).

Once I'd finished my appointments and snatched a quick cup of coffee, I was ready to start. Mandy had Lucy fetch the Schnauzer up from the ward kennels, instructing her to continue with their cleaning and to come up and assist should she be required. The abrupt schoolmarm tone of voice didn't escape my notice and, from the look that Lucy gave Mandy, it didn't escape hers, either.

But Mandy, as ever, swung into action and, in her typically efficient manner, ably assisted in the induction, intubation and preparation of Bo-Bo for her hysterectomy; and it only seemed minutes before I was in the operating theatre, peering into the Schnauzer's open abdomen, beginning to panic when I saw the size of her uterus, as one horn of it bulged out of the incision I'd made.

Knowing the womb, in this dilated state, would be highly susceptible to rupture, I had to be extremely cautious as to how I handled it for fear of tearing open the uterine wall. I gingerly slid my hand in and under the one horn, levering it out; I then stretched my fingers back in and upwards to locate the left ovary and, clasping it between finger and thumb, gradually pulled it towards me, keeping the pressure up until the fat and ligament holding it in place parted, and I was able to access the arterial supply, buried in the fatty tissue, and clamp it. I then ligated the artery.

It was always an anxious moment when you released the forceps and watched the ligated artery sink back into the abdomen, praying that you weren't then going to see a pool of blood well up, which would indicate a slipped ligature – since relocating the bleeding artery, especially in dogs with deep abdominal cavities, was a momentous task and fraught with difficulties.

And I should know; I'd had just such a slipped ligature during one of my early attempts at spaying a dog. The dog in question had been a large, adult Alsatian bitch. I knew from the outset it was going to be difficult. She was deep-chested and overweight so I predicted the ovaries would be buried in a huge wodge of fat way down inside her abdomen, difficult to find, difficult to extract, and difficult to tie off their supply of blood. I was right.

In the struggle to pull the first ovary out, my constant heaving and squeezing of the surrounding fat reduced it to the consistency of semi-liquid blancmange; greasy, slippery, almost impossible to grip, constantly slithering out of my fingers, so that by the time I'd secured what I hoped was a tight enough ligature round the ovarian artery, my fingers were feeling numb with fatigue. I tested the knot with artery forceps, pulling at its end. It seemed secure enough. I let go of the forceps clamped below the knot and watched the ligature in its liquid yellow mass of fat sink out of sight between loops of gut. There was a little blood in the abdominal cavity – inevitable as some had oozed in from the initial incision – and I reached over for a swab and dabbed it over the loops of intestines, mopping up the remnants of that blood. Only, as I did so, more blood seemed to seep up through the bowels. I tossed the first swab – now soaked – onto the instrument trolley and snatched up another, pushing it into the abdominal cavity, withdrawing it in less than a minute, bright red and sodden.

'Christ,' I muttered, a surge of panic welling up in me in much the same way blood was now surging up through the guts and lapping at the edges of the abdominal incision.

Mandy, sitting on a stool, monitoring the anaesthetic machine, looked across and stated the obvious. 'You've got a bleed, Paul,' adding, 'I'll get you some more swabs.'

Of course, that wasn't the answer. I realised I now had a slipped ligature on my hands, the fact verified when the ligature itself floated out on a sea of blood. I think I actually squealed when I saw it, knowing that deep inside the Alsatian, a large artery was pumping out blood at high pressure, and unless I could track that artery down, isolate it and clamp it off, the dog would bleed to death. My hands started to tremble, my heart race. Sheer despair gripped me as I extended the abdominal incision forward in an attempt to access the point of bleeding more easily. I watched as blood poured over the edge and ran down onto the drapes, instantly soaking them.

'I think I'd better get Crystal in,' said Mandy quietly, and ran from the room.

Moments later, Crystal was there, a gown hastily donned, me stepping to one side, splattered in blood, as she snapped on some surgical gloves and plunged in, Mandy next to her, mopping up the constant stream of blood, some of which had trickled under the drapes and was now dripping onto the floor, being smeared into red, slippery puddles by our boots.

'Paul, hold these back,' said Crystal tersely, indicating the coils of intestine she'd heaved out of the wound to give her more space. 'And use those tissue forceps to hold the wound open for me.' She nodded at the trolley. I did as instructed. Crystal was now immersed up to her forearms inside the dog's abdominal cavity. 'Mandy, swab please.'

Mandy had already anticipated her request, having put surgical gloves on to pick up a swab, ready for Crystal's need. It was snatched from her, and another requested almost immediately as Crystal peered up and under the Alsatian's liver.

'Right ... forceps, Mandy.' Crystal held out a hand and the forceps were placed in it. They disappeared into the wound. 'Now let's have some curved artery forceps, please.' Crystal's other hand extended out to one side and the forceps slid onto it without hesitation on Mandy's part. These two clearly worked as a good team. There was the click of the forceps as they were clamped. Another two swabs offered by Mandy were used. The surge of blood stopped.

'Right,' declared Crystal, easing herself up. 'Seems I've got the blighter. Just need to make sure it's tied off more tightly next time, eh, Paul?'

I felt myself go crimson.

She noticed, adding a little more gently, 'It happens to us all at some stage or other,' and proceeded to ligate and release the artery with the skill and ease that comes with practice.

Thank God, no such problems occurred with Bo-Bo – at least with her left ovarian extraction; and so I turned my attention to the right horn of her womb, pulling it out as far as I could and ligating the ovarian artery on that side, breaking the ligaments and fat that were holding the ovary in place so that I could haul the distended two horns of the uterus out onto the drapes where they laid steaming and glistening. The body of the uterus now had to be tracked down to the cervix, and where, on each side, there were prominent arteries, which were engorged and throbbing. I first clamped the whole of the womb just at the entrance to the cervix and then I threaded a curved needle with catgut and carefully slipped a stitch round each artery, anchoring it with a small portion of the uterine wall. Clamping a second set of artery forceps above the others, I cut between the two, severing the whole of the womb to enable me to drag it out and lift it across to the stainless steel dish Mandy was holding out for me. Boy, was it heavy. I checked the interior of the abdominal cavity. There was a little bit of free blood. I dabbed it away with some swabs ... none reappeared. Seems my sutures were secure. Breathing a sigh of relief, I rapidly stitched up the wound, two layers – inner connective tissue and skin. A few drops of blood oozed from the wound. Nothing significant. I stood back, feeling exhausted.

Mandy picked up a dry swab, ran it along my row of sutures then dusted them with antibiotic powder and covered them with a strip of gauze.

She looked across at me and actually smiled. 'Well done, Paul,' she murmured. Wow. Praise indeed.

Although not actually Superman, I was still flying high when, later, I had to turn my attention to Archie's teeth. But tackling that canine grounded me in one fell swoop, as I was to find out after lunch.

As anticipated, with the operation on Bo-Bo taking precedence, the morning's list had spilled over into the afternoon. A little bit tired and more edgy than I cared to admit, I was planning to take a curtailed lunch break when Eric bounced in, having returned from seeing to one of Alex and Jill Ryman's motley assortment of pigs and goats – I knew the Rymans and their two children, Emily and Joshua; I'd attended to their Miss Piggy's farrowing last year.

'Phew,' he exclaimed, standing in the middle of the office, bringing his hands together in a loud clap. 'That goat of Alex's is a right bugger to handle. Fair wore me out trimming his hooves.' He looked over to where I was about to settle in one of the two office armchairs, cup of green tea on the small table beside it. 'I'll get you to do it next time,' he grinned, his face splitting like two halves of a melon while he patted his jacket pockets. 'Which reminds me ...' He pulled out a folded piece of paper. 'Emily did this for you.' He stepped over and handed it to me. 'Seems you're flavour of the month over there. Especially with their little girl.'

Unfolding the paper, I found myself looking at a coloured line drawing which could have done justice to a Lowry painting in that it showed a brown, stick-like figure, clasping in one hand the handle of a black box, which I guess was meant to be a black bag, while the other hand was stretched out holding some sort of stick or pencil drawn in red crayon. The figure had strokes of yellow and brown pencilled round his head (hair?) – and his stick legs were encased in blotches of green (wellingtons?). Next to him were two joined circles, the smaller having ears and large red dots for eyes and nose – the larger having four stick legs, a curly tail, and between them a row of orange marks which I took to be teats, as, although it was a crude representation, the drawing was clearly meant to show a pig – no doubt Miss Piggy.

'Is that supposed to be me?' I asked Eric.

'Yes, of course. Although she forgot your studs.' Eric glanced at my ears. 'Just as well ... you ponce.' But it was said with a smile.

'And what's that in my hand?'

'The thermometer you rammed up Miss Piggy's arse. That made a lasting impression on both Emily and Joshua. Jill says they've never stopped talking about it since.'

I was quite touched that Emily should have bothered to do a drawing of me – even if it was rather anal in its orientation – and vowed to thank her next time I got called over to the Rymans' smallholding.

Meanwhile, Eric was suggesting I joined him for a quick pint over at the Woolpack.

'I really don't think I should,' I said. 'I had quite a difficult pyo to deal with this morning and there's a dental to do before I start my afternoon appointments.

'Oh come on, Paul,' cajoled Eric. 'Just a quickie.'

'Quickie what?' said Beryl, walking stealthily into the office post fag-out-of-back-door. I suspected she'd been listening in at the door. She slid in with that funny way of walking she had – almost a glide – and with her slightly hunched back I often pictured her as a black slug, half expecting to see a trail of slime in her wake. 'You're not going over to the Woolpack, are you?'

Right ... she had been eavesdropping. She gave both of us the benefit of her withering look, and even though it was with just the one eye, it was every bit as effective as if she'd lasered us with two. I certainly felt as if I were being blasted back against the office wall. But Eric seemed to stand his ground.

'Erm ... just for a quick jar, Beryl,' said Eric, running a finger round the collar of his shirt, the top button of which was undone. 'It's been quite a fraught morning for both of us.' He glanced in my direction, his eyebrows curled. 'Hasn't it, Paul?'

Before I could reply, Beryl had butted in. 'It'll be even more fraught this afternoon if you come back the worse for wear.' The withering look remained undimmed. 'Paul's still got Mr Henderson's dental to do ... and he's got a full appointments list later. You're fairly quiet, though.' She stared pointedly at Eric. 'But I'm sure I'll manage to rustle up a few more clients for your evening surgery. So I don't think the Woolpack's a good idea ... do you?'

Eric looked decidedly uncomfortable. 'Well, if you say so, Beryl.'

'I do say so.'

'Who says so?' The question was from Crystal, who had just breezed in and the words hung in the air as did her delicate perfume. We all seemed dumbstruck as no one immediately replied; but then Beryl rallied to and said, 'We were just discussing the workload for this afternoon. There's quite a bit on. So I don't think ...' Her voice trailed off as she realised she was perhaps overstepping the mark.

Crystal wrung her hands together and the bracelets on her wrists tinkled. As did my heart briefly, as I reminded myself of my fantasies about me and Crystal making the Downs alive with the sound of music.

'That's what I think as well,' said Crystal, a lilt in her voice. Really, Crystal? I thought with a sudden jolt. Perhaps I wasn't being a silly little goatherd after all – until I realised she was talking shop, not musicals. 'All the more reason for us to keep a clear head.' She turned and smiled at her husband.

'Of course, dear,' replied Eric, giving Beryl a murderous look before sallying out, only to appear in the archway behind Beryl's desk, raise his arms and, with two fingers forming a V on each hand, viciously claw the air above the back of her head – an action I could see but one he made sure was out of Crystal's view. Beryl swung round suspiciously, just as he ducked out of sight, and we heard him whistling his way down the corridor to the tune of *South Pacific*'s 'Happy Talk'.

I only wished Superman's little dog could have taken his cue from that song, but it wasn't so much 'happy' as 'snappy' talk when the time came to bring him up from the kennels for his dental. A very harassed Lucy, red in the face, out of breath, rushed into the prep room where I was waiting to start – Mandy's role that afternoon was to assist Crystal with her clients in what I termed the 'executive consulting room' – larger and lighter, overlooking the rose garden – whereas the one allocated to me was dingy, its window partially obscured by a rampant Virginia creeper, and overlooked the exercise yard from where the odour of what dogs did when they were exercised would drift in should I dare to open the top vent. Many a time an owner would enter the room and wrinkle his or her nose at me, wondering, no doubt, whether I'd had curry for lunch.

I felt sure Mandy considered dealing with a dog's teeth rather beneath her, hence her apparent willingness that afternoon to abdicate her role as my ops nurse and allow Lucy the privilege of setting up the descaler and having ready the thiopentone to anaesthetise Archie. Well, that was the plan … only Archie had other ideas. Hence the appearance of the harassed Lucy.

'Paul,' she said abruptly, 'Archie's proving impossible to catch.'

I had heard a few snarls emanating up from the ward and did wonder whether Archie had decided to be uncooperative. He must have been a real handful if he had thwarted the attempts of Lucy to catch him. She was a past master at dealing with difficult dogs, the bigger the better it seemed – the Rottweiler down whose throat she'd stuffed a crystal of washing soda after the dog had swallowed a Christmas stocking was a good example of her aptitude in dealing with well-muscled, strong dogs. It was almost as if they were a challenge – something that she relished.

Maybe I should build up my biceps and get her to relish me a bit more, I thought, as I followed her down to the ward, watching the curve of her slim hips, the neat calves encased in their dark stockings. I had an overwhelming desire to take a lunge at her in much the same way Archie had an overwhelming desire to do likewise as I approached his kennel, and he flung himself at the front and bared his teeth, biting the bars, growling. Of course, I'd have taken a much gentler approach in leaping on Lucy. But currently,

105

with the way things were between us, such leapings were an unlikely event.

Stop this, Paul – concentrate on the present. A furious, white ball of foaming pooch. How different to the little dog wearing his red cape that Mr Henderson had dragged in that morning. Perhaps we really did have here a miniature Krypto, the Superdog, ready to save the planet from an alien force, which he clearly thought I was. Archie had been kennelled in one of the smaller, upper cages which served to house cats and small dogs prior to their operations or in-hospital treatment. So that snarling ball of spit was directly level with my face ... and not a pretty sight.

'Now, calm down little fella,' I said in the smoothest of dulcet tones I could muster. Archie's reaction was to lunge at the bars again and clamp one in his jaws with a growl worthy of a dog twice his size.

'Come on, Archie, no one's going to hurt you.' OK, not quite the truth. The dog was going to have a jab and some of his teeth might get yanked out – but he wasn't to know. But then, by the way he re-launched himself at the bars with another savage snarl, I suspect he thought I was a lying toad and one that required annihilation. I began to think, Star Trek-style, that a stun gun might have come in handy to give Archie a quick zap. Whizz – Pow –Bang. One dog flattened, ready for his dental.

'Paul.' It was Lucy, holding a less exotic means of overpowering Archie – a small syringeful of tranquillizer.

There was still the problem of actually catching the dog to administer the sedative; but Lucy had the answer to that in her other hand – a pair of thick, suede gauntlets, usually used for pinning down cats, but applicable to fur balls of the canine variety such as Archie.

With the cage door cautiously opened sufficiently for me to lever in one gauntleted hand, to which Archie immediately latched himself, my dulcet tones rapidly descended into a series of deep and heartfelt utterances – 'Why, you little sod ...', 'Damn you ...' and 'Bloody well behave yourself ...' as I struggled to pin Archie in one corner, with his head squashed against the cage wall and, at the same time, grip one of his flailing back legs to enable Lucy to jab the sedative into his thigh. My voice was quite croaky once we had achieved our aim, and I had released the dog and slammed the door on him, before he had the chance to sink his teeth into my gauntlet again. Oh, what a charming little pooch! I just wondered how many teeth I could legitimately pull out once he was under. The lot? No, that would be unethical. Besides, such was his savagery, he would no doubt still be capable of giving me a severe gumming.

In the event, having carried his inert little body through to the preparation room once he'd succumbed to the sedative, given him his intravenous thiopentone, intubated him to prevent any spray from the descaler trickling into his windpipe, and set to work on descaling his teeth, of which it was only the back molars that were heavily encrusted with tartar, I found I could only justifiably extract two loose incisors. And although I gave his prominent canines a good prod and poke, they were firmly embedded in the gums with no trace of decay, so there was no way I could find a reason to whip them out. 'So, matey,' I said, removing a couple of soggy swabs from the back of his throat and sliding out the endotracheal tube, 'you live to bite another day.'

Lucy grimaced. 'Thank you, *Paul*,' she said as, without looking up, she sponged blood-tinged water from around

Archie's muzzle. Not exactly a term of endearment with its undertone of sarcasm. But at least it was a response. A communication of sorts. It could only get better, surely?

It certainly couldn't get much worse. We still hadn't been speaking to each other for days – apart from the basic necessity to converse to ensure the day-to-day routines were maintained. The banalities of life. Oh dear, I was sounding really jaded. I realised I was clutching at straws to think that we could turn things round easily; and the place to start that process was certainly not a heart-to-heart over Archie's gnashers. I acknowledged Lucy's help with a polite 'Thank you' and peeled off my ops gown and mask – the latter worn to prevent infected droplets from the descaler being inhaled – washed my hands, put on my watch and, seeing there was time for a cup of tea before starting the afternoon's consultations, slipped out into the corridor only to collide with Beryl, who had been lurking there.

'Just on my way down for my afternoon ciggie,' she explained in a guilty whisper, peering round my shoulder into the prep room where Lucy was just picking up Archie to take him back to his kennel. 'Everything, OK?' she added, frowning in Lucy's direction.

'Fine,' I sighed. 'Just fine.'

'If you say so,' replied Beryl, clearly not believing a word I'd said, and hurried on, muttering under her breath.

An hour later, Beryl was a changed woman – not in the sense that she had changed her clothes; mind you, even if she had done, it would probably have been into a similar outfit to the one she always wore – black trousers, black polo-neck sweater and black cardigan draped over her shoulders. No, it was a mood change, brought on by the arrival of Ernie Entwhistle and his new puppy.

I heard her as I walked down the short passageway between my consulting room and reception, passing to my right the door into the waiting room, behind which I could hear the murmur of voices, a plaintive miaow and the panting of a dog. 'Oh, what a sweetie!' I heard her say. 'Just like you,' I heard him reply. Yuck! I stuck my tongue out. Beryl's response was, 'Oh, Ernie, you old devil,' accompanied by a girlish giggle which abruptly stopped as I swung through the door.

'Mr Entwhistle's just arrived,' she said, her manner becoming instantly businesslike the moment she saw me.

'I'm afraid I'm a bit late,' apologised Mr Entwhistle, turning his attention to me as the collie pup he had on a lead pulled towards me, panting and pawing the air in a friendly greeting – what a contrast to Archie.

I awaited Beryl's customary tart response; none was forthcoming. Instead, Mr Entwhistle got a beaming smile and a 'That's no problem ... Mr Mitchell was running late anyway.' She turned to me with what for Beryl was almost an angelic smile. 'Isn't that so, Paul?'

Running late? Was I? Well, maybe a little.

'In fact, he'll be able to see you now.'

I will?

'Won't you, Paul?'

'Yes, Beryl.'

'See you in a bit then,' said Mr Entwhistle, giving Beryl a little wave with his fingers, before he followed me up the passage with his puppy skittering over the vinyl ahead of him.

From my computer in the consulting room, I read that the collie was just under three months old, called Bess, and was due for her first vaccination. Mr Entwhistle hoisted her onto the table where, with a double click of his fingers, she promptly sat down, only to spring up again as I approached to give her a check-over.

'Bess,' said Mr Entwhistle, quietly. 'Sit.'

Bess sat. With a triple click of his fingers, she fidgeted on the table with her front paws, first lifting one, then the other. He clicked again. 'Shake a paw with Mr Mitchell then?' he said. But all I got was an excited lick of my fingers and a frenzied wag of her rump and tail. 'She'll learn soon enough,' he added. And no doubt be as obedient as Ben, I thought – she'd soon be jumping onto the table, sitting and raising a leg for shake-a-paw to the same finger-click commands that Ben used to respond to.

Even without doing shake-a-paw, Bess remained sitting down and allowed me to give her the required vaccination, my needle slipping under the skin of her scruff without her uttering so much as a whimper.

'Wish all my patients were as well behaved as Bess,' I said, thinking of the wretched Archie who would be now coming round from his anaesthetic. Having signed Bess's vaccination card, given Mr Entwhistle an information pack on diet, worming and subsequent boosters, there was one comment I wanted to finish with. It had been going through my mind as I'd been examining Bess. Her markings – the white patch over one side of the head and the white socks – uncannily resembled those of Mr Entwhistle's previous collie. I hesitated, wondering whether it was prudent to remind Mr Entwhistle of Ben. Some owners felt uncomfortable, as if acquiring a new dog was somehow disloyal to the memory of their previous pet. But I decided to take the risk.

'You know, I hope you don't mind me saying,' I said, scratching the puppy's back, causing her to turn and lick me enthusiastically, 'but Bess reminds me a lot of Ben.'

110

Mr Entwhistle's face creased into a smile. 'No surprise there, Mr Mitchell,' he said, reaching down to give Bess a kiss on her head. 'She's Ben's great-great-granddaughter.'

As I watched them walk back down the passage, I anticipated there was going to be a great bond develop there, with many potentially happy years to look forward to. When I heard Mr Entwhistle chortle out in reception and Beryl's titter in response, I wondered whether the same might apply to them as well, although I doubted whether Beryl would jump into bed at the click of a finger. But then you never know.

'What's happened to my 5.50 appointment?' I asked her when Mr Entwhistle finally took his leave with another little wave of his hand and a 'See you soon' directed at Beryl, who was simpering, her rounded cheeks flushed, as she hunched up her shoulders and gave a little wave of her scarlet talons in return.

'Beryl, my 5.50 appointment – the cockatiel?'

'Bye,' said Beryl, softly, as Mr Entwhistle paused, hand on the door, and gave another little wave in her direction.

'Bye,' he whispered.

'Bye,' she echoed, her hand still in the air.

'Beryl.'

'What is it, Paul?' she snapped, dropping her hand once Mr Entwhistle had finally left.

'The cockatiel.'

'Oh, the cockatiel. Mrs Tidy cancelled. I've rebooked it for tomorrow.'

'You didn't tell me.'

'Didn't I? Must have slipped my mind. Now, when is it you're seeing Mr Entwhistle again?'

Clearly *he* hadn't slipped her mind.

I quickly scooted down to the ward to check on Bo-Bo,

who was staying in overnight. She'd come round from the operation OK but was obviously still weak; when she looked up and wagged her tail at me, albeit feebly, I felt she had a good chance of pulling through.

Meanwhile, Superman had flown in and carried off his Archie without anyone getting savaged in the process. I only wished someone would take me under their wing and fly me back to Willow Wren. As it was, with Lucy staying upstairs in the flat to provide emergency cover for that night, I had to transport myself back by more conventional means – the Vauxhall Estate provided by the practice – and microwave a ready-meal; then, later, with no means of clicking my fingers to have a well-trained companion jump to my command, eager to spring into bed with me, the only click heard that night was that of the bedroom light switch being turned off as I decided to turn in early. Probably best anyway, as I'd had quite a day ... and I was out as soon as my head hit the pillow. I might not have slept so well had I known what was going to happen the next day with Mrs Tidy and her cockatiel.

7

CLEAN? NOT BY A LONG SQUAWK

I was woken up at 5.50am by my neighbour's cockatiel.

It had been happening for several weeks now – Eleanor Venable's Wilfred had taken to squawking first thing – with that 'first thing' getting earlier by the day, as spring advanced and first light dawned earlier and earlier. I was beginning to feel a little tense from a constant stream of disturbed nights. OK, had Lucy been curled up next to me, I could have slid my arms round her and lost my tensions immediately in those sleepy, dreamy moments of shared love instead of having to share them with the presence of Wilfred, whose regular interjections were enough to deflate the most hardened man's ardour.

There again, to be honest, Wilfred was only a symptom, not the cause, of my lack of intimate relations since Lucy *was* usually curled up next to me – unless she was doing her rota of night duties over at Prospect House – only she was curled up in an 'OFF LIMITS – KEEP AWAY' sort of position most of the time – back to me, arms folded across her bosom, legs tightly together with knees drawn up. In her more mellow moments, when I suspected an advance from me might go unhindered, I did contemplate attempting a fairly straightforward manoeuvre – the 'sidle-up-and-gradually-ease-into-unbridled-passion' strategy – but the wodge of duvet she drove down between us suggested that that was the only stuffing I was likely to get if I attempted it. So I didn't.

It was no surprise then, later that morning, when I staggered into work after a particularly strident awakening from Wilfred, to have Beryl say, 'Christ, Paul, you look terrible. Did you get called out last night?'

I shook my head, then wished I hadn't as it felt as if my brain was slopping around inside my cranium. If Beryl was then going to suggest my minty breath was from sucking a sweet to disguise the effects of a hangover when it was solely due to my stripy toothpaste, a new tube of which I'd started that morning, then I'd throttle her. That's if I could summon up the strength. I did feel surprisingly more under the weather than a mere early waking would account for. Perhaps I was going down with something. Lucyitis, perhaps?

Beryl was still looking at me rather strangely, no doubt trying to work out why I looked so haggard, so I decided to explain.

'It's Wilfred ... he got me out of bed earlier than I needed to.'

You should have seen Beryl's eye. It nearly popped out of her head while her glass one did a violent jerk upwards. Despite my muzzy head, I flicked a hand through my highlighted hair, gave my left ear stud a tweak, wiggled my hips, and said, 'He can be quite hard on me sometimes.' I then minced out of reception, leaving her gawping and plucking furiously at her mole. Tee-hee.

Crystal and Eric were both down in the office, having, it would seem, an animated discussion, from which they immediately broke off as I entered the room. The sight of Crystal – my incarnation of the perfect English rose – positively glowing with health, in sharp contrast to my pallor, went some way to lifting my flagging spirits.

'Oh, morning, Paul,' she exclaimed, 'we were just talking about you.' She smiled, her cheeks dimpling, her Cupid lips exposing the merest glimpse of her teeth – no nasty Archie-style gnashers there, I thought. She didn't elaborate on the context in which I'd been discussed. It was as if her smile, in its perfection, said it all – nothing to worry about. It was Eric who charged in, putting his foot firmly in the mire.

'Yes,' he said, 'you and Lucy. We've noticed things seem a bit strained between you.' He scratched the side of his bald head with one finger. 'We're just wondering ...' He tailed off, his gaze sliding from me.

'You know our views on this, don't you?' said Crystal crisply, still smiling, although I now felt it a little forced, her steel-blue eyes hardening. Yes, I knew their views – only too well. Crystal had taken me to one side last year and discussed the implications of Lucy and me hitching up. It wasn't a problem for her and Eric, so long as it didn't interfere with the smooth running of the practice and, at the time, it hadn't been a problem. Once, perhaps, there'd been a minor glitch in the 'smooth running' when Eric caught the two of us snogging in the dispensary – he'd rushed in to get some worm tablets and rushed out again muttering about 'tom cats' and 'castration'. Other than that, we'd kept our emotions under control and the day-to-day activities of the practice hadn't been affected. I still felt that situation hadn't changed. OK, Lucy and I were having our differences,

115

going through a bad patch, barely speaking to each other, but I trusted the professional commitment to our work would ensure it didn't interfere with how we carried out our duties. But obviously attitudes had been noticed, things said – Beryl would have been the first to comment – hence the warning finger now being wagged at me by Crystal, albeit a dainty finger with its well-manicured, pink-lacquered nail.

Crystal's voice broke my reverie. 'Paul, are you listening to me?'

'Sorry. Yes.' I went on to reassure both of them that my personal life certainly wouldn't impinge on the working relationships within the hospital.

'I'm glad to hear that,' said Crystal. 'We all get along here extremely well, don't we, Eric?' she added, turning to her husband.

The vexed voice of Beryl ringing out from reception interrupted her. 'Eric, where are you? Your first appointment's been here five minutes already.'

Eric grimaced at me, his lips turning down at the corners. 'We do try to get along, yes,' he said.

'*Eric*!'

Eric sighed deeply, crossed the fingers of both his hands and hurried out with a 'Coming, Beryl.'

My muzziness had cleared by the time I was halfway through my morning consultations, only to be reminded of what had precipitated it in the first place by the sound of screeching that erupted from reception and then continued unabated in the waiting room. It was all too horribly familiar, my eardrums being too well tuned to the discordant notes to be wrong. So there was no self-congratulation to be had in knowing what bird I was to be presented with before it appeared; and when the cockatiel was duly proffered for my inspection, my customary line of introduction stuck in my gullet in much the same way I wished something substantial could be rammed down the bird's.

I did eventually manage a 'So this is Billy, is it?' as the cockatiel's cage was eventually hoisted onto my consulting table, but not before a barrage of squawks from its owner, the competition from which had the effect of shutting the bird up. Temporarily, at least.

Entry into my consulting room had been dramatic. Having called out for a Mrs Tidy, a gargantuan lady had risen from a seat in the waiting room, beckoning to a spindly little man next to her, on whose lap was an enormous cage. Well, at least I guessed it was a cage – its occupant was emitting screeches but couldn't be seen – since the entire container was covered in a close-fitting, zipped, white plastic coat, vented with high windows of fine mesh on two sides, below each of which was a yellow label with a black and yellow biohazard warning symbol on it.

'Come on, George, it's our turn,' she said above the racket emanating from the covered cage. The little man struggled to his feet; the woman, whom I assumed to be his wife, offered him no assistance as she rummaged in the large, plastic shopping bag she was holding and eventually pulled out a bottle with a trigger-spray top containing bright-green liquid. Holding this in front of her like some sort of gun, she advanced towards me, her husband following behind, dwarfed by the cage he was carrying, only the top of his thinning, mousy hair visible.

I took a step back, half turned and attempted to smile and say, 'Do come through,' but my words were drowned by the bird's screeches; so I feebly waved my arm up the passageway, indicating the door opposite.

'You first,' boomed the woman, waving her gun at me. I felt that if I turned away from her she'd prod me in the back and tell me to raise my arms. So I sort of slid away from her, feeling the wall behind me, and edged back into the consulting room where I turned and scooted to the other side of the consulting table, fighting the urge to scream, 'I surrender.'

Mrs Tidy, like some automaton, ground to a halt in the doorway, almost filling its frame, while her husband was left standing out in the passage, still holding the cage. She certainly was a large lady. Her shoulders, even though hidden in the confines of a military-style, navy jacket, were broad, and I could picture them heaving up hod-loads of bricks on a building site with little effort; and her hips and thighs, encased in a tight, navy skirt, could have graced the haunches of a hippo. All of this was topped by a head, square in its proportions, bleached breadboard in its complexion, with a severe cut of platinum-blonde hair swept up like a bottle brush, and eyes that at this moment were scanning the room from behind severe, black-framed glasses.

'You *can* come in,' I ventured to say.

Mrs Tidy took two steps forward which, being giant steps, were enough for her to draw level with the consulting table, at which she directed her spray and with a loud 'pssss ... pssss' engulfed it in a mist of disinfectant.

The tic in my temple began to throb ominously. Cool it, Paul, I thought, and said, 'I do wipe the table down with antiseptic between clients.'

There was another 'pssss ... pssss'.

'Ah, but you can't be too careful,' replied Mrs Tidy. 'You might not be using the right concentration to kill off all those ...' She paused and looked furtively round her before continuing '... those nasty bugs.' She paused again and then, taking a deep breath, spat out the word 'germs', her face filling with loathing as she said it. It was followed by another jerky squeeze of her disinfectant spray. 'They lurk everywhere you know.' Pssss. 'So you can't be too careful.' Pssss ... pssss. 'OK, George, you can bring Billy in now.'

Her half-hidden husband shunted into the room, engulfed by the cage in front of him, and levered it onto the consulting table before standing back to smile nervously at me, his wife towering over him. She, with her hefty limbs, was the epitome of a Mrs Muscle; he, by contrast, lacked any components worth being called 'meaty', his clothes hanging off a spindly frame, his face thin and gaunt, eyes deeply recessed in their sockets – a Yorick in the making.

Mrs Tidy unzipped the pristine plastic cover and handed it over to Mr Tidy to hold. The cage revealed was spotless ... its metal bars gleamed ... its stainless steel feed and water pots glowed. Not one dropping blemished the sand sheet covering the base, above which, on a polished wooden cross perch, sat the occupant – Billy, the cockatiel. Even he was not your normal, common-or-garden variety of cockatiel. No dusty grey plumage for him. He was a Lutino, with pure-white plumage, unmarked save for the yellow head and crest and the characteristic seen in all cockatiels – the orange cheek feathers; though no doubt Mrs Tidy might have had a strong desire to eliminate them by bleaching or plucking, should it have been possible, if she thought it spoilt the hygienic, sterile image she was trying to manufacture within that cage.

I suddenly became acutely conscious of the splattered brown stain on the breast pocket of my lab coat, where my previous client's dog had jettisoned the contents of his anal glands, having missed the cotton wool into which I had been attempting to express them. The way Mrs Tidy was staring at the stain, I felt sure she longed to rip the coat from me and plunge it into biological detergent with me closely following behind – although the thought of her riding rough shod over me with a loofah was more intimidating than intimate. I scrabbled to extract one of the phrases from my mental list, narrowly avoiding saying, 'What can I do for you?' in favour of, 'What a splendid cockatiel you have here,' which I didn't have to shout out since Billy had rapidly gone quiet once the cover had been removed. Perhaps it was the sight of me peering in that did it? Or maybe it was the sickly-sweet tone of my voice, which, frankly, was enough to make any self-respecting pet puke. Anyway, he remained silent. But not still. He suddenly wagged his tail, brought it up and evacuated his bowels onto the unblemished sand sheet beneath him.

Mrs Tidy gave a snort of disgust. 'Sorry about that,' she said.

'No problem,' I replied. 'It's just the call of nature.' I was beginning to wonder why Mrs Tidy owned the bird if she was so neurotic about hygiene. She provided the answer by explaining that Billy actually belonged to her sister who was over in Dubai on a two-year teaching contract and who, before leaving, had extracted a promise from her sister to look after Billy until she returned.

'I do worry about germs, though,' she went on, her fingers playing on the trigger of the disinfectant. 'Don't I, George?' she added, turning to her husband. 'You never know what diseases you might pick up these days. And from whom.' She waved the sprayer matter-of-factly at him. Perhaps she was inferring that her husband was more of a bug in her life than the love of it. He merely gave a nervous nod of his cadaverous head.

She swung back to me and directed a puff at my anal gland stain.

'Germs,' she reiterated. 'They could be the death of us.'

I coughed as the mist of disinfectant got up my nose – much like Mrs Tidy's manner. And still she hadn't finished. 'They're everywhere,' she went on in a conspiratorial whisper, leaning forward, looking from left to right as if afraid of being overheard. Maybe she thought the room was bugged. Whatever, she was certainly bugging me.

'They are?'

'Oh, yes. You'd be surprised.' She narrowed her eyes. 'And they're liable to strike at any time.' Mrs Tidy drew herself up to her full height and with her spare hand executed a karate chop through the air. 'You could be cut down before you knew it. Salmonella ... E. coli ... the MRSA bug. Nasty bit of work that one.' The word provoked another 'pssss' of her sprayer. 'Not to mention the likes of swine 'flu.' More 'pssss ... pssssings'.

'Yes, I quite understand your concerns,' I interjected, 'but what have you actually brought Billy in for?'

'I want you to give him the full works.'

'Sorry. I'm not sure I understand. The full works?'

'That's what I said, yes. I want you to carry out a full screening to check he's not carrying any nasty bugs. I read on the Internet that birds can carry salmonella and something called ...' She paused. 'What was it called, George?' she went on, turning to her husband.

'Chlamydia, dear,' he murmured.

'Yes, that's the one.' She turned back to me. 'Charmid ear. You must have heard of it, you being a vet.'

'Chlamydia. It's a condition birds can get, yes.'

'And we can catch it too, so I understand.'

'There is a possibility, if the bird is carrying it.'

'Well, there you are then,' exclaimed Mrs Tidy with another 'pssss'. 'That's why I want Billy to have the full works, in case he's carrying one of those nasty bugs.' Mrs Tidy had obviously done her homework since she went on to explain that she required a 'charmid ear' screen and a culture of the throat and vent.

I gulped.

Billy scuttled to the other end of his perch and raised his crest, emitting a muted squawk – no doubt alarmed at the prospect of having a swab rammed up his cloaca.

'Right,' I said, a little peeved that Mrs Tidy was taking charge of proceedings. But if that's what she wanted ... 'I'll get Billy booked in then,' I continued.

'We'd rather we had it done now,' declared Mrs Tidy emphatically. 'Wouldn't we, George?'

'Yes, dear.'

'See? My husband thinks it would be best done now.'

'Well, it's just that we have got our morning's ops lined up to do.' And, I thought, Mandy lined up to make sure I did them to order. I didn't fancy crossing her, but then, gazing up into the ever-hardening features of Mrs Tidy, her eyes glinting menacingly, I wondered which would be the lesser of the two evils. 'I'll get the swabs,' I said.

As Billy was my last appointment of the morning, at least I didn't have the worry of getting behind with my consultations, although it did mean missing out on my coffee break in order to be ready for the ops Mandy would push through up to lunchtime.

It didn't take long to winkle Billy out of his cage in a green drape. Yes, I'd reassured Mrs Tidy, it was a sterile one – bug free. And yes, as she saw, I'd put on surgical gloves entirely for her benefit, before swaddling him. And no worries, the forceps I used to prise open his beak to get the throat swab were clean. And, of course, the swabs were sterile in the first place as there wouldn't be any point in using them otherwise *would there*?

When I'd finished, I instructed Mrs Tidy to make an appointment to return in a week's time, when all the results would be back from the diagnostic laboratory.

'What's the point in that?' she queried, brusquely.

Actually, she had a good point. There wasn't much point – unless there was a problem to be discussed. However, it had been instilled in me by Crystal that clients were to be encouraged to come back in order to go through the laboratory results with them; but I suspected it was more to do with charging an extra consultation fee, rather than the expediency of seeing the patient again. Evidently, Mrs Tidy thought likewise and stated, 'That's rubbish, if you don't mind me saying. I'll either phone up at the end of next week or pop in if I'm passing. Less cost to me and, besides which, there'll be less risk of Billy picking something up from here if I don't bring him in.'

Who was I to argue? I looked across at Mr Tidy and felt a wave of sympathy for him as he staggered out under two burdens in his life – a large, heavy cage and his large, heavy wife.

No one could fail to hear Mrs Tidy when, later in the week, she decided to 'pop in' on her way through to Westcott's new shopping precinct. This was the pride of the town, opened a year earlier with a civic reception; first, music from the Sussex Stompers – a local, balding band that had been doing the rounds for many years and were now getting a bit long in the tooth to stomp without stooping; followed by a parade by the Westcott majorettes – the young ladies in their short, frilly skirts always attracted a large crowd – elderly gentlemen, in particular, seemed roused by the whirl and toss of their batons; lastly, a triumphant opening proclamation by the town crier – one hired specially for the day – whose cries were drowned out by council workmen drilling in an adjacent road. The mayor fared no better. Those standing in the first two rows could just about hear him extol the delights of the brick-paved, pedestrianised High Street, with its concrete, vandal-proof planters, wrought-iron lamp posts and, lining each side of the street, the standard, brand-named stores interspersed with charity shops and building society offices. Despite the claim of worthy Westcotteans that the revamped High Street gave the town an individuality all of its own, the bland uniformity engendered was one shared by countless shopping precincts up and down the country, making Westcott's 'uniqueness' one of many. So it was to this that Mrs Tidy was heading; but, having decided to call in at Prospect House on the off-chance Billy's lab results were through, she was now standing in reception, confronting Beryl. That was a mistake. She should have headed straight for the shopping precinct.

I was in the office and had just finished my Bert's baguette – today's was tuna salad with his special mayonnaise – and was sipping my mug of green tea – when the strident tones of Mrs Tidy echoed down from reception. Oh Lord, I thought, that's the last thing I need. But then I felt sure Beryl would be able to cope with the woman; I needn't be involved. Nevertheless, I still found myself standing just inside the office door, mug in hand, listening – purely for professional reasons, of course.

'I've come in about my Billy's lab results,' I heard Mrs Tidy saying.

'Oh yes, I remember,' said Beryl. 'The cockatiel. Just let me check whether they've come back yet.' There followed the clicking of her keyboard. I knew the results were back as I'd been studying them the day before. And I knew damned well that Beryl also knew as she'd updated Mrs Tidy's records with them the same afternoon. She was just playing for time, making Mrs Tidy wait.

'Yes, here we are,' she said.

'Well?' exclaimed Mrs Tidy.

'Well, what?' said Beryl.

'The results, what are they? Has Billy got the all-clear?'

There was an indignant intake of breath. 'Oh, I can't possibly let you have them. You'll need to see Mr Mitchell. I'll make you an appointment, shall I?'

I took another swig of my tea, relishing every moment of the drama unfolding. I could just picture the two of them, one each side of the reception desk, squaring up like a couple of boxers waiting to see which one was going to throw the first punch.

Kapow! It was Mrs Tidy. 'I demand you give me the results now.'

'You can demand all you like, Mrs Tidy. I am not releasing them.'

Momentarily there was silence. Was Mrs Tidy jigging back and forth in front of the reception desk, her muscly arms up in front of her, fists curled, ready to land a punch on Beryl's nose. Unlikely. Mrs Tidy was too heavy to jig; pound perhaps, but definitely not jig. Come on, come on … you've surely got a bit more up your sleeve, Mrs Tidy.

Bam! Yes – another verbal jab. 'In which case, I insist on seeing one of the vets. Whoever's on duty will do. But I want to see them now and register a complaint.'

'I'm sorry, but the best I can do is to make an appointment for you to see Mr Mitchell.'

'That's not good enough.' Mrs Tidy's voice had risen to

a crescendo. 'I demand to see someone this instant. And I won't leave until I do.' Wow, this was fighting talk indeed. Thank goodness I wasn't out there in the thick of it as I felt sure I'd get pummelled. I heard the front door swing open and Eric's cheerful voice ring out.

'Hello there ... have we a problem?'

It was Mrs Tidy who got in before Beryl. 'Are you one of the vets here?'

'Yes, indeed. Do you need to see one then?' Eric still sounded hopelessly bubbly. Poor man. Couldn't he sense the acrimony up there? Waves of it were hitting me and I was yards away from its epicentre.

'I most certainly do,' said Mrs Tidy, her voice grating ominously.

'Well, let Beryl here book you an appointment then,' said Eric, oblivious to the fact that he was about to be hit by a pile driver. I cringed.

The assault came swiftly. 'This woman here ...'

'You mean our receptionist ... Beryl?'

'Yes, that woman has already tried to do just that.'

'Well, what's all the fuss about then?'

I winced ... and swigged another mouthful of tea.

'I'm demanding to be seen now.'

'I'm afraid it's by appointment only.'

I hunched my shoulders and grinned to myself. Lovely stuff.

'That's what I've already told Mrs Tidy,' Beryl said at last.

'Well, there we go then,' said Eric breezily. 'Speaking of which, I must get going. Byee.' I heard the inner door open and suddenly there was Eric bouncing down the steps towards me before I had a chance to duck back into the office and out of sight.

'Hi, Paul,' he exclaimed, as he sailed past, 'hope you

126

don't have too hectic an afternoon,' and disappeared in the direction of the prep room whistling a tune from *Oh! What a Lovely War.*

'Paul?' That was Beryl calling from reception.

'Mr Mitchell?' That was Mrs Tidy.

'Can we have a word?' That was the two of them.

I finished the dregs of my tea, put the mug on the office desk and reluctantly dragged myself up to reception to face my own lovely war.

'Mrs Tidy wants to know the results of the lab tests on Billy,' said Beryl the moment I appeared.

'Oh, does she?' I said, all innocence, as I turned to Mrs Tidy, whom I could see now was seething like a volcano – any minute I expected a fountain of molten rock to explode from her cranium; as it was, she had a very red face with cheeks like glowing lava.

'Mr Mitchell,' she said, her voice trembling as she fought to control herself, 'we agreed that I could phone through for the results or pop in. Am I correct?'

I looked across at Beryl before answering. She was also beginning to seethe and I wondered which one would erupt first. Either way, I wasn't going to escape unscathed and decided to take my chances with the volcanic lump that was Mrs Tidy.

'You're quite right, Mrs Tidy. We did agree on that.' I walked over to Beryl. 'I think we've got the results, haven't we?' I gave her the sweetest smile I could muster. 'Perhaps you could just pop them up on the screen.'

Beryl's long scarlet talons hovered above the keyboard, her bony fingers trembling, before, with great reluctance, they descended and she brought up the cockatiel's clinical history and the lab results that had been entered. I bent over the screen and made a pretence of scanning them before stretching back up, to slowly turn and address Mrs Tidy, who was still glowing like a gigantic ember in the middle of the reception area.

'They're fine,' I eventually said. 'No pathogens detected.'

'You're sure?' queried Mrs Tidy.

'Positive. All the tests were clear.'

Mrs Tidy sniffed, the reddening of her cheeks beginning to recede. 'Well, I suppose that's a relief,' she said.

I found the remark puzzling. It was almost with regret that it was said – as if she'd have been happier to have had confirmed some of the 'nasty bugs' she was so paranoid about. Perhaps then it would have given her the excuse to get rid of Billy, and find him a new home. But there we go. I'd never know. What I did know, or at least discovered a few days later, was that I hadn't got rid of Mrs Tidy.

'I'm sorry, Paul, but I've had that woman on the phone,' said Beryl, who, having returned from her coffee-break fag by the back door, was now hovering in the office before going back up to reception. 'You know the one I mean.'

For a moment I couldn't think. There'd been that medium, Madam Mountjoy, insisting on a house visit because her cat had been spooked – I was still wondering if the love spell I'd spotted on that little table of hers in the Wiccan Shoppe was ever going to take effect. I certainly hadn't given her any thought since – erotically or otherwise.

Then there'd been Francesca Cavendish – the 'resting' actress with whom I'd had an argy-bargy over her Maltese – but that had been ages ago and, again, I hadn't heard from her since.

'It's Mrs Tidy, that cockatiel owner,' Beryl went on, 'she's requesting a visit.'

For a moment, I wondered why. Maybe it was Beryl. I

could imagine Mrs Tidy wouldn't relish another confrontation with her. But the reason given was that Mrs Tidy didn't want to run the risk of Billy passing any bugs on to us if she came into the surgery.

'You sure you've got that right, Beryl? Bugs being passed on to us, not the other way round?'

Seemed that was correct. Billy had come down with a tummy upset and Mrs Tidy didn't want to run the risk of spreading the infection. Hence the request for a house call.

'Well, in that case, I suppose you'd better book it in.'

'Mmm, I'm not sure Crystal would approve.' Beryl had stuffed her packet of cigarettes back in her black bag and was still hovering in the doorway, scratching her mole, when Crystal came trotting down the steps behind her and stopped in the doorway next to her.

'What's that, Beryl?' she said.

'Oh, it's a client wanting a visit from Paul.'

'So?'

'Well, it's practice policy to discourage house calls wherever possible.'

'Quite right. Yes.' Crystal stepped past Beryl into the office and turned in front of the desk. 'Now you come to mention it, I have noticed he's been doing rather more house visits than I'd have thought necessary.' She threw a look at me. 'Isn't that so, Paul?'

I squirmed on the spot, averting my gaze from those steely-blue eyes of hers and mumbled something about only doing them if clients were adamant.

'From what I gather, you see these clients here and then the next thing they're demanding a visit from you. I'm not sure what's going on but, whatever it is, just remember that such visits are to be discouraged wherever possible.'

Beryl was listening in her customary, vaguely astonished

way, mouth slightly open, head tilted forward and to one side, good eye wide open, giving the impression of a half-blind owl that had just been clobbered by a brick.

Watching her as Crystal did her little rant, I came up with a brilliant strategy of which Eric would have been proud. Once Crystal had finished, I continued to look at Beryl and said, 'I'm sure Beryl here does her utmost to discourage such visits, don't you?'

'Well, that's part of her job, of course,' Crystal said. 'Isn't it?' she added, swinging sharply round to her.

Beryl's jaw tightened, her good eye contracted and her head jerked up. 'Well, of course, I do my best,' she stuttered, clearly puzzled as to why attention had suddenly switched to her. As if it were now somehow her fault.

'Let's say no more on the matter then,' concluded Crystal, with a dismissive wave of her hand.

But it didn't let me off the hook regarding Mrs Tidy; and half an hour later, I found myself driving through the estate of bungalows on the other side of the Green. There was a uniformity about these bungalows that I found depressing – all were of red brick – save for one or two brave souls who had stepped out of rank to render theirs white. One even sported a light-pink wash, something I suspected wouldn't wash with the majority of the neighbours. All had that dull, red-brown, pantile roofing, although a degree of change had crept in over the years, whereby some now sprouted dormers. In fact, in one road, there was a whole row of loft conversions, as if the spores of one had spread to the next and had then mushroomed up through the tiles like some fungal growth, creeping from roof to roof.

The new rooms with a view – the dormers opposite – were hidden from view of each other by cascades of net curtaining. Indeed, this was the land of nets, where I suspected that curious malady I termed 'net curtain twitch' was rife. I sensed eyes following me from behind a string of nets as I cruised slowly along Downs View Drive – the name of the road into the estate a misnomer, since there was no view of the Downs to be seen – Bungalow Boulevard would have been more apt and would at least have commemorated the almond trees lining the road, the pink buds of which were just peeping through. Reminders of the time when this patch of Sussex was occupied by meadows grazed by sheep were reflected in Drovers Drive, the first left turning I took ... Lark Rise, the fourth right ... and finally Shepherd's Close, where having driven slowly round three-quarters of the cul-de-sac, an action that provoked a series of twitches from One, Two and Five, I came to a halt outside Number Seven, my destination.

It was no surprise to find I'd arrived at a very neat, well-ordered bungalow, whose white, wrought-iron gates gleamed, matched by a white lacework of wrought iron over a spotless, white garage door, with a similar gate in white leading down the side to a pristine UPVC front door – also white. The front garden was completely devoid of vegetation. If there used to be patches of lawn each side of the drive like the neighbours, then they'd long since been covered by mock-brick paving slabs; and although most of the close had neat privet or escallonia hedges dividing their gardens, Number Seven had a no-nonsense low, concrete wall down each side – rendered in white, of course. The only concession to nature was a couple of wooden tubs beneath the front window, which contained splashes of multicoloured garden centre primroses and a few mauve-and-black winter pansies.

It was Mr Tidy who answered the door when I rang the bell.

I seemed to recall the only word I'd had out of him to date was 'chlamydia' – or, in his wife's words, 'charmid ear' – one of the bugs that could be carried by birds and passed on to humans. This time, he was more effusive and uttered two words: 'Come in.' But at least it was accompanied by a smile – albeit somewhat forced – which revealed a set of gleaming white teeth so uniform in their appearance they could only have been dentures, a fact confirmed by the way 'Come in' was accompanied by a whistle of air through his gnashers and a rattle of dental plates. No wonder he was a man of few words. But his reticence was more than made up for by Mrs Tidy, who bustled out into the hall and, with an 'I'm pleased you could visit,' ushered me into the front room where, on a shiny, white, Formica-topped table in one corner, was Billy's cage with the cockatiel on his perch inside, looking rather subdued. There was certainly no raised crest or scuttling along the perch as I approached. He just sat there, feathers ruffled.

'He's gone very quiet these last 24 hours,' said Mrs Tidy. 'There hasn't been a peep out of him … has there, George?' She turned to her husband who had followed us in and was standing behind his wife, half hidden by her. He poked his head round her and shook it. I swear I heard his dentures rattling against his jaws. Alas, poor Yorick.

'And what's more,' she went on, 'he's got loose.'

For a second I thought she meant he'd escaped. However, my momentarily blank look didn't escape her notice as, with an exasperated and emphatic 'tut' which signalled her great reluctance to use the language of the lavatory, she said, 'He's got the runs …' and shuddered.

This was backed up with a helpful interjection by George, whose supportive 'Squits …' whistled through his teeth.

I looked into Billy's cage and saw that his sand sheet was unsoiled. 'I've just cleaned him out,' said Mrs Tidy. 'Can't be having that sort of thing lying around. All those ...' She took one of the deep breaths with which I was becoming familiar, before she'd utter a word of which she disapproved, then, out it came, with the full force of her loathing: '*Bugs.*'

There was another pause ... another intake of breath ... followed by, 'I think he might have picked something up from your consulting room last week. He'd been perfectly all right up to then. But now, those germs could be everywhere.' She raised her arms like the prongs of a forklift truck about to dump a pile of bricks on me, just as Billy did his own dump of a pile of diarrhoea. Splat! The liquid mass splashed down onto the sand sheet at high velocity. 'There! See what I mean? We could be exposing ourselves to untold contamination.' Mrs Tidy side-stepped and swung round on her husband, pumping a muscular arm up and down. 'George, do the honours please.' She pointed to a tea trolley covered with a small, white tablecloth, on which there was a box of clear plastic gloves, a white, moulded face mask and a stack of sand sheets; under the trolley was a black plastic bag.

Mr Tidy scurried forward, clamped the mask to his face, looping its elastic fastening over his skull, rummaged in the carton to extract two plastic gloves and, having donned these, he pulled out the black bag, undid its tie and propped it open against the table; he then yanked Billy's tray far enough out for him to extract the sand sheet, which, as he withdrew it, he carefully folded over back into itself, and then quickly lifted it free and popped it into the adjacent black bag. A clean sand sheet was slid onto the tray and the tray pushed back in, the gloves peeled off and tossed into the bag, and the bag firmly sealed with its tie before you could say 'George's your uncle'. Mr Tidy then sank back behind his wife – silent, save for the quiet clatter of his teeth over a job well done.

Having watched, spellbound, this finely executed performance, I tried to collect my thoughts as to what might have precipitated Billy's condition. I was a bit puzzled, especially as the laboratory screening had been clear. I reminded Mrs Tidy of those negative results.

'Ah, but there are some bugs you can miss,' said Mrs Tidy. 'George found that out on the Internet, didn't you, George?'

He nodded, with a muted whistle, as if about to speak.

'There's one in particular that you might not pick up unless you take several samples. Isn't that right, George?'

There was another whistle.

'George may not say much but he's very good at finding things out on Google, aren't you, George?'

Whistle. Whistle.

'The name of that … *bug* (a shudder here) … er … "camp" something or other. What was it, George?'

George had, by now, cranked up a sufficient head of steam to set his dentures in motion. He blew the word out: 'Campylobacter.'

'There you go. That's the one. Heard of it?' said Mrs Tidy, addressing me.

I had heard of it. Campylobacter was a bacterium that could be carried by dogs, cats and birds. But it could also be carried by quite a high percentage of humans, without symptoms being shown. That was the limit of my knowledge. As to its detection, well, I assumed it could be picked up by faecal screening, though, from what Mrs Tidy was telling me, that could be missed if only one sample was taken. But then if detected, so what? It was carried by animals without symptoms being shown. Ah, yes, but Billy *was* showing symptoms, wasn't he? But then not symptoms of any serious illness – he was bright-eyed and bushy-tailed. Well, feather-tailed, to be more precise. Oh dear, I was beginning to tie myself in knots here.

I questioned Mrs Tidy further and was able to verify that Billy, indeed, was still bright and perky, eating and drinking as normal.

A little bell started to ring in my brain. Eating ... appetite ... food.

'What exactly do you give him to eat?' I ventured to ask, prompted by further sparking in my neurons.

'Come through and I'll show you,' replied Mrs Tidy, and marched me through a scrupulously clean kitchen to an extension at the back which served as a utility room – washing machine, boiler, Belfast sink and scrubbed draining board, with wall and floor units to each side. Mrs Tidy flung open the wall unit to the left of the sink. There, displayed on two shelves, were large, white, plastic containers, with screw tops, each neatly labelled with its contents – peanuts, sunflower seed, sesame seed, millet. 'I make sure they're all washed and dust free before I give them to Billy,' said Mrs Tidy, proudly.

I could picture her sitting at the kitchen table, dusting and polishing each single seed, lining them up in ranks for inspection to see if they would pass muster.

'What about fruit?' I asked.

'Yes, of course.' Mrs Tidy bent down and swung open one of the units next to the sink. 'I keep most of it down here.' She pointed to the white, plastic vegetable rack wedged inside. Each of its three tiers held a different fruit or vegetable. Shiny red apples in the top rack, pears in the middle and sprouts at the bottom. 'I steam the lot of them,' she added, straightening up. 'I feel happier doing that. At least it lessens the chances of Billy picking up one of those you-know-whats.' Her lips drew into a thin line at her oblique reference to the bugs, which she seemed convinced were ever-present, constantly threatening to invade and exterminate all life on Earth.

It was at that point I decided to take the risk and challenge her misconceptions; and just hoped it would be the right move.

'Mrs Tidy,' I started tentatively, 'I've a feeling that Billy's environment is maybe just a little too sterile.' I saw her eyebrows begin to rise, her eyes narrow, but, undaunted, I went on: 'He needs a few bugs around to build up his immunity.' Her eyebrows continued to rise, only stopping when the creases on her forehead looked as if a tyre had just driven across it. I ploughed on: 'He needs a more down-to-earth diet.'

Perhaps I should have chosen my words a little more carefully as I saw Mrs Tidy visibly flinch. Her response to 'bug' was no surprise, but the flinch detected at the mention of 'earth' was a bit worrying. It seemed this lady really did have a problem with her concepts of hygiene; but I dug my heels in and stuck to my guns, even though it meant being subjected to great shovelfuls of scepticism from her. But my persistence paid off and, eventually, I managed to get her to acquiesce. I left, having got her to promise to feed Billy a more natural diet without resorting to scrubbing and steaming every morsel of his food.

Mind you, as I negotiated my way out of Shepherd's Close, Lark Rise, Drovers Drive and Downs View Drive, I wasn't entirely convinced I was on the right track in my diagnosis of Billy's condition. I could be heading up a blind alley in much the same way I found myself in a dead end when I took the wrong turning out of Drovers Drive and ended up having to reverse out of a Downside Close, whose name I hoped didn't reflect on what was going to happen next.

They say you shouldn't take your work home with you, but I just couldn't get Billy out of my mind; and that evening, I found myself in front of the computer, bringing up Google and typing in a search for diseases transmitted from birds to humans. I tapped into the first one shown, and up came a very simple summary of bacteria that could be carried by dogs, cats and birds and which could be passed to humans, with the symptoms to be seen should a human contract the disease. It might have been a simple summary but, even without explicit details, it was enough to make me scared witless, so I could just imagine how Mrs Tidy must have felt, as I was sure her husband would have shown it to her, his dentures all of a rattle as he did so. Diarrhoea ... vomiting ... abdominal pains ... fever. All of these symptoms were attributable to campylobacter if caught from dogs, cats or birds. And Mr Tidy had been right – faecal screening for the bug could be inconclusive unless a series of tests were carried out. I felt my bowels contract on reading that. Oh Lord ... perhaps my diagnosis had been wrong. Heaven help me if the Tidys also went down with enteritis. But hang on, that was highly unlikely as they were so thorough in their cleaning of Billy's cage. As for Billy, we'd have to see. I had left instructions with Mrs Tidy to get in contact should things not improve and, as a week passed and I heard nothing, I assumed he was on the mend. Until the parcel arrived.

'It's addressed to you,' said Beryl, sorting through the morning's stack of mail. She slid the parcel across the counter. 'Looks a bit suspicious if you ask me.'

I wasn't asking her but it did look a little unusual all the same. It was a standard A4 Jiffy bag, but there was nothing standard about the way it was taped all round its edges and had a biohazard label back and front and a handwritten 'Handle with Care' next to my name, an unintentional juxtaposition I felt sure. The bag bulged in its centre so there was clearly more in it than just paperwork.

Beryl adopted her 'eye-wide-open, jaw-dropped, brick-bashed-owl' look as she contemplated me holding the packet. 'I wouldn't open it if I were you, Paul,' she warned, giving a little shake of her head. 'Don't you remember the letter bomb in that London office last year. It blew the bloke's hand off.'

My hand, which had been holding the parcel, rapidly detached itself from said packet and I hastily replaced the suspect package back on the counter, an action which had Beryl spring from her chair, her wings of lacquered hair flapping. She backed rapidly through the archway and bumped into Eric, who was just bouncing up the steps from the office. As usual, he'd been going at a rate of knots, so the velocity of their impact was considerable. So was the point of their impact. In her startled state, Beryl had backed away with one hand in front of her and one behind. It was the one behind, with its plethora of spiky talons, that drove straight into Eric's genitals.

'Bloody hell, Beryl,' he gasped, his face going puce with pain. 'I'm knackered enough as it is without you grabbing my goolies.'

'I'm sorry,' said Beryl, pulling her hand away as she swung round. 'It's just that we've got a letter bomb on the counter there.' She directed a talon at the parcel next to which I was still standing.

'What?' shouted Eric, looking over Beryl's shoulder and

spotting the parcel. 'Oh my God,' he added anxiously. 'Paul, don't be a prat. Move away ... NOW!'

'What's going on up there?' It was the sharp, clear tone of Crystal's voice echoing up the corridor from the kennels where she'd been doing her ward round with Mandy, checking her orthopaedic ops from the previous day.

'Nothing to worry about, dear,' Eric cried in response. 'We've just got a bomb in reception.'

'Christ, Eric, what on earth are you talking about? What bomb?' Crystal's voice came closer, until I could see her squeezing her way between Eric and Beryl, the three of them now crammed in the archway. Then the top of Mandy's head with its starched cap hove into view behind them, swiftly followed by a flash of blonde as Lucy joined her from the dispensary. If what I had in front of me was indeed a bomb, then with one quick rip of the Jiffy bag being opened I could have blown the entire staff of Prospect House to smithereens in one fell swoop.

'Shall I nip down to the office and call the police?' I heard Mandy say.

'Just hang on a minute,' declared Crystal. 'Just let's see what we're talking about here.' She was about to move forward when Beryl put out a restraining hand and, in a hushed voice, turned to dramatically remind everyone of the arm that had been blown off by the London letter bomb. Uhmm, I thought, give her yet another chance to recall the story and it would be a torso blown to smithereens; then perhaps a leg or two tossed in as well.

'Paul,' Eric called out. 'Did you touch the device?'

It was Beryl who answered. 'Yes, he did. And he was about to peel it open, when I reminded him about the man who got blown to smithereens by that London letter bomb.'

There, what did I tell you?

'Mmm,' said Eric. 'In which case, it could now be unstable. Liable to go off at any minute.' It was a statement which hung in the air for a few seconds – enough time for the five figures to vanish from the archway, Crystal being pulled out of sight by Eric. Sounds of a heated discussion followed.

'We can't be too careful,' I heard Eric saying. 'Remember that vet friend of ours who worked at Porton Down?'

'So? What of it?' That was Crystal, her tone irritated. 'And do let go of me Eric, for heaven's sake.'

'Sorry, love, but I don't want you taking any chances. And there was that vet who had one under her car. She scrabbled out just in time before it blew up.'

'Really?' That was Beryl. 'Well, I'll be blowed.' An unfortunate choice of verb, I thought, considering current circumstances.

'It's like those thingies in Iraq,' Mandy had chipped in.

'You mean IEDs.' Lucy this time.

'Step on one of those, you'd know it.' Mandy again.

'We'd better watch our step then.' Beryl once more.

'Er, excuse me,' I called out, a hand raised.

Beryl's head popped round the corner. 'What is it, Paul?'

'Er ... well ...' I pointed down at the package. 'Are we going to ... er ... do something about this?'

'We most certainly are,' said Crystal, appearing in the archway, smoothing out the creases on the jacket sleeve to which Eric had been clinging. She stepped forward with a determined look on her face, while the other four members of her bomb disposal unit jostled for best viewing position behind her, ready to scarper if she gave the word.

She reached the counter and, with her forefinger, eased the package round to face her and read the label. 'It's addressed to you,' she said, looking up at me. 'It's nothing you were expecting?'

I shook my head.

With finger and thumb, she lifted the package and turned it over – an action which evoked an admiring gasp from her onlookers, apart from me. I was in the front line, hardly daring to breathe. She prodded the bag gently, evoking another admiring gasp. 'Can't see this being a bomb,' she continued. 'Let's see what's inside.'

Her admirers gave a final gasp and vanished. Crystal carefully eased one of her dainty fingernails under the flap and slid it along until the seal loosened and she was able to lift it up and peer inside. 'There seems to be another package in here,' she said, tilting the Jiffy bag to allow its contents to slip onto the counter. Between us now lay a cylindrical parcel about the length of a biro, heavily encased in bubble wrap. As on the outside of the Jiffy bag, this had a label, although smaller, but with what appeared to be similar-styled handwriting on it, although I couldn't read what it said as it was facing away from me. Crystal did the honours. 'It says "Billy Tidy".' She looked across at me. 'Billy Tidy ...' she repeated. 'Does that mean anything to you?'

I nodded glumly. It seems we didn't have a bomb here; nevertheless, those two words detonated an explosion of emotions in my mind as I acknowledged that the words did, indeed, mean something to me. 'It's a patient of mine,' I said.

'Ex-patient now by the looks of things,' I heard Beryl mutter.

Thank you, Beryl.

I had reached my metaphorical Downside Close – a dead end – a cockatiel's corpse buried beneath layers of bubble wrap. I picked up the packet, peeled off the sticky tape and slowly began to unravel the body. But Mrs Tidy, in true belt-and-braces mode, hadn't simply been satisfied with one layer of mummification. I discovered that when the last of the bubble wrap had been removed, I was left with an opaque, cigar-shaped, plastic tube with a plastic screw cap, secured in place with more sticky tape. The tape I removed, to unscrew the lid, which I began to do very slowly and with a very heavy heart, until reminded by Crystal that the reception counter was not quite the right place to unwrap a dead bird.

Her comment was apt as, at that moment, the first of the morning's appointments walked in through the front door – a gentleman carrying a budgerigar cage with a chirping occupant. 'My Billy's come in to have his beak and nails trimmed,' he said brightly. 'I've told him it's nothing to worry about.' His cheery countenance dissolved into bewilderment as he watched the assembled staff of Prospect House disperse rapidly. Only Beryl was brave enough to confront him, but even she was not quite able to rid herself of her brick-bashed-owl look, saying, 'Somebody will be with you soon,' as I snatched up Billy's body and dodged out, while his namesake in the gentleman's cage gave an optimistic chirrup.

Down in the prep room I continued where I'd left off, under the watchful eye of Mandy, who had supplied a kidney dish into which I was instructed to deposit the corpse. Having unscrewed the cap, I tipped up the container expecting Billy the stiff to slip out. Only Billy didn't slip out, due to the fact that he wasn't the prize in this particularly macabre game of pass-the-parcel. What emerged was a neatly cut out, long, rectangular section of sand sheet, in the middle of which was a solid dropping –

green-grey with streaks of white. The perfect poo. Elation shot through me. 'Whoopee,' I cried, realising that Billy's bowels must have returned to normal.

Mandy gave me a withering look which clearly stated, 'What a sad git you are to get so excited over bird shit.'

But I didn't care. I was delighted since I now knew that in any future dealings with Mrs Tidy, my advice wouldn't be pooh-poohed.

8
REIGNING CATS
AND DOG

I might have told Crystal and Eric that things weren't too bad between Lucy and me – certainly nothing that would affect our working relationship in Prospect House – but outside the practice it was a different story. I just felt we'd reached a stalemate and that things weren't going anywhere. But then did I want them to go anywhere? Was I looking for a long-term relationship – the type of commitment that would end up with a mortgage and 2.1 children?

Perhaps it was just the mood I was in. It wasn't helped by an article I'd read recently in one of the Sunday papers, about when married couples are at their happiest. According to a poll of 4,000 couples conducted by a wedding website, they reach the 'zenith of their contentment after 2 years, 11 months and 8 days together'. Hmm … Lucy and I reached ours within 20 minutes of tumbling into bed. No – only joking. But this poll stated that at that point in time, the couples were happy with each other's bad habits.

As for my bad habits ... well, I'm not sure I had any. I didn't leave underpants lying around on the floor – only in the early, eager days of our relationship when they were left under the bed for the duration of activities going on above them. Now, my pants were neatly piled with socks and T-shirts, prior to being placed in our wicker laundry basket – what could one read into that, I wondered? And I didn't leave the toilet seat up after use. The poll also stated that 'three years after walking down the aisle, everything seems to come together – making each other laugh and cuddling up in front of the TV ... and making gestures like offering to cook dinner and help with the washing up.' Oh dear. We were already doing that – out of necessity, really. We were both stretched with our jobs, and so domestic duties had to be shared, including the cooking. A top-notch supermarket had recently opened on the outskirts of Westcott, on my route home to Ashton, and they did such a marvellous selection of à la carte ready-meals that it seemed a shame not to sample them. It was just a coincidence that we usually sampled them on those days when I was due to cook.

That report made me think that Lucy and I, although not married, may have peaked 2 years, 11 months and 8 days too early in our relationship, and that a stalemate had now been reached.

I realised I should have been discussing it with Lucy but somehow there never seemed to be the right time. OK, I admit it ... that was more likely just an excuse. If the truth be known, I was probably just ducking out of the issue. For her part, Lucy seemed to be on autopilot, ticking over ... getting through the daily routines. Her night duties were spent at Prospect House, using the spare room in the nurses' flat above the practice where currently only Mandy

146

lived, although there was enough space for three people to live quite comfortably together.

At the start of our affair, Lucy didn't relish those nights – not so much the fact of having to be ready to take any calls, but more the fact she was away from me. Ah, what passion. The full moon of love. But, like the moon, passion can wane and it seemed this was happening – I sensed those nights away were almost welcomed by Lucy now. At least, that's the impression I was getting of late. I half expected her to move out of Willow Wren and return to Prospect House on a permanent basis, except for one thing – her animals. Or, more accurately, *our* animals, since apart from Queenie, acquired by Lucy at Prospect House, and a couple of guinea pigs and a rabbit which she'd kept in a hutch out in the back garden of the practice – and which had been a constant source of interest to the dogs being exercised out there – the menagerie at Willow Wren was one collected over the five months or so we'd been together. And although I felt she could cope with a split from me, her attachment to our pets was too strong to make that break ... up until now.

You hear of couples staying together for the sake of the children. Replace them with pets, and you had our situation in a nutshell. Someone or something would have to give. But then perhaps things would turn around and we'd be back where we started, love blossoming again like the emerging buds of spring. In the event, it was Nelson who precipitated events and in a catastrophic way.

I have to blame Mildred Millichip for introducing the little Jack Russell into our lives in the first place. She was what I termed the 'would-be-vet' I'd encountered during my first six months at Prospect House. From the word go, I'd had constant battles with her over the treatment of her collection of dogs and cats; she was always trying medications gleaned from a very ancient and very out-of-date veterinary dictionary, with me having to insist that most of her treatments were doing more harm than good. She had quite a commanding presence, in the sense that she had the build of a Sherman tank, topped by a gun turret of wiry, grey hair, wisps of which blew round her face, escaping the clutch of elastic bands and broken-toothed combs which secured the rest of it. Many's the time I heard her say, 'Always wanted to be a vet, ever since I was a mere slip of a girl.'

Er ... that must have been many years ago. Mildred Millichip's now generous proportions had long since engulfed the shadow of her former self.

Mildred's centre of operations was the kitchen of her bungalow – her 'brain centre'. Here her strategies, battle plans and their execution were carried out amidst what, to the uninitiated eye, could only be described as a war zone – a battlefield of growth charts; peeling, out-of-date veterinary drug company calendars; shelves sagging under the weight of faded 'How to' books on animal husbandry. In the middle of this ramshackle miscellany stood her main weapon of war – her kitchen table, a substantial pine affair with chunky legs and wide boarded top; although not antique, the table was sufficiently aged to have warped and split, so there were gaps between the boards into which, over the years, the detritus – hair, nail clippings, dandruff, flea dirt – of countless animals had settled and impacted. Although Mildred Millichip still ate off the table, its foremost use was for the examination and treatment of her cats and dogs. It was on that table I first met Nelson.

I'd just had a preliminary skirmish with her over a cat with a sore mouth. 'Teeth, I reckon,' she declared, having hoisted the cat onto the pine table, where it sat cowering and dribbling under her massive hands, while she ran a finger and thumb under the upper lip on one side of its mouth, peeling it back to reveal molars covered in tartar, gums that were bleeding and the reek of bad breath. She picked at a tooth and dislodged a lump of yellow deposit which dropped from the cat's mouth and disappeared down a crack in the table top. 'Guess Monica needs a dental, eh?' she said. I agreed and a date was fixed for her to bring Monica in for descaling. 'Now,' she went on, wiping her fingers along the edge of the table, 'would you like a cup of tea before you go?'

I declined.

'In that case could I just get you to check over a terrier that's just been brought in? He's a real sweetie but he's got a thing about cats. And as you know I've loads here.' Indeed, I did know. Usually her kitchen was full of them, sitting on and along the top of the sofa, curled up in front of the range, peeking down from the tops of the shelves and stalking round the kitchen table, tails raised in expectation of dinner being served. But today there were no felines on the prowl – in fact, no animals other than Monica and an elderly-looking dog, stretched out on the hearth, gently snoring. 'They're all keeping their distance,' Miss Millichip went on, pointing to the window where a row of cats sat, peering in, 'because of him.' She gestured at the sleeping dog and then walked over to him. 'Come on, Nelson. Wakey wakey.'

She knelt down and gently prodded him. 'Oi, wake up.'

The dog opened an eye and raised his head.

'Yes, you,' she said and turned to me. 'He's a bit deaf. And his eyesight's not so good either.' She slid her arm under his chest and lifted him up. 'Come on, you daft old thing, let's get you checked over.'

Once on the kitchen table, I was presented with a terrier whom I suppose you could have called a Jack Russell. But only just. He was small, short-haired, with a solid, stocky body, stumpy, bowed legs, one ear that flopped over, one that stood up, and a tail a foot high that stuck up ramrod straight. There was a large patch of black over his left eye, echoed by one over his left hip; otherwise he was white – which made the black pigmentation encircling each eye like a thick layer of eyeliner all the more startling. The little chap yawned and sat down, turning to blink at me, his eyes milky.

'You can see he's got cataracts,' said Miss Millichip, reconfirming her 'would-be-vet' status. 'And I'd suspect he's got some fluid in his tummy ... wouldn't you?' She reached over and cupped her hand under his pendulous abdomen.

Once having palpated Nelson's abdomen myself, I was able to confirm Miss Millichip's observations.

'Could be his heart I suppose,' she was saying, 'although he hasn't been coughing or getting out of breath. So it's unlikely.'

Having listened through my stethoscope to Nelson's heart, all seemed pretty normal, no murmurs, no arrhythmias, so I had to agree with Miss Millichip. Again.

'He's got good teeth for a 12-year-old, hasn't he?' remarked Miss Millichip as I opened his mouth. 'All his incisors are still present and there doesn't appear to be anything wrong with his back molars, does there?'

Yes. For the third time, I had to agree.

'And he didn't object when I felt his lower lumbar spine and his hips,' she went on as I was about to start my own examination of them. 'So no obvious problems with arthritis, then.'

'No,' I said, finishing my own rotation and palpation of Nelson's hips, wondering whether it was worth me bothering to go on.

Throughout, Nelson was a model patient, stoically standing or sitting when requested. Only towards the end of my examination did he start to pant a little, his large, pink tongue lolling out of the side of his mouth.

'Well done, old fella,' I said, as I finally finished and tickled him at the base of his ear. It was an action that immediately had him twist his head to one side and produced the biggest grin I'd ever seen in such a small dog, his lips curling back to almost lose themselves behind his ears.

It certainly made me smile and Miss Millichip was quick to notice.

'He needs a good home,' she said, going on to explain that she couldn't cope with his anti-cat stance. I liked Jack Russells, didn't I? Just look at the way Nelson had taken to me – that winsome grin of his, so appealing, wasn't it? And he was in good nick for his age, didn't I think? He just needed a loving, caring home with someone to deal with any problems as they arose. Yes?

Her battering tirade persisted until I began to buckle and, with one final push, saying I was just the sort of owner he needed, all my defences were breached. I surrendered ... and found myself driving home that evening with Nelson sitting on the seat next to me. Although not grinning now, he certainly seemed to have a very pleased expression on his face – who was the stupid mutt, me or him?

But I'd forgotten one thing. And as I turned off the lane down to Willow Wren and eased the car round into the hard standing in front of the garage, I suddenly realised that I'd capitulated in the face of Miss Millichip's onslaught only to land myself with a far greater battle ahead. For some inexplicable reason, I'd totally forgotten one thing in agreeing to take on this smiley old mutt who, the minute I stopped, brought his head up level with the bottom of the window and started sniffing with inordinate and rather troubling interest. Although there was the barrier of the car and the thickness of Willow Wren's walls, it seemed that Nelson's radar was so finely tuned that he could already sense what lay within those walls and what was, no doubt, reclining with regal grace on her favourite armchair – Queenie, Lucy's cat.

'Wait there, old chap,' I whispered, slipping out of the car and going round to the side gate, entering the cottage as if I was about to commit a heinous crime. Which I suppose, in a way, I was.

'Luce?' I said softly, tiptoeing into the living room. She wasn't there. But Queenie was. She looked across from her throne (our settee) where she was stretched out along its back in all her regal, green-eyed splendour, her long, silky, white-and-grey robes (fur) flowing down the front of the settee while the tip of her sceptre (tail) curled up at the sight of me. It was like a regal staff summoning me over. I had to fight the urge to hurry forward and prostrate myself on the red carpet before her, begging to have my sins forgiven by royal pardon.

'Paul? What's up?' It was Lucy coming down the narrow stairs, looking over the banister to where I was standing in the middle of the living room, staring at Queenie, thighs squeezed together, hands wedged between them, ready to drop to the ground in supplication. 'Do you need the loo?' she added, curious at my stance. Although, at that stage, Lucy and I had only been living together less than six weeks, it had been long enough for me to suss out that she had what is termed by some as 'a woman's intuition', and Lucy had it in bucket-loads.

Many a time she observed what I was saying or doing – or maybe not saying or doing – and with uncanny accuracy knew immediately the reasons behind my actions, almost as if she could read my mind. More than a touch of the Madam Mountjoys, there, I thought. Quite unnerving really. She'd shown that intuition when I acquired Gertie, the goose, and this evening I knew the moment she clamped her eyes on me that she'd twigged something was afoot. Maybe my feet were indeed the giveaway – the way they were nervously padding up and down in the middle of the room, rather like a tom cat's hind-legs dance just before he ejects a stream of urine up a wall. Fortunately I wasn't that nervous, and so there was no danger of wetting myself or the living room wall.

'Paul.' Lucy took a step nearer. I lowered my head, my eyes sliding from her glance – a glance which clearly said, 'I know exactly what you've done.'

'You haven't, have you?' she continued.

'What, love?' I said, all innocence, trying to smother the guilt in my voice – a hopeless task with Lucy's radar on full scan.

'Brought home another animal.' Now, had she said that unaided, then I truly would have thought her a mind reader; but just at that moment, Nelson decided he'd waited long enough in the car and let out a mournful howl. On hearing it, she was quick to elaborate. 'And a dog by the sound of it.' Well, at least it saved me the task of telling her the nature of the beast. Lucy took a deep breath and then sighed. 'Well, I trust it likes cats.' She arched an eyebrow at me.

I looked across at her and said, with as much conviction as possible, 'Cats? Oh, he adores cats.' Well, that was true up to a point. Nelson did adore cats – adored chasing them. No good. Lucy's intuition revealed itself with excruciating clarity. 'Bloody hell, Paul. Don't tell me – he hates them.'

I didn't think it fair to reach that conclusion based on the fact that she could read my mind. For all she knew, the 12 or so cats I had in mind, trembling outside Miss Millichip's kitchen windows and doors, fearful to step inside while Nelson was in there, may just have been a figment of my imagination. But I knew they weren't ... and so did Lucy.

'OK ... OK,' I admitted. 'Nelson's not *too* keen on cats. But I'm sure Queenie will soon put him in his place.' I looked across at her royal highness as I spoke; judging from the disdain etched on her face, that place had already been decided – the Tower of London, ready for the chop.

The meeting between the two wasn't as dramatic as I feared. Sure, Nelson trotted in, full of jauntiness, his flagpole tail erect and quivering; and as soon as he spotted Queenie, he raced across the living room, braking to a halt at the settee, then springing onto it with remarkable agility considering his 12 years. Was he expecting Queenie to shoot away, giving him the excuse to give chase? If so, he was sorely disappointed. She'd already stood up when he'd entered the room, and, as he approached, had arched her back and given a warning hiss. All those warning signs were missed by Nelson. But then he was deaf and poor-sighted – or maybe just plain dumb. So by the time he was on the settee with his paws on its back, her own back was well up, arched ready to give him a mighty biff on his nose. Which she did with royal aplomb, as if knighting him.

With an almighty yelp, he reeled back, fell sideways onto the seat of the settee, and then rolled off onto the carpet, where he struggled to his feet and, with a distinct air of disbelief, shook himself, before, his tail erect once more, he trotted out into the kitchen, discovered the remains of Queenie's supper and devoured the lot in a couple of gulps.

Her royal highness, meanwhile, watched him disappear, and then set about rearranging her robes with a good lick of her tongue. And that was the end of the matter. The uprising had been quelled and no further disturbances (apart from those between Lucy and me) were to mar Queenie's reign, Nelson making sure he kept a respectful distance whenever he was in her presence.

I only wished some of the other residents of Willow Wren could have kept their respectful distance. Along with the cottage, we seemed to have inherited a colony of mice, which wasn't in the inventory I'd checked through with Eric and Crystal before settling in. They were a happy band of rodents who, on our arrival, welcomed us with open paws, and a cheery twitch of their whiskers, showing their interest in us by immediately delving into all and sundry, trekking across the loft at night, popping down to rummage through the drawers in the kitchen, with the occasional squeak of delight at having found a tasty morsel – Camembert, Brie and Roquefort were particular favourites. It made me wonder whether we'd inherited a special breed that had smuggled their way in under the cover of one of those French farmers' markets that periodically invaded Westcott – stall holders dressed in berets and blue-and-white jerseys, displaying their strings of onions and stacks of baguettes with plenty of 'Bonjours' and 'Saluts' in the pedestrianised High Street, much to the bewilderment of the old dears trying to get to the Co-op.

These mice certainly had the *sangfroid* of the French and I half expected to encounter one eventually, leaning against

155

our pine dresser, a Gauloise rakishly stuck in the corner of his mouth while watching his mates play boules with some salted peanuts we'd forgotten to put away that evening. They were certainly quite brazen in their comings and goings; often, when I was sitting on the toilet, one would come pattering across the floor, nut rather than ciggie in mouth, to dart into the gap between the lavatory pan and the floorboards.

One even developed a routine whereby he or she would visit me when I was in bed – at the time, I had rather a slovenly habit of having snacks in bed just before going to sleep, which meant a plate with crumbs and often an apple core were left on the bedside cabinet overnight. That is until a mouse discovered my unsavoury habit, and I began finding an empty, scoured plate there the next morning. The rodent's visits got earlier and earlier until, one evening, I'd only just put the plate down when onto the cabinet he skipped, sat up, whiskers aquiver, barely a foot from me and then lifted the apple core between his paws, spun it round as if checking for palatability before sinking his teeth into its centre and scuttling off with it.

'People will think you a bit weird,' Lucy warned me one night as she walked into the bedroom to find me sprawled on the bed in my boxer shorts, digital camera mounted on a tripod with extension release pointing at the cabinet, while I waited to get a flash photo of my core-nicking friend. And, yes, I did get one ... and a few rather more racy shots of Lucy and me later, so in one evening I managed to capture two sides to the wildlife in our bedroom.

'We're really going to have to do something about these mice,' declared Lucy the next morning as she rummaged in her knicker drawer and pulled out a pair in soft-cream satin with dainty, lace trim round the waist – I'd bought them at the Christmas sales, all the racy red satin numbers in size ten had gone. She held them up, stretched between her hands, turning to show them to me. 'See? Just look at that. Completely ruined.' And just to emphasise the point, she stuck a finger through the hole in the gusset where a mouse had chewed it.

I had thought the presence of Queenie might have deterred the hordes of mice.

'You must be joking,' Lucy told me. 'That's not her thing.'

Queenie's thing, it seemed, was to cast a regal eye over the mousy proceedings without batting an eyelid at their frequent toings and froings across her empire. She would not stoop to conquer; not for her Boudicca-style charges to snatch a rodent or two. The likes of next door's Tammy could catch and bring in her spoils of war should she choose to, but for Queenie that was far beneath her, far too demeaning. In fact, the opposite was true of her – she expected the spoils of war to be brought to her … or rather, the spoils of our cooking.

'She's bloody faddy,' I once declared, as she padded over to the bowl of gourmet, tinned food I'd forked out for her, gave it one cursory sniff and then walked over to the fridge, sat down and patted the door with a paw.

'She's got good taste, that's all,' said Lucy opening the door to take out the remains of our chicken casserole, spoon a portion into a dish and put it down for Queenie, who immediately tucked in with great relish.

'Hey, I was saving that for our dinner tomorrow,' I cried.

Lucy shrugged. 'You'll just have to find something else.'

I looked down at the pile of untouched gourmet chicken and liver cat food and wondered if I could curry it.

Queenie's indifference to the mice was one reason Lucy and I didn't discourage Garfield when he first made his appearance. It was a late summer's evening as I was returning from an emergency appointment at Prospect House – an evening when Lucy had been the nurse on duty and so was sleeping in the flat that night, reluctantly, as we were still nuts about each other at the time; in fact, had it not been for the animals to be seen to at Willow Wren, I would have stayed in the spare room with her, even though it risked Mandy overhearing our lovemaking, which could be noisy at times. It was something I kept forgetting at Willow Wren, wondering the next morning as we got woken by Wilfred's screeches penetrating the dividing wall whether our equally vocal 'aaargghs' and 'uurrrffs' of the previous evening, accompanied by the rhythmic pounding of bedsprings, ever impinged on Eleanor's sleeping patterns. Nothing was ever said. But then how could a genteel lady whose son was a vicar broach such a subject? She could hardly say, 'Would you mind being a little less zealous in your bonking?'

It was getting dark as I drew up outside Willow Wren. Eleanor's lights were on, glowing through the curtains she'd already drawn. It had been a warm day, so as I walked down the side of the cottage, I could feel that warmth radiate out from the walls and, on reaching the little wrought-iron gate opening onto the metre or so of brick path that led up to the front door, I stopped and put a hand on the corner of the wall, curling my fingers round the edge, allowing the warmth to seep into them while I gazed down the darkening garden, silhouetted against pencils of cloud that now scored the western sky in deep pinks and indigos. And that's when I saw him – or rather, at first – *heard* him.

There was a rustle in the ivy that grew in a wide, heavy band up the south side of the cottage, fanning out from a dense clump right in the corner where the extension jutted out, and which was now deep in shadow as I strained to see what was causing the rustling. I had once seen a hedgehog snuffling about in the mulch of dead leaves that I deliberately left piled under the ivy to encourage insects and grubs for just such visitors; but instead of the hedgehog I was now expecting, out stepped a cat. He was a small, ginger-and-white creature, and from what I could see of him in the gloom, spindly and thin. As I opened the gate, he spat at me, his teeth gleaming in the twilight, and then he charged off down the garden. The next I saw of him was the following evening when a ginger nose was pressed to the lower pane of the kitchen window at roughly the same time as the previous night.

Unlike the unnamed tortoiseshell that was to adopt us for a few weeks later in September, and which Lucy took against, her reaction on seeing the little ginger-and-white cat was very positive. Perhaps she saw it as a means to an end – the end of mice nibbling at her gussets – since she exclaimed, 'Paul, look … there's a sweet little cat peering in. He looks like a miniature Garfield.' That became his adoptive name.

Over the ensuing days, Lucy did her level best to entice the cat indoors with a constant stream of 'Puss … puss … puu-uuss …' but he was having none of it, preferring to take up residence at the back of the garage where we stored a couple of bales of straw for Bugsie and the guinea pigs; the gap between the two provided sufficient shelter and safety for him.

Unlike Queenie, he wasn't too fussed about what he was given to eat and gratefully tucked into whatever tinned cat food I churned out for him, purring as he settled down to eat it, having waited until I had stepped a safe distance away; and drink-wise he seemed happy enough with the water I provided, although over the months, at Lucy's behest, the water was first replaced with water with a dash of milk in it, then half and half, and eventually progressed from skimmed through semi to full cream. And although both the food and water bowl – or rather the cream dish as it eventually became – were positioned daily closer and closer to the kitchen door, Garfield never saw his way to placing a paw within the cottage. No doubt, once he had caught sight of Queenie parading round inside, he realised a lowly peasant such as himself would not be fit to grace her presence.

The same applied to another scrawny-looking cat, this time black, who turned up in much the same way as Garfield – a sudden appearance one evening; and he, too, stayed, but chose as his living quarters the shed further down the garden, the back panel of which was loose and which he learnt to lift with his paw and sneak in. Hence his adoptive name of Push-in. The shed served as Gertie the goose's night-time shelter, but his new roomie didn't deter Push-in, who used a shelf out of bill range as his bed, supplemented by an old pillow which ironically was stuffed with goose feathers.

Of course, any hopes of domesticating either Garfield or Push-in were well and truly dashed by the arrival of Nelson, who saw to it that the house was off limits, and they had to keep to their chosen territories – the garage for Garfield, and the shed for Push-in. They both often had to make beelines for their respective quarters – their flights hastened by a snapping terrier at one or other of their heels. I eventually kept a window at the back of the garage ajar, while the loose panel on the back of the shed I nailed up so that both cats could escape unscathed.

At least some sort of order was established between the cats and dog living at Willow Wren, which was more than could be said for the human occupants. Garfield and Push-in had their bolt-holes – it seemed that the spare room in the flat over the surgery was to become more and more of a bolt-hole for Lucy. But what was she escaping from and why?

9

SHOW ME
THE BUNNY!

The rabbit that Lucy brought with her to Willow Wren was a black-and-white creature called Bugsie. To tell you the truth, I didn't take much notice of him, never having been enamoured by lagomorphs.

As a child, my mother had brandished Beatrix Potter books over my bed at story-time, and I had to endure endless recounting of the shenanigans of Flopsy, Mopsy and Cottontail, not to mention the exploits of Benjamin Bunny. This was all reinforced a year or so later by the playing of Happy Families, Snap and Pairs with Beatrix's ghastly little friends depicted on the cards. One Peter Rabbit card had a creased corner, so when the cards were spread out over the floor, their backs up, and I turned up an unmarked Peter Rabbit, I could quickly pick out his bent partner to make a pair. Perhaps, deep down in my psyche, I developed an aversion to rabbits, reasoning – irrationally – that if I were to get too up close and personal to such a creature, I might become damaged goods as well. Guys named Peter have a similar effect on me – I must see a psychiatrist about it one of these days. Meanwhile, Bugsie stayed low on my list of favourite animals that had come to live at Willow Wren. Until, that is, the day Beryl booked me an appointment to see a certain Mr Grimaldi – a magician who had a sick rabbit.

'Sorry,' apologised Beryl, 'but the man was in quite a state on the phone and insisted he be seen as soon as possible. So I've had to squeeze him in before you take your tea break this afternoon.'

Beryl was right about his state. Mr Grimaldi was certainly in a flap, and his demeanour suggested that, even in his calmer moments, he was still a bit of a flapper, there being a certain girlishness about him in the way he waltzed in, all of a tizz, and proceeded to enlighten me as to his concerns in an Italian-accented, sing-songy voice that had nasal undercurrents reminiscent of Kenneth Williams in *Carry on Cleo*. However camp his manner might have been, though, his looks suggested something quite different. He was short – barely coming up to my shoulders – with a paunch which a dark-blue, velvet jacket did nothing to disguise; and he had ginger-brown hair slicked back from a receding hairline and tied in a ponytail. There were no remarkable facial features apart from one to which my eye was irrepressibly drawn – an enormous, droopy moustache that dropped from the corners of his mouth to hang like two ginger tassels either side of his chin. The intention, perhaps, was to lend himself a rather cavalier air, but unlike Frans Hal's masterpiece, this particular cavalier was a little less butch, and definitely not laughing.

'I'm so thankful you're able to see me at such short notice,' he shrilled, hoisting onto the consulting table a white plastic carrying cage in which huddled a white rabbit. 'It's my Tzarina, you see. She's ill, very sick.' Mr

Grimaldi's voice rose a pitch and, in true artistic style, he reached into his trouser pocket and pulled out a long blue, red and yellow silk handkerchief, which he proceeded to wave to and fro in front of me before bunching it up to dab at the tears now spilling from his eyes. Oh, what a drama queen.

Mind you, the cause of his anguish, Tzarina, the white rabbit in the cage on the table, did, indeed, look very sick. You didn't need five years at veterinary school to realise that. Nor were those intensive years really necessary to ascertain that Tzarina was suffering from a condition called snuffles. The rabbit's half-closed eyes, gummed up with greenish-yellow pus, and the similar encrustations round her nose were pretty conclusive. Nevertheless, I did my statutory duty and slid the holding pin out of the lid of the cage and lifted the moribund rabbit onto the table, where she continued to sit hunched up, her rib cage heaving like a pair of bellows. I reached for my stethoscope and listened to her lungs – they sounded like an un-oiled wheelbarrow being dragged across a cobbled yard. Taking her temperature, it was 102°C – way above normal.

'We've a very sick rabbit here,' I said as I finished my examination, realising as I said it how pathetically obvious that sounded. Mr Grimaldi thought so as well. His multicoloured silk flew above his head in an exasperated gesture and he said excitedly, 'I know ... I know ... That's why I've brought her in. It's for you to make her better.'

'Well, I'm not sure ...'

'Oh but you must, you must,' interrupted the little man, the tassels of his moustache swinging wildly from side to side. 'Tzarina's part of my show.'

'Show?'

'My magic show. I'm a magician. Grimaldi the Great ...

at your service.' He deftly tossed his silk handkerchief from one hand to the other and, as it sailed across, its colours changed to green, orange and white. 'And I need Tzarina for my show on Friday,' he went on. 'It's a special show for a little girl. She's just come out of hospital.'

I took a deep breath. 'I'm sorry, Mr Grimaldi. I really don't think I can make your rabbit better in time for your show. I'm suggesting we have her in for a course of antibiotic injections, so that will be at least five days. It's Wednesday now ...'

I was interrupted by a wail from Mr Grimaldi. Clutching his silk to his mouth, he shuddered; then snatching the hanky away, he gasped, 'What am I to do? What am I to do?'

What a to-do, I thought, but out loud said, 'Perhaps you've another rabbit you could use?' That was an unwise comment as it evoked a sharp intake of breath from the magician and a rolling of his eyes heavenwards.

'Oh, Mr Mitchell, how could you possibly say that?' he squealed. 'How could you?' He threw his arms wide in an exaggerated display of despair. 'Tzarina's my one and only. No other rabbit could possibly replace her. You must make her better in time.'

I felt the tic in my temple begin its customary throb. This little man just didn't seem to appreciate how sick his rabbit was. Short of my waving a magic wand – or asking Mr Grimaldi to waggle his – there was no way Tzarina would be fit for his Friday show.

'Look,' I said firmly, 'the important thing is for us to try to save Tzarina.'

'Save? What do you mean "save"?' There was another wild flap of silk.

Whoops, we were off again.

'Rabbits with snuffles often don't make it. But we will do our best for Tzarina. Now just leave her with us.' I gestured at the door and mentally waved my magic wand. Abracadabra ... vamoose ... scram. It had the desired effect as Mr Grimaldi seemed to calm down a little and allowed himself to be escorted through to reception, where he meekly signed the admittance form and, with a final bow, a swish of his ponytail and a click of his heels, he vanished out of the front door.

Beryl watched his departing figure, her face lowered, eye peering up suspiciously at his ponytail. 'Right pansy there,' she said once he'd gone. 'Never did with ponytails on a man.'

'Now, now, Beryl. Each to his own,' I remonstrated.

But I was reminded of my student days when one of our year, a slight, nondescript youth, who sported a luxuriant ponytail that stretched down to his waist, was standing in a small group, all of whom were wearing brown coats, watching our Professor of Surgery during a practical session in a barn. The Prof was explaining the mechanics of doing a Caesarean on a cow and the equipment you could use to make the task easier; having finished his discourse, he turned to the youth and declared, 'So even a slip of a girl like you should be able to manage.'

I smiled inwardly, and explained to Beryl, 'He's upset because he was wanting to use his rabbit for a show he's doing this Friday.'

'And he can't use another one?'

'Apparently not.'

'Well, if it's that important, I can't see why he couldn't at least try,' mused Beryl, absent-mindedly scratching her mole. 'Lucy's got that rabbit she used to keep out the back somewhere.'

'You mean Bugsie? Yes, he's over at Willow Wren now.'
I looked quizzically at Beryl. 'Why? Do you think he'd be suitable?'

Beryl shrugged. 'Don't ask me. Ask Lucy. Just thought it a possibility.'

So I did ask Lucy that evening once we'd polished off the lasagne I'd lovingly chosen from the supermarket ready-meal shelf on the way home. At the time, we were still basking in the delights of living at Willow Wren and the delights of living with each other, so there was no problem in having a tête-à-tête, especially if it was supplemented with a glass or two of white wine.

Having each polished off a second glass, as we sat snuggled up to each other on the settee, Queenie gazing down from her throne, I filled Lucy in on my consultation with Mr Grimaldi and how Beryl had suggested that Bugsie might do as a replacement for Tzarina.

'Well, he's certainly a placid enough little rabbit,' Lucy remarked when I'd finished. 'Rather depends on what's involved. If he's just to be winkled out of the magician's cloak, then I don't see why he couldn't be used. But you'd need to try him out first.'

I had my arm round Lucy's shoulder, my fingers running through her hair, gently pushing her head towards me, my tongue ready to lick her left earlobe, thinking what I could winkle out for her. 'You'd also have to convince Mr Grimaldi that Bugsie's up for the job,' I murmured, nuzzling her neck.

'Seems you're up for the job,' giggled Lucy, running a hand up my thigh. She suddenly sat up, pulling herself away from me. 'But seriously, though. I've just thought of a way you could convince him ...' She went on to elaborate, getting more enthusiastic as she spoke. 'It's certainly worth a try, especially if it means that little girl will get to see a rabbit in the show,' she concluded, her eyes sparkling.

I listened, my heart sinking the more I heard about her plan. 'Honestly, Luce, I really think that's taking things too far.'

'Nonsense,' she retorted, visibly hardening while I found myself going in the opposite direction, passion killed. 'There's nothing lost by doing it.'

Only my self-respect and professional dignity, I thought miserably.

But Lucy being Lucy, I felt obliged to go along with her; so the following day found me down in Westcott town centre during my lunch break, standing nervously in 'Let's Party', the fancy-dress shop tucked away down a side street, waiting to collect the magician's outfit – black cape with red satin lining and secret pockets, magic wand and top hat – that Lucy had phoned up about and which had been put by for me to collect.

'What are you going to conjure up then?' joked the assistant, as she popped the items in a large carrier bag.

You might well ask, I thought, giving her a wan smile and a non-committal reply.

Once back at Prospect House, I sneaked down into the office thankful that no one was around to see me, and secreted the carrier bag behind an armchair. But, as if by magic, the office suddenly filled up. First Beryl, up from her lunchtime fag by the back door.

'Oh, you're back,' she said, staring suspiciously round the room. 'Lucy asked me to book an appointment for that magician chappie this afternoon. He's coming in at 4.00pm, just after your tea break.' She looked at me quizzically. 'What's this all about then?'

'Er … nothing really. Just something I wanted to discuss with Mr Grimaldi, that's all.'

Next, in bounced Eric, clapping his hands together. 'Hear we're in for a bit of a treat this afternoon, Paul,' he said heartily.

'What treat?' queried Beryl, turning to him.

'Overheard Mandy quizzing Lucy about the rabbit she's brought back. Bugsie, I think. Seems there's going to be a bit of a show this afternoon. So where's the outfit then?' Eric raised a questioning eyebrow at me.

'Outfit?' queried Beryl, swinging round on me.

'What's this about an outfit?' another voice asked. It was Crystal – she'd just marched in.

Oh Gawd. I now had the three of them gawping at me. Keeping things under wraps in this place was impossible; so I dragged out the carrier bag and explained what I intended to do. Crystal and Eric looked at one another and shook their heads in disbelief while Beryl's features rapidly set in their bashed-with-a-brick-owl mode. 'You're barmy,' she muttered over her hunched shoulder as she slithered, slug-like, back up to reception.

I guessed I probably did have a screw loose; but I blamed it all on Lucy's determination to give it a whirl. And a whirl I did give, feeling an absolute prat, as I flounced round the consulting room wearing the cloak. I stopped short of donning the top hat – it was too small in any case – and had the satisfaction, at least, of seeing Mr Grimaldi mesmerised by my appalling attempt to magic Bugsie from the cloak's deep inner pocket.

Bugsie was quite unperturbed as I fished him out. It was me who struggled to keep my balance and, more importantly, my composure; I could feel myself going red with embarrassment as I finally managed to lever Bugsie onto the consulting table, where he sat, his nose twitching, making no attempt to hop away.

Mr Grimaldi magicked a red silk hanky from his sleeve and dabbed at the tears running down his cheeks – this time tears of laughter. 'Oh my dear boy,' he cried, 'you're utterly useless.'

Thanks a bunch, mate, I thought crossly. I'm only trying to do my best.

Which is what Mr Grimaldi reiterated, saying I had tried to do my best – there was a stifled snigger at that point – which sort of ruined his sentiment. But he controlled himself, and said he genuinely appreciated the effort I'd made to convince him that Bugsie might be suitable. And, indeed, he could see the little chap seemed remarkably unfazed by everything that had gone on. So, yes, he was quite happy to give him a go, and he promised to return with Bugsie after the show, on Friday evening, if that suited.

So it was with some trepidation that, on Friday, I hung on after evening surgery had finished, wondering, as I waited, how the show had gone.

At ten past six, in breezed Mr Grimaldi, still in his full party regalia, very much in the pink – literally. Pink satin cape ... pink top hat ... shiny pink shirt and baggy pink trousers. He looked like a stick of candy floss with a 'tache. He was holding out in front of him what appeared to be an empty cage, his other hand clutching the middle of a large pink and white cane; he trotted purposefully into the consulting room and placed the cage on the table, stepping back to twirl his cane.

'Mr Mitchell,' he announced triumphantly, 'your Bugsie was a real star turn. Did everything required of him.' He put his free hand to his mouth and blew a kiss in the air. 'An absolute poppet. Oh yes, indeed-e-oh.'

'But where is he?' I queried, staring at the empty cage.

Mr Grimaldi slipped a hand in his right trouser pocket and pulled out a long, green silk, which, having put down his wand, he unfurled to reveal a square, the centre of which depicted a white rabbit with the words 'The End' beneath it in red letters.

For one horrible moment I thought it meant Bugsie was no longer with us, that somehow he'd departed from this world, done a Madam Mountjoy and been embodied in some other being. I watched intently as Mr Grimaldi lifted the silk square – held at its upper two corners by finger and thumb – over the cage and allowed it to float gently down and cover it. He picked up his pink wand and flashed it one … two … three times over the cage and then tapped the top. 'Bugsie!' he proclaimed with as much dramatic resonation his tremulous voice could muster; and whipped the silk away with one hand to reveal the rabbit sitting quietly in the cage.

I was gobsmacked, lost for words, but eventually managed to croak, 'How on earth did you do that?'

'Sheer magic, my dear chap … sheer magic.' Mr Grimaldi leaned over the cage and kissed the top of it. 'Now, don't tell on me, will you, sweetie-pie. Let's keep it a little secret between you and me.' I wondered who he was referring to – me or Bugsie. Thankfully, it was the rabbit, as he went on, 'And as you've been so good, here's a little treat for you.' There was a flash and whirl of the silk, and suddenly in his hand there was a large, well-scrubbed carrot. The magician placed it on the table with a little giggle. 'Who can tell what I've got up my sleeve,' he continued, stepping back to look at me and smirk. He paused and then added, 'Or down my trousers. You could be in for a big surprise there.' He turned his head slightly and gave an exaggerated wink. Oh, so very Kenneth Williams.

'Very impressive,' I said, still wondering how on earth he'd managed to transfer Bugsie into the cage with such deft sleight of hand.

'You haven't seen anything yet,' said Mr Grimaldi, his voice so full of innuendo I wondered whether I should terminate the discussion there and then, before anything else got exposed. But it was just my filthy mind working overtime as Mr Grimaldi went on, 'I understand your girlfriend put you up to this – and that Bugsie's her rabbit?' I nodded ruefully.

'Then I think she deserves this.' There was another flourish of the silk draped over his right wrist, and his left hand appeared from under it holding a bouquet of red roses which he held out with a little bow; but he snatched them away as I reached to take them. 'Sorry,' he apologised, 'they're actually my trick silk ones. But I do have some real roses in the car which I insist you give to your girlfriend with my warmest wishes.'

I assured him I would do just that. I was also able to tell him Tzarina was making good progress, responding well to her antibiotic therapy, and that with any luck he could have her home on Monday.

'Well, there you go,' Mr Grimaldi declared, with a squeal of delight. 'You've been able to work your own magic. I don't know how to thank you.'

'Don't worry, Mr Grimaldi. That's what we're here for,' I said, while at the same time thinking he could try conjuring up something for me; not a rabbit out of a hat, something more to my taste. But I thought better of suggesting it when the magician stretched across the table and patted my hand, saying, with an exaggerated wink, 'I'll come up with something for *you* later.' And then he added, 'My name's Peter, by the way.'

10
RUNNING OUT
OF TIME

At least, now, Bugsie had made his mark; and, as a result, he was able to join the ranks of the animals at Willow Wren with much higher esteem than might otherwise have been the case.

But, for me, the favourite of the bunch, far outranking Queenie and co. or Gertie, had to be dear old Nelson. That lopsided grin of his, first noticed when I tickled him on Mildred Millichip's kitchen table, had endeared him to me then, and continued to do so throughout those first six months or so at Willow Wren.

More often than not, his daily constitutional consisted of a toddle round Ashton's recreation ground; but there were days when he seemed eager to explore further afield and so, if time permitted – off-duty weekends, and those weekdays when evening appointments finished early – I started to take him across the nearby meadows, a stile leading to which was only 100 metres or so to the west of the cottage. The footpath took you along the southern boundary of Ashton Manor, a large, timber-framed farmhouse which now – according to the Spencers, who used to live next door, and who kept Lucy and me fully informed before their move to Gloucestershire – was owned by a couple, the husband having made his money in fish paste. The interior had been gutted in much the same manner as the shoals of fish that would have passed through the husband's factory.

You could see little of the house from the fields as a dense thicket of now very overgrown leylandii prevented anyone from gawping into the garden; and I would have needed more than a pile of bricks to enable me to peer over – not that I would have wanted to pry – besides, when I tried prising back some of the lower branches, I discovered a second rank of conifers blocked my view into the grounds.

The footpath meandered over to the far corner of the meadow where a metal field gate gave access to a farm track bounded by hawthorn hedges. The heatwave of that first summer had covered the track with hard-baked ruts of clay that zig-zagged down into a lightly wooded area of oak and ash; the dappled shade created a welcome relief from the burning heat of those August days.

Nelson loved that wood. Along its edge were thickets of brambles, intertwined with pink tresses of dog roses; and in the autumn, the brambles were laden with large crops of blackberries, ripening on those secluded banks, to produce heavy, succulent fruits that were savoured on the grassy slopes below them, picked and passed between lips as Lucy and I lay there, our purple tongues exploring each other's mouths while Nelson sat waiting for the odd berry to be chucked his way. He didn't get many.

Besides watching our grassy tumblings, there were other distractions for Nelson. Under the canopy of the trees, the ground was carpeted in bluebells, which, when we first discovered the wood in August, consisted of spent flower stalks and yellowing spikes of leaves, semi-collapsed from the drought, but through which it was easy to pick out many narrow paths worn down to the bare earth. Nelson would speed down these tracks, his rudder tail swishing from side to side as he picked up the scent of whatever animal had passed along them. Apart from roe deer and badgers, I suspected rabbits were the number-one users. They could often be seen out during the day, grazing at the edges of the meadow, only to retreat rapidly into the wood, their scuts up in alarm, exposing their white under-fur as Nelson set off in hot pursuit of them. His excited squeals would erupt from the brambles, accompanied by much crashing around in the undergrowth.

Only once did he ever succeed in catching one, and, on that occasion, he emerged with it triumphantly clamped in his jaws, the rabbit half dead, its limbs twitching. Lucy pinned him down while I attempted to prise his mouth open. He was a stubborn little dog with powerful jaws, so it was a real struggle to get him to let go; but, eventually, with many entreaties of 'Give it here …' he did release his grip and I was left holding his trophy – no Peter Rabbit lookalike but a mangy specimen with bulging, pus-covered eyes, suffering from myxomatosis. I quickly put it out of its misery.

During those outings, I imagined how the wood would look come the following spring with its carpet of blue, and relished the thought of being able to walk through it, hand in hand with Lucy, Nelson trotting at our side.

How wrong I was. Not that the wood failed to live up to my expectations that April – it did. My parents had a reproduction of a Vernon Coles painting in the hall of their bungalow down in Bournemouth. It had been on that wall for all the years I lived there before going to university – some seven of them. I felt I'd grown up with it. It was a classic woodland scene – a glade of beech trees, their buds having just unfurled into a mantle of soft greens; while beneath, the glade was a sea of bluebells with just the hint of a track to draw the eye in. It was a bog-standard painting, but skilfully executed to ensure it was easy on the eye.

The one jarring note was the unflattering frame in which it was mounted – a surround of white-painted wood. I could have held that frame up in the wood where Lucy, Nelson and I walked and the view through it would almost have been identical – the tracery of fresh green; the bluebells merging into a blur of blue; and the emptiness. The emptiness in my heart, that is, for I walked there these days accompanied only by Nelson; Lucy, although invited on several occasions, declined to come with me, excuses being offered or, more often, just a cursory 'No thanks', as if the notion of walking hand in hand with her partner through a magical, woodland glade was an abhorrence to her. So I started to venture out alone with Nelson. At least he appreciated my company, and I his.

They say having a pet helps to reduce stress; studies in which people have been monitored while they are stroking pets have shown that it helps to reduce blood pressure. That, of course, may rather depend on the sort of pet being stroked – somehow I don't think stroking a spitting cat or attempting to tickle a snarling Doberman under the chin would be conducive to anything other than your heart rate going through the roof. And as for talking to your pet, well, that's fine. Although discussing your prostate problems with a stick insect might be seen as taking things a bit too far, and you could run the risk of being dragged off to the funny farm.

I resisted the urge to gossip with Bugsie and, instead, found taking Nelson for a stroll into the woods the best way to unwind from a hectic day at Prospect House. On so many early evenings that April, I would be over there, savouring the serenity of the glade now full of bluebells, their delicate scent drifting in the light, evening breeze as the rays of the setting sun sank down under the canopy of leaves and sent rods of gold flashing between the tree trunks. But then I did start talking to Nelson. Not the usual 'Come here' and 'Sit' sort of conversation with which we're all familiar, but more the 'What do you think's going on?' and 'I don't know how this is all going to pan out, do you?' variety. Nelson was quite tactful when I was in that sort of mood, and carried on ahead of me, head down, sniffing the path for rabbits, pretending he hadn't heard me. There again, he was rather deaf, so I suppose it was unfair of me to expect any other response; but it didn't stop me from ranting on, and I certainly felt marginally better for doing so.

At the far end of the wood, the land fell away across a rolling countryside dotted with a patchwork of maize and wheat, criss-crossed with acres of rapeseed, already showing traces of the vibrant yellow with which those fields would soon be emblazoned. Far in the distance, you could just make out the meandering course of the River Avon, which, at this time of the evening, caught and reflected the setting sun in a ribbon of orange. The scene was one which made you want to stop and meditate – sit with one's back resting against the warm bark of an oak, and watch the evening melt into night. And that's what we did. Not me and Lucy – me and Nelson. He, sitting by my side, that large, soppy grin on his face, as I gently caressed his nape, me nattering away, getting things off my chest.

Those evenings together certainly helped to reduce the tension in me and instil a sense of calmness and serenity.

'Maybe we can't put the world to rights,' I said on one such evening, looking down at him, my hand caressing his ear in the fading, golden light. 'But we can have a damned good try.'

He looked up with that wonderful grin of his, and I couldn't help but smile in return. What great buddies we were.

So what happened two days later was all the more traumatic and heart-wrenching, and will remain indelibly etched in my mind.

Lucy and I both had the Saturday off. It started off peacefully enough, being woken by the soft coo-cooing of collared doves in the silver birch trees out the front and one or two muted caws from the rookery. No screeches from Eleanor's cockatiel next door. His morning vocals had finally got the better of her, and the bird had been despatched to live with her son over in Chawcombe.

I padded down to the kitchen, stopping to say hello to Nelson – when I say Nelson, I actually mean the mountain of blankets atop a beanbag in front of the Aga, under which, I assumed, was the dog. Occasionally, I made the wrong assumption and found I was really greeting a pile of blankets, and I often continued to talk to it until much later when, having lifted one corner of them, I discovered an absence of dog, Nelson having slipped out during the night to find a cooler spot in the living room where he'd still be flat out, snoring, not having heard me come down.

This morning, my 'Hello' was rewarded by a slight movement of one end of the blankets and the emergence of Nelson's flag-pole tail, which raised itself to half-mast and gave one wag before flopping down again. I pulled back the layers of blankets and said, 'Morning. How are you today?'

Nelson's response was the same every day when in residence under the blankets. He'd stretch out and squirm on the beanbag until he'd managed to manoeuvre himself onto his back and then lie there, back legs splayed out, front legs folded in at the ankles as if begging, his distended tummy ballooning out like a half-inflated ball. A perfect 'I'm fine … give me a scratch please' position; and I would duly oblige, evoking a facial expression of sheer bliss as his eyes closed again and his lips curled back in that grin of his, all front teeth exposed.

Nelson's constitutional, first thing, usually consisted of an amble round the back garden, which would be notched up a gear if Garfield or Push-in happened to be about; later, if we were at home, he was allowed to wander round to the front of the cottage where the mid-morning sun hit a patch of sheltered lawn and hard standing, turning it into the perfect spot for a bit of canine sunbathing. It was here that Nelson would snooze contentedly for a while before the shadow of the cottage crept round to cover it and so force him to move.

That Saturday was a bright, sunny one. Sipping my green tea while standing by the open kitchen door, I could already feel the warmth of the sun as it appeared over the top of the willows and shone down in my face; a sharp contrast to the chilly atmosphere inside the cottage, where I'd taken a mug of tea and two biscuits up to Lucy who had still been asleep. As with Nelson, all I could see of her was a mound of duvet. But unlike with him, I didn't pull the duvet back, as I knew that, had I done so, she wouldn't have responded by rolling onto her back and splaying her legs out – much as I may have wanted her to. In your dreams, mate, I thought, putting the mug and biscuits down on the cabinet next to her and walking away.

I usually cooked breakfast, and today was no exception – boiled eggs for the two of us. I liked mine lightly boiled, Lucy liked hers harder. So I usually left hers in the pan a minute longer than mine, making sure I kept a careful eye on the kitchen clock throughout so as not to over-boil either of them. I was dipping a soldier of toast into mine – the yolk nice and runny – when she came down with her tea half drunk and plonked herself at the table with a rather abrupt 'Morning ...' But at least I had to be thankful she was acknowledging my presence.

I echoed her 'Morning ...' with one of my own, which I hope sounded a little more cheerful, adding, 'What are you going to be doing today?'

'What's it to you?' was her reply.

Oh dear. I thrust my soldier deep into my egg. She cracked hers sharply with a spoon, splintering the shell in two taps, jerking off the pieces with her finger and thumb; then, having tossed them down in an untidy heap on the plate, she stabbed the top of the egg and levered off a spoonful of white and yolk. Both were rock hard. It was to set the scene for the day: me feeling I was forever treading on eggshells when in her presence; she feeling hard done by.

So I escaped into the garden; there, I had a different battle on my hands – waging war on the weeds that were shooting up now that the warmer weather had arrived. I had a quick word with Nelson, apologising for the atmosphere indoors, before he slunk off round to the front of the cottage. And when I saw the top of Eleanor's grey head over the fence, I nipped onto my pile of bricks to exchange a few pleasantries about how the gardens were looking and all the work that had to be done.

Eleanor waved a yellow, rubber-gloved hand at her borders to emphasis the point, adding, 'But it's such a relief to be able to get out of doors.'

I nodded my head vigorously. So true ... so true. I didn't need reminding, and I turned to observe Lucy come marching out to see to the animals: Gertie to be let out; Push-in's and Garfield's feed and water bowls to be cleaned and refilled; and Bugsie and the two guinea pigs to be fed. All of them were reasons for her to continue living at Willow Wren. As for me? I wasn't too sure where I came in the pecking order – I suspected quite low down, the way things were at present – but at least I still did get fed and watered.

It was just before 11.00am and I was thinking in terms of a cup of cappuccino and a Danish pastry – I'd bought a couple of apricot crowns the previous day over at Bert's Bakery and had covered them with cling-film overnight to make sure they didn't go stale – when I decided to heave up one more clump of weeds before stopping. It turned out to be a particularly tough clump and I really did have to push the fork deep into its centre, rocking it from side to side to loosen the roots – of what, I wasn't sure – and that was my downfall.

Lucy had been walking back up the garden from Gertie's shed and had drawn level with me. 'What on earth are you doing, Paul?' she said, coming to a halt, to look down at the two large lumps of roots which I'd now managed to heave out, leaving two deep craters in the border.

I thought it was obvious, but being acutely aware of Lucy's hedgehog prickliness, I thought it wise not to state the obvious too obviously and attempted to think of a rational explanation that had no trace of sarcasm liable to inflate Lucy's mood to porcupine proportions. I needn't have bothered, as clearly she'd already jumped to a conclusion of her own. Her face twisted to the left and, at the same time, her mouth curved up on that side, an action which caused her left eye to half close and gave the impression of a knowing wink executed by someone who had lost their marbles. But she hadn't lost hers – far from it.

'Idiot,' she seethed, kicking one of the clumps. 'You've just dug up the Michaelmas daisies that attracted all those butterflies last autumn. Don't you remember?'

Now she mentioned it, I did remember. Well, let's say I could recall there being several patches of purple-flowering daisies which, indeed, had attracted many Red Admirals and a few Peacocks, but, as to where those clumps had been, I had obviously forgotten, otherwise why would I be bothering to yank out these thick clumps of what I'd been about to call weeds?

At that point, I saw Eleanor's head reappear over the fence, this time all of it – perhaps she now had her own pile of bricks to stand on. 'Hello, dears,' she said affably, as Lucy's features rapidly composed themselves into some degree of normality and she swung round to smile.

Eleanor looked past her to where I was standing, a boot on top of the fork's head, the fork still embedded in one of the clumps of weeds ... er ... Michaelmas daisies. 'Paul's been busy, I see,' she continued. 'Good idea to divide up the perennials this time of year. Keeps them healthy. And if you've got some spare clumps of those Michaelmas daisies, do let me have them. It's so nice to be able to encourage the butterflies, don't you think?'

I swear there was the briefest of winks in my direction before, with a little wave of her yellow-gloved fingers, she dropped back out of sight.

'Coffee time,' I said to Lucy. 'I've got some apricot crowns.' And, without further ado, I nipped inside, suppressing the grin that threatened to break out on my face. Good old Eleanor.

But Lucy remained prickly. If it wasn't going to be me mistaking perennials for weeds, then I felt she'd find some other excuse to have a go at me. It didn't take her long. By then, we'd finished our pastries and coffee, having had them on the patio, and I, at least, was enjoying the warmth of the morning sun, praying that it might help to improve Lucy's mood as we continued to sit either side of the patio table, each of us on a cushioned lounger. Between us was Nelson, who had joined us from the front garden to hoover up any crumbs, before stretching out at my feet to continue his morning siesta on the now pleasantly warmed-up bricks.

What a peaceful, restful scene. A blackbird was singing in the forsythia, his gleaming plumage haloed by bowers of yellow; two blue tits fussily flitted in and out of a hole up under the eaves – I could hear the burr of their wings, their chirrups, as they investigated a possible nesting site. Minutes later, they were chased away by a pair of starlings that descended with raucous cries; one stayed perched on the gutter while the other slipped into the hole to look at the possibilities of it being a des res, appearing minutes later with a strident call to his mate suggesting that, indeed, it was going to be the ideal home to rear their family.

I half opened my eyes and looked across at Lucy, wondering what sort of home would be ideal for her to raise a family. I closed my eyes again. For a start, I dreamt it would have to have plenty of room for animals. But not only animals. I could see Lucy with a large family of her own. She was that sort of girl – the homely, meal-ready-on-the table-for-hubby sort of woman – soft-natured, warm and sensual, yielding willingly to the wants of her husband whenever he desired them, allowing him to bury himself in her warm, sensuous body.

'Paul.'

I was dimly aware of Lucy's voice.

'Paul. I want you to do something for me.'

'Yes, my love,' I murmured sleepily, easing myself up the chair a little – it had suddenly become quite hard. 'Whatever you want.'

'*Paul.*' The tone was more strident and woke me fully.

'What is it?' I snapped, luscious Lucy receding rapidly.

'Bugsie's out of pellets. Go and get some for me, will you?'

I'm not sure why I reacted in the way I did. I often look back and try to work it out, to offer the reasons for my response, to attempt to justify it, because the consequences were so devastating, so appalling, I would have given my right arm to have put the clock back and stopped them.

Was I still half asleep, not really with it enough to realise the consequences of my reply? Was it discovering the reality was so different to my dream? Maybe I was trying to cover the embarrassment of my erotic reaction to that dream, so my mind wasn't on my reply? Perhaps it was because I was being asked to do something for a rabbit – even though he wasn't called Peter?

Or … I just hated Lucy.

I said, 'Get them yourself …'

Those three words had been loaded like shells in a revolver. Each was deliberately fired at Lucy and each scored a direct hit. But there was no shouting and screaming, no throwing of mugs – Lucy just jumped to her feet and said, 'Well, you can bloody well get your own lunch then, you bastard.' But that one sentence was said with such vitriol that she might as well have poured a flask of sulphuric acid over me and watched it etch into my skin in much the way her acid words were wounding me now.

Nelson, too, felt, or at least sensed, their acidity, since he quickly scrabbled to his feet and trotted out of the gate to seek refuge round the front of the cottage.

I sat up, swinging my legs off the side of my lounger, and watched Lucy flounce into the kitchen, heard the chink of the car keys being picked up from the glass dish on the window sill where both sets were kept and, minutes later, she reappeared, jacket on, bag over her shoulder and stormed out of the gate, banging it back on its hinges.

Oh boy. What a mess. I anticipated that a walk over into the bluebell woods with Nelson to discuss the matter was going to be an essential ingredient of my afternoon's activities.

Still sitting on the lounger, I heard the slam of her car door, followed moments later by the rev of the Fiesta's engine, and then a sound which will forever be seared in my memory – a long, heart-rending howl. Christ. What had happened?

I sprang up as the car engine died, a door opened and Lucy screamed, 'Oh my God!' Racing out of the gate and up the side of the cottage, I met Lucy staggering towards me, her face rigid with fear and, in her arms, the body of Nelson. Distraught, she held him out, howling, 'I've run him over … but he's still alive … please, dear God, say he is.'

I could feel the tears well up in me, my throat constricting, my body beginning to shake as Lucy pushed Nelson into my arms and we ran inside where I slid him onto the kitchen table. He lay there, his sides erratically heaving, eyes glazing over, blood trickling from one nostril. At the top of my voice, I yelled, 'You've bloody well killed him ...' and pulled Nelson to me as he gave one last, long, shuddering gasp and died in my arms. I couldn't stop the tears. They blurred my vision, streamed down my cheeks and coursed over Nelson's face – a face that would no longer grin at me, the lips slowly setting in a mask of death.

And Lucy's reaction? Stunned silence. There were no tears ... just agony etched on her face. Only after minutes of watching my uncontrollable sobbing did she reach out, put a hand on my shoulder and hoarsely whisper, 'I'm so, so sorry, Paul.'

Of course it was an accident – there was no way Lucy would have deliberately run Nelson over. He'd gone back to his patch by the front lawn but had moved across to the hard standing when the sun had edged round, and there had fallen asleep. Being deaf, he hadn't heard Lucy get into the car. She, for her part, had been in such an agitated state that she hadn't stopped to think that maybe Nelson was behind the car, and had reversed over him.

It was an event that marked a turning point in our relationship; and although we were to continue living together – and, indeed, Nelson's death brought about a temporary reconciliation of sorts – it was as if Lucy was only doing that as atonement for what had occurred. The real passion and commitment in our relationship died with that little terrier.

11
NOTHING TO SNARL ABOUT

The following Monday morning saw me driving over the Downs to Westcott with a heavy heart; the rush-hour traffic, with the bumper-to-bumper congestion between the two roundabouts on the outskirts of the town which I had to negotiate to get to Prospect House, did nothing to alleviate my mood.

Just why am I doing this? I thought, inching forward another couple of metres to brake and wait another few minutes. Well, I did know why; it was all to do with being a vet. I remember Cynthia Paget, the divorcee in whose house I had stayed when I first started at the practice, saying how she admired my dedication to the job and was ready to give a helping hand whenever I needed it. She'd been standing at the top of her stairs at the time, cigarette in the corner of her mouth, housecoat half open, staring down at me in the hallway as I answered a night-time call on her phone. My mobile wouldn't pick up any signal in my bedroom (her front room converted into a bedsit), and I'd refused her offer to try it out in hers. I was just wearing boxer shorts and felt that the leery look on her face and the apparent lack of clothing beneath the housecoat suggested that, whatever the quality of the phone signal, I'd be guaranteed a warm reception.

Thinking of her reminded me of the savage little Chihuahua she owned – Chico. He was forever lunging at my toes and springing up to grab the bottom of my boxer shorts when I was trying to dash up to the bathroom first thing, making it imperative to wear footwear and ensure that a protective hand was over my crotch. That little blighter had been much loved by Mrs Paget. She would suddenly appear when Chico was making a beeline for my privates and rush to pick him up and clasp him to her bosom, admonishing him first, and then turning, with a questioning look, to ask if he'd got me anywhere and, if so, was there anything she could put on it for me? I swear the two of them were in cahoots – both wanting to rip my boxer shorts off and attack my genitals.

As I slowly approached the second roundabout, just off which was the entrance to the practice, I recalled that it was about here that Chico had been run over; he'd been rushed in by a panic-stricken Mrs Paget, and the little chap was taken into the operating theatre, still just alive, to be put on emergency oxygen, but he had died on the table. Mrs Paget had been distraught. I now knew exactly how she'd felt, and took a deep breath to prevent my emotions surfacing again at the thought of poor Nelson's demise as I finally managed to leave the queue of traffic and turn into the drive of Prospect House.

Beryl looked up from her computer when I rushed into reception, late for my appointments. 'Blimey, Paul. You look glum,' she said. 'Traffic bad?'

I just nodded. It wasn't the time or place to explain.

Besides, I could hear the shuffle of feet and paws in the waiting room and wanted to get cracking before too much of a backlog built up; and being a Monday morning, it was the sort of thing that was liable to happen – people leaving it till after the weekend before deciding their pets needed to be seen.

'You are quite busy,' warned Beryl as I made a dash for the consulting room, struggling into my white coat on the way. And so it proved, the first patient setting the scene for the whole morning – a corgi called Carl. In theory, it should have been a quick and simple appointment; the dog just needed his claws clipped. But the case notes on the computer screen were punctuated with typed warnings. 'Take care' when seen last year by Crystal and 'Vicious bugger' when seen by Eric just after Christmas, some three months back. Now it was my turn to assess the dog's temperament.

I went through to the waiting room to find two people in there. There was a lady with a wicker cat basket on the chair next to her and, on the opposite side of the room, a gentleman with a corgi sitting placidly by his side. 'Mr Holder?' I enquired.

The man nodded and got to his feet, addressing the dog, 'Your turn, Carl.' His dog stood up and trotted into the consulting room at the side of Mr Holder without a murmur and, when picked up and put on the table by his owner, he sat there, panting slightly, but otherwise looking at me quite unperturbed, no shaking or quivering, very relaxed. Take care? Vicious bugger? Surely not. But to be on the safe side, I thought it best to make a few overtures of friendship to the corgi. Test the water, so to speak. I held out the back of my hand, ready to snatch it away if necessary, and said, 'Hello, Carl. How are you then?'

His response was to look up at Mr Holder and give a little growl.

'He says he's fine,' said Mr Holder. 'Just wants to have his claws clipped. They're getting a bit long. Aren't they, matey?' As if to prove the point, he held up one paw to show me. The claws were long – but looked as if they'd be easy to clip, with no danger of cutting the pink quick as it was clearly visible in each nail. It was just this temperament issue ... according to his notes, that was.

Conscious of time ticking on, I reached round for the nail clippers, turning back to see Carl look at me and give another soft growl. I admit I was already in a foul mood from the weekend's upsetting events, and didn't want it made worse by being bitten, so I said, 'Look, Mr Holder, I think I'd better muzzle Carl, just to be on the safe side.'

'It really shouldn't be necessary. Carl's never bitten anyone,' Mr Holder replied, looking aghast. The corgi swung his head up to stare at his owner and growled again. 'This is just Carl's way of talking.' He ruffled the dog's neck. 'You're not vicious are you, Carl?'

There was another rumble from the corgi's throat. Hmm. I wasn't convinced. And those notes did say ... Yep. I made up my mind.

'Sorry, but I'm going to muzzle him,' I insisted.

'He's *never* had to be muzzled before,' said Mr Holder emphatically. 'It could really stress him.' His podgy face was beginning to turn red with indignation.

Not half as much as it would stress me if I got bitten, I thought, and grabbed the length of bandage coiled on the glass trolley next to the boxes of needles and syringes, tied it in a loop, and advanced on Carl, having told Mr Holder to put his arm under the dog's neck and hold him against his chest. Once he'd reluctantly done as instructed, I lassoed

Carl's snout and then quickly tightened the bandage, clamping his jaws together.

It was at that point all hell let loose. Carl started scrabbling with both front and back paws, wriggling in Mr Holder's arms, gradually slipping from his grip, his head writhing from side to side, his front claws coming up to hook into the bandage, his eyes rolling upwards, the whites showing; and in this frenzy, saliva bubbled and foamed from between his clenched teeth, and he began to emit a high-pitched whine of savage fury.

'My God, he's having a fit,' shouted Mr Holder, still hanging on to him.

'No, no,' I tried to reassure him. 'It's only Carl resisting. Just keep holding on. You're doing a grand job.' I grabbed the clippers, and tugged the dog's left front paw free of the bandage, whereby his leg started to thrash around and I had to force it still by pinning it to the table before I could attempt to clip the first claw. I had done three, during which time Carl continued his frenzied snorting and snuffling, his whole body convulsing in his efforts to break free. I was just on his fourth, when his whole body suddenly went limp on me. There was a sickening rattle in his throat and his head lolled over Mr Holder's arm.

'My God, you've killed him,' screamed Mr Holder, easing Carl down onto the table.

I, too, was screaming – internally, silently – his words reverberating through me. Outwardly, my feelings contracted into one word: 'Shit!' I snatched a pair of scissors off the trolley and cut the bandage off, yanking it away. I quickly prised his mouth open, a sticky stream of saliva pouring out as I did so. His tongue was flopped back, engorged and blue. I reached in and pulled it forward. Behind, there was a pool of mucus. Still holding the tongue, I stretched across to the adjacent trolley and jerked a wodge of cotton wool from its glass container, which, in my haste, caused it to tip over and be dragged to the edge of the trolley, toppling over to smash on the floor. I snapped at Mr Holder, 'Here, hold the upper jaw,' instructing him how to do it, while I pulled downwards on Carl's tongue, forcing his mouth to open wider, thereby allowing me to reach into the back of the throat with the ball of cotton wool and scoop out the accumulated mucus that had been blocking his epiglottis, preventing him from breathing. I prayed there would be a sudden intake of breath. There wasn't. Shit!

Quickly checking his airway was now clear, I let go of his tongue, told Mr Holder to still hang on to Carl's muzzle to help keep his neck extended, and moved round to his chest. I executed a quick, firm push with both hands down on his chest. There was a gurgle as air and some fluid was forced out of his lungs. I hoped there would be a reflex intake of air. There wasn't. Damn! Damn! Damn! I checked his tongue. It was getting bluer. Sod it! I slid a finger and thumb each side of his chest. No heartbeat. Bloody hell! I almost squealed with panic.

I shifted my finger and thumb back a little. Was that something? Yes ... a heartbeat ... feeble ... but a heartbeat. Carl was still alive. Just. I picked him up in my arms. 'I'm taking him down to the theatre,' I gabbled, pushing past a distraught Mr Holder. 'You wait here.'

'Mandy,' I cried out loud, leaping down the steps and tearing down the corridor. 'Mandy, where are you? I need help.' I elbowed my way into the prep room where she was setting up the instruments for the morning's ops. 'Mandy. Get me a tube. Quick.'

She dropped the pack of instruments she was holding,

and ran round to pull open the drawer of endotracheal tubes, decisively picking out one and rapidly smearing it with grease. I snatched it out of her hand. She, without the need to be instructed, swiftly manoeuvred the corgi's head round and opened his jaws to allow me to pull his tongue forward, expose the epiglottis and push the tube through it into the windpipe. Only it wouldn't go. It slid over the top of the epiglottis and started to disappear down the corgi's throat. I tried again. Same thing happened. Shit! Shit! Shit!

'Paul,' said Mandy quietly, 'just take your time. You're an expert at doing this.'

I drew a deep breath, controlled myself, and slipped the tube once more over Carl's tongue. This time, it engaged with the top of his trachea and I was able to slide it down his windpipe. Mandy was ready with the blue plastic connector and fitted it without a word.

'Right, into the theatre,' I said. 'Quick. Quick.'

Mandy ran ahead of me across to the anaesthetic machine and twisted the oxygen knob to 'On'. I almost threw Carl's inert body on the table. She connected him to the oxygen supply and I gave his chest a pump. We waited. Nothing. I gave his chest another pump. 'Come on ... come on ... breathe, you bugger,' I urged.

'His colour's getting better,' said Mandy, rolling back his tongue.

But still nothing. I felt his chest. His heartbeat was stronger.

'Come on, you sod, breathe,' I repeated.

There was a slight movement of Carl's chest. A twitch ... a tremor of muscles. Suddenly, there was an almighty expansion of his ribcage as he took a large gulp of oxygen. There was another gulp. And another. Then, gradually, his breathing settled into a steady rhythm. 'Thank God for that,' I gasped.

Leaving him under the watchful eye of Mandy, with instructions to disconnect him from the anaesthetics machine and transfer him to a kennel for observation, I raced back up to the consulting room, my heart still thudding, my whole body still shaking, to inform an equally agitated Mr Holder that his corgi would be OK.

The look of relief on his face was quickly replaced by a scowl, his forehead wrinkling, as he exclaimed, 'You're not going to hear the last of this, young man. I consider your handling of Carl abominable. Disgraceful. Completely incompetent.'

'I'm sorry but ...' I got no further as Mr Holder threw out his arm, pushed me to one side, and marched off down to reception, where I heard him tackle Beryl, demanding to be seen by one of the senior partners. I scurried after him, but stopped in the doorway behind him, Beryl catching my eye over his shoulder, with a look that said, 'Let me deal with this, Paul. You get on with your appointments.'

With the waiting room noisy with yowls, snarls, dogs panting and the occasional chirrup, I thought it best to take her advice, but throughout the next hour, as I dealt with a couple of booster vaccinations, a case of otitis – the dog frantically flapping his ears as he was dragged in – and some post-operative removal of stitches, I was all the while thinking of what was going to happen over my handling of Carl.

The backlog of clients to be seen meant I over-ran into my coffee break, and it wasn't until nearly 11.20am that I managed to see the last case for the morning. Feeling very apprehensive, I made my way back down to the office.

Crystal was there, sitting behind the desk, mug of coffee, half drunk, in front of her, flicking through a *Daily Telegraph*, which she neatly folded and placed on the desk as I entered. There was no sign of Beryl. And Eric, I knew, was out on a visit.

She saw me look round. 'I told Beryl to go and have another cigarette,' she said. 'Take a seat, Paul.'

I glanced at my watch, knowing I was expected down in the prep room to start the morning's routine ops. 'Mandy's still keeping an eye on Mr Holder's corgi,' she added, as if reading my mind. 'An unfortunate business that. Tell me exactly what happened.'

I slid onto the seat opposite, feeling like some errant schoolboy about to get the cane – in more sunny circumstances, such a thrashing might have been quite a pleasurable experience in Crystal's dainty hands – but not under the dark cloud currently hovering over me. I explained about the warning notes on the dog's case history and how I felt it prudent to restrain the corgi by muzzling him. Only he'd swallowed his tongue and nearly asphyxiated.

'Mr Holder is saying that muzzling shouldn't have been necessary,' said Crystal when I'd finished. 'According to him, Carl's always been a well-behaved dog.' She looked across, her steely-blue eyes fixed on me. I felt like an entomological specimen, squirming in front of her, about to be pinned down. 'But,' she went on, 'I do accept it was up to you to make a professional judgement. Perhaps in this case, it was the wrong one.' A cough just outside the office door made her pause. 'Beryl, is that you?' she called out.

Beryl slithered into view. 'Was just going back up to reception,' she said, with another little cough. This time, one of embarrassment at having been caught eavesdropping.

'Well, as you were no doubt listening,' said Crystal, 'you might as well come in and tell Paul yourself about the mix-up.'

Mix-up? What mix-up? I thought, swinging round in the seat and rising to my feet.

Beryl shuffled in, one hand stuffing her packet of cigarettes back in her bag. She stood there looking extremely uncomfortable, shoulders hunched under the black cardigan, hanging loosely from them as usual. I guessed from the deep, uniform colour of her raven-black hair that she'd recently re-dyed it; now it had the effect of highlighting her pasty, white face with startling intensity, a face ill-disguised by the thick layer of make-up trowelled over forehead and cheeks. She looked at me, her face lowered, her good eye focusing, it seemed, on my feet, while her glass eye swung upwards to gaze at the ceiling. Disconcerting, as always. Although more disconcerting was what she said. 'I'm sorry, Paul. Seems there was a bit of a mix-up over the records. I gave you the case history of Carl junior, the corgi that can be vicious, whereas you actually saw Carl senior, his placid dad.' Beryl gave a little shake of her head. 'I really am sorry, Paul. It's not like me.'

Crystal looked across at her. 'Well, these things happen, Beryl. But not often, I might add,' she continued, switching her gaze to me. 'Beryl's been here ... what ...'

'Over 12 years,' interrupted Beryl, a note of pride creeping into her voice.

'Yes, 12 years,' echoed Crystal, 'and is very well known and respected by our regular clients. In fact, I'm not sure what we'd do without her.'

'She'd be missed terribly,' said a voice behind Beryl, and a young woman appeared, slid her arms round Beryl's waist and drew her back to squeeze her tightly, digging her chin into her right shoulder.

Beryl squirmed sideways as the young woman let go, and turned to exclaim in a delighted voice, 'Jodie. What a wonderful surprise. I didn't know you were back.'

Although still to be introduced, this Jodie was a wonderful surprise for me, too. A young lady in her early twenties, slim, of average height, pert nose, freckles, and two features that gave her identity away– cornflower-blue eyes and a halo of Pre-Raphaelite copper curls – Crystal, her mum, to a tee.

Crystal got up and came round the side of the desk and the two of them kissed. 'You managed to get some sleep then,' she said. 'Jodie's just flown in from Costa Rica,' she added, by way of explanation to Beryl and me.

'Fine … yes … no problem,' replied Jodie, her eyes sparkling with curiosity as she smiled across at me.

Crystal stepped back. 'Sorry, darling, this is Paul. Paul, my daughter, Jodie.'

Jodie and I both held out our hands and, as they touched, and I looked into those wonderful eyes of hers, I was instantly smitten, holding her hand a fraction longer than etiquette demanded.

'Oh, right, so this is the new vet?' said Jodie, with another dazzling smile. 'Hope Mum's not putting you through the mill too much,' she went on, staring at me mischievously. 'We all know she can be a bit of a dragon.'

'No, no, not at all,' I stuttered, feeling myself go red, like some love-sick, knock-kneed schoolboy and averted my gaze.

Jodie gave Beryl another hug, with the promise to catch up with her later, and told her mother she'd just pop into Westcott and then return home to sort herself out. 'Nice to have met you, Paul,' she added, her cheeks dimpling. 'I'll be around for a while so maybe you and I could get together over a glass of wine and you can spill the beans on how they've been treating you.' She smiled again, and waved delicately, 'Bye for now.' With that, she whirled out of the office.

Physically, I remained rooted to the spot, glowing; but, mentally, I was already skipping up onto the Downs clutching the hand of the new 'Maria' in my life. Odl-lay-ee ... Would the hills ever resound to the sound of our music? I wondered.

The clipped tones of Crystal soon had me rapidly descending from my Down-land dream as she referred back to my encounter with Mr Holder, telling me that he'd calmed down enough not to pursue his original intention of reporting me to the Royal Veterinary College, but would instead make sure I never set eyes on his dogs again by switching to the rival practice on the other side of town. Ouch. Duly chastised, I finished my morning, working through the list of spays and castrates, my mind wandering at times to images of frolicking on the Downs with Jodie, as I grappled with yet another set of reproductive organs.

That lunchtime, Beryl and I ate our Bert's baguettes out in the back garden where there was a rickety wooden bench, sheltered from the wind but positioned in quite a suntrap. A pleasant enough spot, providing you watched where you trod as you walked over to it, since it was on the main exercise path for the hospitalised dogs; and each end of the bench was a scenting stop for the dogs, so daily got liberally showered with urine, making the bench reek. But smell and faeces apart, it was at least somewhere for Beryl to sit and have a smoke when the weather permitted.

I was two-thirds of the way through my cheese and

pickle baguette before I asked the question. 'I guess you've known Jodie a long time?'

Beryl, having finished hers, had her mouth open, and was picking at her bottom molars with one of her red talons, attempting to extricate a lump of cheddar. Having successfully dislodged it, she flicked it onto the worn grass before answering. 'Goodness, yes. Ever since she was eight years of age. Lovely little girl. And still is, of course. Has set many a young man's heart on fire.'

Too true, Beryl, too true, I thought, mine smouldering away in my chest. With a little gentle probing, which I hoped didn't sound too obvious, I learnt that Jodie was the Sharpe's only child. She'd been given a private education, first at St Bartholomew's in Westcott and then over at Brigstock's College for Girls, before going on to Exeter University, where she studied English Literature, gaining a 2:2.

I asked Beryl whether Jodie had ever wished to be a vet, and Beryl shook her head, saying that there had been the usual run of family pets and she did have a pony at livery when she was in her early teens, but then lost interest. Boys had taken over. It seems she did do the rounds with her dad and had helped in the hospital, cleaning out kennels, exercising dogs when they were short-staffed, so knew a thing or two about the routines. She'd even helped on a couple of emergency call-outs, so Beryl believed. But her passion was more for books.

She'd just come back from Central America, as I'd heard her say. Some place in Costa Rica, where she'd spent a year teaching in a school way out in the jungle. Couldn't imagine her staying in Westcott too long, mused Beryl, lighting up her second cigarette. Too high-spirited a girl. Beryl took a deep drag on the cigarette and exhaled sharply, her gaze fixed on the towering clump of rhododendrons through which the path to the Green tunnelled, and which looked magnificent, laden, this time of year, with deep violet blooms. That bank of rhododendrons was a remnant of when Prospect House had more formal grounds, rather than the scraggly rose beds out the front, bordering the drive, or the block of flats adjacent to the main house, built on the site of the old Victorian coach house, long since demolished.

She paused, tapped some ash off her cigarette against the side of the bench and said, 'I'm sorry about this morning, Paul. Not like me to make such a mistake.'

I tried to reassure her that I didn't hold any hard feelings against her, thinking privately that I'd rather save those for Jodie. But she wasn't that convinced. Nor was I – about Jodie that is. From what I'd just heard, she'd be way out of my league, even if there was a chance to get to know her better. But that chance did come, and not so far in the future, as it happened. And the rhododendrons, at which I was now staring, played their part. A really big part.

Meanwhile, there was Lucy. Literally, there was Lucy. She'd appeared from the kennels with Carl on a lead, walking him slowly towards us, and stopped as she drew level with us.

'How is he now?' I asked, looking up at her, screwing my eyes against the sun, shading them with a hand. I couldn't really see her face but her voice sounded pretty glum when she answered, 'Seems to have recovered,' before moving on.

Beryl took another drag on her cigarette and then held it to one side, as, with her left finger and thumb, she picked off a bit of baguette stuck to her tongue. 'Ooo-er,' she commented, staring at Lucy's receding figure. 'Bit down in the dumps, aren't we?'

'Well, it's to be expected,' I said with a rush, surprising myself at my sudden support for Lucy, and went on to explain what had happened to Nelson. Of course, Beryl was full of sympathy and again apologised for adding to my woes with that morning's mix-up, concluding with the hope that the rest of the day would go better. It didn't.

For a start, just before geeing myself up to start the afternoon list of appointments, I bumped into Mr Holder who had come to collect his corgi. I knew then what 'looking daggers' really meant. The look he gave me as I walked into reception, unaware that he was waiting there, consisted of a whole canteen of high-quality, finely-honed, razor-sharp implements hurled with deadly accuracy in my direction. I reeled back, mentally lacerated, and spun round to disappear down to the consulting room, expecting any minute a real dagger to come whistling after me and lodge between my shoulder blades.

The appointments weren't exactly easy either, and I had great difficulty in assessing what the problems were in several cases – none of which helped my battered self-confidence. All very depressing.

The Standard poodle was a good example. There was an inauspicious start, when the owner, a Mrs Stanton, informed me in rather an imperious manner, 'I usually see the lady doctor, but, as she's fully booked, I've been forced to see you instead.'

Forced, eh? Charming. What a morale booster.

The poodle was limping. I thought it was lame in its right hind-leg as it walked round the consulting table. The owner said she thought Mimi was favouring the left one, although I should know as I was the vet. When I flexed

Mimi's right knee there was no reaction; but when I did the same with her left one, she yelped. Mmm.

'Seems there's a problem in her left knee,' I said. 'Possibly a rupture of the ligaments.'

'Possibly?' she queried, her tone rather sarcastic.

I ignored her.

Mimi was given an anti-inflammatory injection and a course of pills, with instructions to book an appointment with me in a week's time – with a view to surgery if there was no improvement. I heard her out in reception making her appointment – categorically stating it had to be with Dr Sharpe, and not that young vet, thank you very much.

Thank *you* very much.

Then there was the cat that was drinking a lot.

'For how long?' his owner was asked.

'This past two weeks.'

'Eating OK?'

'Ravenous.'

'Losing weight?'

'A bit.'

'Could be diabetes.'

'It is.'

'Sorry?' I queried.

The owner explained she was a nurse, had used one of the health centre's test sticks on a sample of her cat's urine, and this had proved positive for glucose; having completed an exhaustive search of the Internet on diabetes in cats, she had come up with a list of what had to be done – insulin, obviously, but also hospitalisation to monitor blood glucose levels to ensure the daily dose of insulin given was correct. So would it be all right to leave the cat with me now, please?

I couldn't argue. Didn't dare.

I got home that evening completely demoralised, fed up to the back teeth and drained. All I could think of was collapsing on the sofa, feet up, watching the TV, regardless of what was on. I did get a few crumbs of comfort from Lucy. That was a turn-up for the books. The guilty conscience over Nelson was clearly working overtime.

'Guess you've had a rotten day,' she said, clearing the dishes after a supper of spaghetti bolognese, her standard quickie meal when we'd both been working a long day. She'd just flopped into the armchair next to me when the phone rang.

I visibly jumped, such was the state of my nerves.

'Leave it,' said Lucy firmly, seeing me about to get up. 'You're not on duty. Let the answerphone kick in.'

I sank back, failing to suppress completely the mild attack of jitters provoked whenever the phone rang, regardless of whether I was on duty or not. A sort of Pavlovian response. But instead of salivating, I would start sweating, my armpits getting drenched within seconds of the first ring. I could feel the wetness seep through my shirt as a woman's voice issued from the answerphone: 'Hello. I'm sorry to trouble you this time of night, but I was wondering if you could help. I'm Sandra Coles, your neighbour over at Ashton Manor. I understand you're a vet and just want some advice really. One of our Boxers is acting really strange. If you could possibly give me a ring back I'd be very grateful.' The message ended with a telephone number, repeated twice.

I swung my feet off the settee.

'What do you think you're doing?' asked Lucy sternly.

'Ringing the woman back.'

'You'll do no such thing.' Lucy's voice was adamant.

'You're not on duty. Let her ring the surgery and get Eric to deal with it. He's on tonight.'

'But she's only after some advice.'

'Paul. Leave it.' Lucy's tone had become more strident.

I sat for a moment on the edge of the settee, and then lay back again to watch the TV screen blankly, careful not to say anything to provoke her. But it didn't do the slightest bit of good; Lucy had the bit between her teeth now. 'This is typical of you, Paul. You're getting far too wrapped up in your work. Nothing else matters.'

Ah, did I detect an inkling of what was the matter with Lucy? That she felt I was putting myself and my work before our relationship. Maybe she did have a point. Maybe I was too obsessed with putting all my energies into ensuring I was as competent a vet as I could be. Today's performance suggested I still had a long way to go. All the more reason, then, for her to realise I was still learning my trade. Perhaps she didn't have the capacity to see that. Unlike someone like ... Well, someone like ... Jodie Sharpe. A knot tightened in my stomach as I realised the implications of what I was thinking.

That really wasn't fair on poor Lucy. She was a good sort in her own way. I cringed again at my train of thought. 'A good sort in her own way ...' How condescending that sounded. How patronising. But the niggles had begun to surface. Perhaps Lucy was sensing them ... and sensing I was losing my respect for her. If so, no wonder her manner had changed towards me. But for the life of me, I couldn't see how I could alter my ways, express more appreciation of her, be less self-centred, if that's what she thought I was, unless – and this was the nub of the matter – unless it genuinely came from the heart. And I had to acknowledge, no matter how much I regretted it, that my heart was not truly in it. Not for the long run, at least.

Lucy fell silent. I thought I heard a sob – or was it just a sniff – above the babble of voices on the box, and wondered whether it would be wise, as a conciliatory gesture, to go across and give her a hug, say how much I was still fond of her (I wasn't certain I could use the word 'love'), and that things would sort themselves out. Yes. I decided it would be a good idea and went to lever myself up just as a car's headlights lit up the front curtains, quickly followed by the sound of car doors slamming.

Lucy sprung up first to answer the door when the bell chimed, a voice outside immediately apologising for disturbing us, but would it be possible to have a word with the vet? It was the voice of the woman on the answerphone. 'I'm afraid he's off duty,' Lucy was saying. 'But if you phone through to the hospital someone will be able to help you. I'll give you the number if you like.' There was the murmur of anxious voices outside ... a muted 'Sorry to have troubled you.'

It was no good; I couldn't let it be, and jumped to my feet, calling, 'Lucy, just a minute.' She turned and scowled as I drew level with her and peered out of the door. It was dark, but in the light from the porch stood two people; they were in their mid-forties, the woman solid-framed, mousy, short hair, wearing an oilskin jacket, and the man in a similar jacket, of similar physique with receding hair. The faces of both were creased with concern.

When I asked what the problem was, it was the woman who spoke first, introducing herself as Sandra Coles, and the man next to her as John, her husband. 'We really are sorry for disturbing you, but it's Henry, one of our Boxers. He seems to be really stressed.'

Her husband butted in, shifting uncomfortably from one foot to the other. 'I know it's a bit of a liberty ...' He paused and gave an embarrassed smile. 'But as we live just across the back there ...' He raised his hand and vaguely waved in the direction of Ashton Manor '... we thought perhaps ...' His voice trailed off.

'We've got Henry in the back of the car,' said the woman. 'If you could possibly have a quick look we'd be most grateful.'

'Much the best thing if you get him to a vet,' said Lucy icily.

'Bring him round,' I said, ignoring her.

'Thank you,' said Mr Coles, and instantly both he and his wife turned on their heels and ran back up the side of the cottage.

'Typical of you,' seethed Lucy, storming back into the living room, in what I considered to be a completely unreasonable frame of mind. But then maybe she'd just been trying to protect me from myself. Whatever, the appearance of the Boxer in the porch instantly concentrated my mind on the problem I was being presented with. The Coles were right to be concerned – Henry was a very sick dog. Supported by Mr Coles, kneeling next to him, holding his collar, the Boxer stood splay-legged like a rocking horse, his chin out, froth round his muzzle, strings of saliva hanging down from his jowls, his breathing shallow. When asked, the Coles told me he'd been like it for the past 30 minutes or so.

'He's just so restless,' said Mrs Coles. 'Can't seem to settle.'

'And he keeps trying to be sick but not bringing anything up,' said her husband, stroking the Boxer's head. 'Don't you, Henry?' He kissed the top of the dog's head.

Sandra Coles stepped round the side of the Boxer and ran a hand down his left flank, gently patting it. 'And see here – his tummy looks really swollen, if you ask me.'

I didn't have to ask her. I could see. Henry's abdomen was indeed swollen. Grossly dilated. I bent over and tapped it. As suspected, it was tympanic – tight as a drum. I lifted his upper lip. Even though the porch light was poor, it was sufficient for me to see that the gums were extremely pale, and just to prove the point that the dog was in circulatory collapse, I pressed on the upper margin. It stayed white when I removed my thumb. There was no doubt in my mind as to what was happening.

I straightened up and said, 'We've got a gastric torsion here. He's going to need emergency surgery if we're to save him.'

Both the Coles' faces blanched to the pallor of Henry's gums.

'You'll need to get him over to the hospital straight away. I'll ring them for you now.'

'I've just done it, Paul,' said Lucy, appearing at the doorway, obviously having listened in to the drama unfolding. 'Mandy will be expecting them.' She got hold of my sleeve and pulled me in to say in a lowered voice, 'But there is a problem. Eric's out on an emergency calving and won't be back for at least another hour.' Hell's bells. Henry was unlikely to survive that long.

'I'll just have to go in then,' I declared. I saw Lucy's look. 'Well, there's no other choice, is there?' and added with a whispered hiss, 'Otherwise, we'll have a dead dog on our hands.'

I stepped back outside and instructed the Coles to get going, telling them I'd follow on behind.

'Are you sure?' they queried.

'Yes, yes. Be as quick as you can. And I'll see you there.'

'That's so kind of you,' gushed Sandra Coles as her husband lifted and carried Henry back to the car.

They were already sitting in the waiting room when I arrived at Prospect House. 'Your nurse has taken Henry through,' they informed me. They both vigorously nodded their heads when I told them they could stay there if they wished. I then charged down to the operating theatre where Mandy had the – by now collapsed – Boxer on the table, his abdomen already shaved, a drip set up ready to be connected, the anaesthetic machine to hand, emergency instruments on the trolley. Brilliant. What a great nurse.

With Henry anaesthetised, I did wonder about stomach-tubing him, but Mandy had already anticipated that and handed me one from the anaesthetic trolley with a 'Thought you might want this.' I slid the tube down, but, as suspected with the stomach twisted round on itself, it wouldn't pass through the pyloric sphincter. I needed to get into the abdomen and turn the stomach on its axis before that could be done. No easy task ... especially as it was the first gastric torsion I'd ever encountered, and I only knew from my college notes that such a twist of the stomach – with the resulting build-up of trapped gas causing the extended stomach to press on the diaphragm – would gradually stop the dog from breathing and lead to circulatory collapse and death.

The operation went better than anticipated, although I was tired and anxious. At one point, when wrestling with the inflated stomach, trying my best not to rupture it, I did wonder whether I was manoeuvring it the right way – in gastric torsions did the stomach twist clockwise or anticlockwise? And was that looking towards the dog's head or towards the dog's tail? For a panicky moment, I couldn't decide which, until Mandy came to my help.

'Paul,' she said, 'I'll push down on the stomach tube as you turn.'

Yep. Good idea. And it worked. I knew the stomach was correctly positioned when the tube slid through the untwisted pyloric sphincter and the trapped gases seeped out, the stomach gradually reducing to its normal size without any visible damage to its walls or adjacent organs. Once again, my thanks, Mandy.

Despite still being shocked, the imminent danger of dying had been prevented and immediately Henry's colour started to return to normal and his breathing eased. So, too, did my colour and breathing. So, too, did the Coles' when I told them Henry had survived the crisis; both of them burst out crying with relief. I almost joined them.

All in all, it had been a horrendous day. A challenge to my abilities as a vet. A roller coaster. One moment I was down, full of self-doubt, and then up again, as now, pleased as punch that I'd been able to save Henry.

The Coles brought the Boxer over to Willow Wren ten days to the day after the op, to have his stitches removed. Against house rules really, as he should have been seen at the hospital, but what the heck.

And what a different dog I was presented with this time. A Boxer full of high spirits, haunches swinging from side to side in a frenzied greeting, jowls this time slobbering with delight and not fear. Nevertheless, he lay down in our hallway and, with John Coles' restraining hand on his chest, allowed me to remove the stitches without a murmur, while Sandra stood to one side, holding in her hand a thin, rectangular parcel wrapped in green-and-gold paper. She handed the parcel to her husband as he got to his feet.

'This is for you,' he said, proffering it to me. 'A thank you from both of us. And of course, Henry.' The Boxer had sat up, and was looking at me, head on one side.

'That's very kind of you,' I said, holding it between my hands. 'May I open it now?'

Both John and Sandra shrugged. 'Please do, if you wish,' said Sandra.

Henry whined.

'Seems Henry wants you to,' said John, with a grin.

'In that case ...' I said, and began to tear off the paper, gradually revealing a framed watercolour. Even before I had removed the last vestiges of the wrapping, I could feel the tears begin to well up, and it was with a supreme effort that I kept them at bay as the portrait was fully revealed.

'How did you ... how did you ...' I faltered, still fighting to keep my composure.

John Coles explained. He was a bit of an artist, dabbled in his spare time, especially animal portraits, and had seen me on occasion taking a terrier for a walk over in the bluebell wood. He'd then asked Lucy if there was a picture of the dog he could borrow, and she'd emailed him one of my digital snaps. This was the result. He hoped I didn't mind.

I could only shake my head, biting my lower lip. How could I ever mind? There, sitting among the bluebells, one ear up, one ear down, looking at me questioningly, as if to say, 'Are you coming, mate?' was Nelson, my darling terrier, wearing that wonderful, lopsided grin of his.

12
A-ROVING HOME
WITH REYNARD

In my walks over to the bluebell wood with Nelson, and the subsequent ones without him, I would often find evidence of creatures that had passed along the tracks winding through the trees: uprooted bulbs and small pits dug out with excrement in them indicated badgers; bark nibbled off the lower trunks, rabbits and squirrels; areas of bark worn away higher up and almost encircling the younger trees' trunks, roe deer rubbing their antlers and ripping off strips of bark. And distinct among all those signs, there was a smell. A particularly pungent smell. The unforgettable smell of fox. A vixen or dog that had slipped through the brambles, maybe scenting their territory as they went, urinating or, more obviously, depositing black, pointed-ended faeces on the edges of the paths.

So that May morning when I entered Prospect House and sniffed the air, I recognised the smell instantly – the acrid scent of fox. Presumably to another fox this was as attractive as the pheromones that used to spur me into fevered activity with Lucy on our ancient bed, forgetting, in the passion of the moment, that Eleanor Venables, next door, would have been privy to every ping of the springs. Sad to think that those springs hadn't pinged for what seemed ages.

'It's not me, if that's what you're thinking,' said Beryl stiffly, from behind the reception desk, while aiming a squirt of 'Springtime Blossom' in my direction.

'Good Lord, I should hope not,' I replied, adding, 'smells like fox.' I wrinkled my nose. 'Yes, definitely fox.' I left reception with the sound of another squirt of spray being ejected behind me. The smell grew stronger as I headed down the corridor, and the ward positively reeked when I entered it. Even if the air hadn't been polluted, there was definitely an atmosphere in there, and the spring in my step faltered as I caught sight of Eric and Mandy in the middle of a heated discussion outside one of the kennels.

'Look,' Eric was saying, his face a gleaming ball of sweat, 'I'm sure one of those rescue centres would take it.' He looked up as I approached. 'Or even Paul, here.' His face cried, 'Help, Mandy's having a go at me.' And he waved a clenched fist behind her as she turned and said, 'Morning, Paul ...' with a tight smile.

I looked through the bars, expecting to see a fox, but all I saw was a wooden crate, not much larger than an orange box, with two rusty bands holding the sides together and a twist of wire looped over a nail, holding the top down. Through the slats, I glimpsed the shadow of something, a wisp of muddy-brown fur, a blur of white. But there was little else to suggest that the crate held a fox ... except the smell. Seems the crate had been dumped overnight next to Eric's car, with a note pinned to it – 'Found by side of road. Hit by car perhaps?' – and had been discovered by Eric

214

when he set out to work that morning. Still alive, as he'd heard it moving around, he told me. But he didn't want to open the crate in case it 'vamoosed'. Mandy was clearly displeased that one of her kennels had been taken up, not to mention the smell that was now pervading her nice, antiseptically clean hospital.

'I was telling Mandy that we'd better check it over,' said Eric, 'before we send it off to one of those rescue centres, that is. Don't you agree, Paul?' His face screamed, 'Help me out, you sod, and I'll buy you a drink later.'

I decided to throw caution to the wind and wade in on Eric's side. 'Would seem sensible,' I said. 'After all, it wouldn't look too good if it had a broken leg or something, and we hadn't done anything about it.'

'We're not a wildlife sanctuary you know,' retorted Mandy, clearly lacking any spring-like movement in her body, her features fixed and rigid. What she needed was a good squirt of oil to loosen her up. What she got was support from Crystal who, at that moment, strode in, wrinkled her pert little nose, and demanded to know what the smell was as it was all round the hospital.

'It's Eric,' said Mandy, without a trace of irony, merely lowering her long, sable eyelashes as she looked down at the crate.

'Well, not *actually* me,' corrected Eric with a little laugh, glancing murderously at Mandy before addressing his wife. 'It was next to my car this morning. Didn't think you'd want it messing up *your* car, so I brought it in.' He cocked his head and gave a hesitant smile as if to say, 'Wasn't I a considerate fella?'

It didn't cut the mustard with his wife, and his face fell sharply when she said, 'Then do something about it. I want it out of here as soon as possible. Understand?' She looked first at her husband and then at Mandy, adding, 'We're not a wildlife sanctuary you know.'

Mandy smiled and flickered her lashes at Eric and me. 'That's what I told them,' she said as if butter wouldn't melt in her mouth.

Eric's look suggested a ball of suet rather than butter should have been rammed into her mouth, but he cleared his throat and went on to say, 'Paul thought it wise to check it over first, though.'

What ... me? Hang on a minute.

'Fine,' said Crystal, turning to me. 'So get on with it now before you start your appointments.'

It was my turn to throw a dagger at Eric, who merely gave me a sheepish smile and bounced towards the ward's exit door, whistling the tune of 'Onward Christian Soldiers'.

Mandy also looked as if she'd love to lob a scalpel or two in his direction; but I couldn't really blame her. With Lucy being off for the day, visiting her mother over in Eastbourne, Mandy was having to cope single-handedly, seeing to the incoming cats and dogs booked for routine ops and cleaning and feeding the animals that were already hospitalised for treatment. The snap and crackle of her uniform was beginning to sound a bit more snappy and crackly than normal.

Crystal also realised the problem, since she abruptly called out after her husband's disappearing figure, 'Just a minute, Eric, where do you think you're going?'

He stopped and turned, the whistle of ' ... *marching off to war* ...' faltering on his lips. 'Best if you give Paul a hand here,' Crystal advised. 'Mandy's got enough on her plate as it is.' There was no mistaking the sharp edge to her voice.

Eric did a smart turnabout and retraced his steps,

looking like a punctured ball, his bounce lost, an impression his baggy trousers, belted below the paunch of his belly, and the loose shirt escaping from them, did nothing to allay. Crystal gave Mandy a nod and instructed her to get on with her jobs; she then excused herself to us all with a little wave of her dainty, perfectly manicured fingers and a haughty, almost regal look, informing us she was due to visit Lady Derwent. The ring of the bell in reception was Mandy's excuse to slip away with a big wave of her squat, stubby-nailed digits and a 'Told you so' look which provoked, from Eric, a two-fingered gesture at her retreating figure and a snort of disgruntlement.

'Now, now,' I said, 'I'm sure this won't take long. So which one of us is going to do the honours?'

'Guess I should catch the blighter as I brought it in,' replied Eric, striding over to the sink unit and rummaging in the cupboard under it, saying that there should be some gauntlets in there somewhere; he eventually pulled out a grey, suede pair that had seen better days, the stitching on the edges of several fingers having come apart, leaving gaps down the sides through which sharp teeth could easily slip. 'Better than nothing,' he said, holding them up. 'We're going to have to be careful, though,' he added, as I slipped the bolt on the kennel door and swung it open. 'The last thing we want is the critter making a dash for it.'

He stepped in. I followed, and swung the door closed and bolted it again, shaking the bars to make sure it was securely shut. 'Mind you, if it's injured I don't suppose it will be going far.' He stepped over to the crate and donned the gauntlets while I bent down and untwisted the wire over the nail holding the lid down. He, too, bent down. 'OK … let's see what we've got.'

I cautiously lifted the lid a fraction. There was a slight

movement inside and, in the gap between the lid and the crate, I could just make out the features of a fox – the intense yellow eyes, dark-brown ears, the long muzzle, white under the chin, its hindquarters backed up to my end of the crate like a coiled spring. For some reason – maybe because it was in a small, wooden crate – I'd been expecting a cub, possibly still in its woolly, infant grey coat, but this fox appeared to be older by several months, the red-brown of the adult coat beginning to show through.

'Steady, Paul, steady,' warned Eric as I inched the lid open a bit more. 'Now put your arm across your end of the gap and just open the lid sufficient for me to get my hand in, OK?'

I nodded and did as instructed, the lid creaking open a little bit more. Still no movement from within. Eric grasped his end of the lid with one gauntleted hand and cautiously eased the other inside, peering into the interior as he did so. 'Think it's up your end,' he hissed. 'It's not moving. Must be shocked. Right … ready? I'm going to pounce.' He thrust his arm in, causing the lid to jerk open even more. In an instant, there was the blur of reddish fur, the somersault of limbs, a flash of teeth sinking into a gauntlet and a 'Bloody hell!' from Eric as he yanked his arm out, a young dog fox fastened to it.

The fox thrashed all four limbs against Eric's arm and the gauntlet sailed off in his teeth, leaving Eric with a hand from which blood splattered in the air. 'Damn!' he cried, slamming his hand against his chest, his eyes rolling with pain, while the fox shook its head violently, an action which caused the gauntlet to go flying across the kennel. He then shot off the top of the crate, flinging himself against the back wall, his claws scrabbling against it, before he slid down and streaked round the side, hurling himself at the kennel door, the bars rattling as he pounded time and time against them.

'Paul, here, give me that gauntlet, quick,' shouted Eric, and I leapt across, picked it up and he snatched it from me. 'I'll get the blighter yet.'

As he spoke, the fox twisted his head to one side and pushed it between two bars; within seconds, the rest of his body had somehow squeezed through, and the creature was now fast disappearing down the corridor.

'Why, the little bugger ...' seethed Eric, ramming back the door's bolt and running down the corridor after him. 'At least the ward door's closed, thank God,' he shouted back to me, as I watched him come to a halt, both gauntlets now on, and crouch down to creep stealthily towards the fox just as Mandy walked in and screamed as it shot between her legs. Eric disappeared after him and I hastily followed, pushing past a thunderstruck Mandy with a spluttered 'Sorry about this' to see Eric at the top end of the corridor leaping up the steps as another scream reverberated from reception – only this scream tailed off to be followed by the sharp tones of Beryl reprimanding Eric.

I arrived just as all hell was let loose and the waiting room erupted in a cacophony of howls and yowls. In the doorway, a tall, white-haired gentleman, whom I recognised as Major Fitzherbert, a retired Army Officer client of mine, appeared and proceeded to wave his stick at the three of us.

'I say, you lot,' he harrumphed, 'never guess what I've just seen race through your waiting room. It was a bally fox, if I wasn't much mistaken.'

He chortled, his thick, white moustache and matching eyebrows bobbing up and down like demented caterpillars. 'Takes me back to my hunting days. Tally ho and all that.

Not that I can do much of that since my accident.' He tapped the side of his thigh with his walking stick. We all knew what he was referring to. He'd told us many times how he'd been gored by a rhino during his time out in East Africa, on one of his many safari trips hunting big game. Only we also knew – Beryl having been informed on good authority – that he'd incurred the limp through tripping over a loose paving slab in Westcott's High Street before it was pedestrianised. 'The varmint went through that away.' He raised his cane and pointed up the corridor towards my consulting room. 'How're you going to catch the little sod then?' The caterpillar eyebrows arched.

'Erm ....' Eric shot me a look.

I was thinking of my trusty 'cat catcher' – the noose on the end of a pole that I'd used to restrain Major Fitzherbert's Leo, a semi-wild cat I'd been called in to treat in his greenhouse. The Major was obviously thinking along the same lines since he barked, 'This young laddie here used that contraption on a pole to nail Leo. Much better if he'd darted him. Easier all round, don't you think?' The eyebrows wiggled at Eric.

He flapped his hands helplessly. 'I'm afraid we don't have such a thing as a dart gun.'

'More's the pity, I say,' said the Major with a loud harrumph. 'Good bit of sport to be had there.' He raised his cane and slid a hand along it, pushing the crook against his shoulder to peer down its length. 'Pow. Pow. I'd get the little blighter. Used to be a cracking good shot you know.'

'Cat catcher, Paul?' questioned Eric, turning to me with a shrug of his shoulders, his arms spread out.

'I've got it here.' We all turned to see Mandy in the archway, holding out the pole.

'Splendid. Right then,' spluttered Eric, gesticulating at

me with one hand, the other pointing at the pole. 'You're probably better at this sort of thing than I am.'

Thanks, mate.

There was an excited murmur of anticipation from the onlookers – clients now crowding round the waiting-room door, fascinated by the unfolding drama taking place in reception. Two people, with their dogs, who had just entered through the front door, shuffled alongside Major Fitzherbert and, in excited whispers, asked what was going on. A third lady squeezed in with a cat basket and was told a savage wild animal was rampaging through the hospital and that the young vet over there was going to track it down and lasso it. I was? The buzz of expectation grew higher as I took the cat catcher from Mandy while one lady told another in a loud whisper that lions could be very dangerous when cornered, and that her Tibbles would stay in his basket until she was given the all-clear.

Suddenly, another voice cut across the babble with a 'Hey, what's going on here, Dad?' as Jodie squeezed her way through the gaggle of clients and drew level with her father. 'A lion on the loose?' She turned a questioning face in my direction. 'And you're going to try and catch it with that?' She looked incredulously at the cat catcher I was waving around in front of me as another wave of excited murmurings rippled through the crowd of spectators.

'Go on, get in there,' urged one elderly lady, her glasses misting up, while Major Fitzherbert was recounting a story about a lion he'd bagged to the owner of Tibbles, who asked if she could sit down as it was all getting a bit too much for her cat. I was beginning to feel rather gladiatorial – Ben Hur (Paul Mitchell) about to be cajoled along the underground passageway (corridor) into the amphitheatre (consulting room) to do battle with the lion (young fox).

Eric explained to his daughter what had happened and then turned to me and asked if I'd mind if he left me to get on with it as he was due over at the Stockwells to see about a sick sheep of theirs and was late already. Before I could answer, he wished me luck and eased himself through the throng to disappear out of the front door. Jodie apologised on her father's behalf and Major Fitzherbert suggested I enlist his help in following the critter's spoor and track him down to his lair, where we could then plan our strategy for bagging him. Jodie looked at me as he spoke, a twinkle in her eyes, and volunteered her own support, a suggestion I quickly accepted.

So, minutes later, having closed the doors to reception and the waiting room behind us in case the fox tried to do another bunk, it was just the two of us, tiptoeing down the corridor towards my consulting room, me clutching the cat catcher, its handle slippery with the sweat that was oozing from my palms, Jodie close behind, clutching the gauntlets her father had shoved in her hands before his hurried departure.

'This is rather fun, Paul,' whispered Jodie. 'On safari in Prospect House.'

I wasn't so sure, although the close proximity of Crystal's daughter and my awareness of how I used to fantasise about her mother did act as a pleasant diversion as images of crisp, white blouses, tight, corduroy safari trousers and long, leather whips cracking against firm thighs slipped through my mind, to be replaced by a fox's fangs and putrid anal secretions the instant we got to the door of the consulting room. We stopped … and cautiously peered in.

The room was empty … but the fox had been in there. The smell and smear of faeces across the floor meant that it didn't require Major Fitzherbert's expertise to realise the creature had come and gone.

'Must have scarpered down there then,' said Jodie, turning to point down the back corridor, which crossed behind the waiting room to connect with the other consulting room, and off which was the dispensary, a windowless small room, currently in darkness, its door open, an obvious bolt-hole for a frightened fox. 'Bet you it's in there,' Jodie continued as we reached the dispensary door, her lips slightly open, the pink tip of her tongue delicately tracing the outline of her Cupid's bow. 'Are you going to go in?'

The invitation, and her lips, were irresistible.

'Paul, what are you doing?'

I found my tongue was hanging out, so I quickly retracted it to say I was giving her ... it ... some thought.

'Well, it's obviously been in there,' said Jodie, turning sideways to reach past me, her T-shirt and the words emblazoned on it – 'I'm always hungry for more' – fuelling my appetite as they slid past my chest. She wrinkled her nose over my shoulder, her right earlobe only inches from my tongue. Oh, what a pert little nose, just like her mother's. Oh, what a dainty earlobe, just like ...

'I've a feeling it's in there,' she whispered hoarsely, her soft breath caressing my right earlobe. 'What do you think?'

Oh, how could I possibly tell her what I was thinking when her chest was pressed hard up against me, her thighs practically fused against mine in that doorway. 'Yes, it could well be in there,' I murmured, easing my pole away from her.

'I tell you what,' declared Jodie, still in a low voice. 'I could get it out for you.'

'Sorry?' I said, my mind boggling.

'The fox, Paul,' said Jodie giving me a funny look. 'The room's too small for both of us to squeeze in, especially with you swinging that pole of yours around.'

Mmm ... if only.

She elaborated: 'If I go in and flush it out, you could lasso it as it comes through the doorway. And if you don't get it first time ... well, no sweat ...' Jodie shrugged. 'There's nowhere else for it to go as the doors down the corridor are closed. So you could have another go.'

Oh yes please, I thought.

'Don't worry, Paul. I'm quite used to this sort of thing.'

You are? I thought. Wow.

'Like a bit of a challenge.'

Oh really? Mmm.

'Used to go round with Mum and Dad on some of their visits. And helped out in the hospital when they were short-staffed.'

Ah. Yes. Of course.

'So let's get on with it then,' concluded Jodie, her brisk, Crystal-like tone shaking me out of my reverie. With that, she pushed the dispensary door open even wider, and snapped on the light inside to reveal the interior lined with shelves on three sides, all packed with bottled medicines, cartons of pills, boxes of syringes, needles, cotton wool and bandages, while on the floor, in one corner, stood a fridge, alongside which were three rows of sacks, each row three deep, each a different variety of specialised canine dietary feed, the back sack resting with its top touching the wall, the bottom a few centimetres out, leaving a gap big enough for a young fox to slip into.

'Bet he's behind those,' said Jodie in a loud whisper, pointing at the sacks. 'If I pull out the three nearest the wall he'd probably bolt out the other end. So be ready at the door.' With that, Jodie pulled on the gauntlets she'd been carrying, stepped over and dragged the first sack forward. Nothing stirred. Then came the second sack. Still nothing. Then the third.

Whoosh. A streak of brown fur bombed out of the end of the row, turned sharply and zoomed towards me. I blindly swept the pole out with its noose open, and pulled at the end of the cord laced through the pole's centre; I felt the noose tighten as, more by luck than judgement, I saw I'd caught the fox round its neck. So I continued to pull, pushing the pole down, until the fox was pinned in a squirming, foaming ball on the floor.

Jodie whipped round and fell to her knees, grasping the hind-legs together and pushing them out while doing the same with the front ones, stretching the fox's body.

'OK, Paul, I've got him,' she said. 'You can release the noose a touch now. We don't want to garrotte the little chap.'

I eased the tension on the cord and pulled the cat catcher out of the dispensary, with Jodie, still on her knees, sliding the fox in front of her until she and the fox were both out in the corridor with me.

The young fox lay stretched between her hands, breathing rapidly but otherwise still. Jodie looked up at me. 'Doesn't seem to be much wrong with him, if you ask me,' she said.

I thought the same. Certainly no broken limbs. And when I knelt down beside her and checked him more closely, there didn't seem to be any superficial injuries either; no open wounds, no abrasions or broken claws. If he had been hit by a car, there was no evidence.

'Lucky escape then,' commented Jodie when I finished my examination and sat back resting on my heels. 'So what now?'

Seeing as the fox hadn't suffered any obvious injuries, I thought the easiest solution would be to release him.

'But not around here, surely?' remarked Jodie when I told her. 'Might get hit by another car.'

I'd already thought of that and decided the best bet – and here I took a deep breath – would be to re-crate the fox and take it back to Willow Wren; once there, I'd let it go over in the woods. At least then it would have a better chance of survival.

Once I'd re-tensioned the noose, Jodie released her grip on the fox's legs and I kept the fox pinned to the floor, with one foot firmly on his hindquarters, while she ran down to the ward and quickly returned with the orange box. Gripping the fox's legs once more, she lifted him into the crate as I let the noose slip off him. Then expertly keeping her right gauntleted hand pressed to his head, she released her grip on his hind-legs and, as I pressed down on the lid, slipped her right hand out before the fox had a chance to escape again. What a performance. It had certainly impressed me. Oh, to be a young fox in her hands. I'd willingly be hounded by her any day.

It meant the fox having to stay cooped up until later that day when I finished early, and could then get back to Willow Wren to release him. Not ideal, but the best I could do under the circumstances.

After the excitement of the chase, it was difficult to switch back into routine appointment mode. I ploughed through the morning's crop of vaccinations, dirty ears and blocked anal glands in need of expression, followed by the routine spays and castrates, of which there weren't too many that morning – just as well, as it gave me a chance to catch up with things after the delays caused by the fox's flying visit.

My mood remained quite buoyant during the afternoon's session of appointments. If only I'd realised how it was all going to change for the worse that evening. Oh boy.

I was feeling quite happy as I headed over the Downs with the young fox in his crate, stowed in the boot of the car. Mandy had told me she'd fixed a drinking bottle to the side of the crate with its nozzle pushed through one of the slats, and it seemed Foxy had taken a drink from it during the day, so at least he wouldn't have got too dehydrated prior to me releasing him – something I intended to do as soon as I got home. So, yes, I was feeling happy and even sang along to the car radio, a rare occurrence for me. But that happiness was to be short-lived. Quite brutally snuffed out.

I somehow sensed it was going to happen as soon as I drew up behind Lucy's car outside the front of Willow Wren. For a start, she was back from her visit to her mother's earlier than normal. Always a bad omen. She and Margaret didn't get on too well. And although Lucy went over to Eastbourne at least twice a month, sometimes staying overnight if not on duty, there were often times when she'd return in a foul mood, declaring that her mother was an impossible woman to deal with and she didn't know why she bothered to put up with her cantankerous ways. 'Well, she is your mother,' I'd say. 'Blood's thicker than water, and all that ...' And at 52, you'd expect an old person to be set in her ways. But she's so rude with it, Lucy would fume, vowing not to bother contacting her. 'Let her phone me,' she'd say. Then, a few days later, I'd hear her ring through and they'd end up deep in conversation together for hours – usually talking trivia – but Lucy occasionally having to express sympathy for the latest of Margaret's tales of woe. I had met Margaret once.

It was just after Christmas, and Lucy had been made to feel guilty at not having seen her mother over the Christmas period. Margaret had been invited to Christmas lunch at the house of her best friend's daughter – this was apparently the third year in a row, and it was becoming a bit of a tradition; on Boxing Day, she had gone, with two other long-standing friends, to the sales in Eastbourne and had had a buffet lunch out with them – yet despite that, she managed to convey the feeling to Lucy that she'd been 'abandoned by her daughter' over the festive period. Hence the visit over to Westcott two days after Christmas, and I've no doubt Margaret saw it as an ideal opportunity to suss me out and see whether I was 'worthy' of her daughter.

They say 'like mother, like daughter', so I, too, was intrigued to meet this woman and see how Lucy might turn out in 33 years or so – whether I would still be with her or not didn't come into it. I was just curious. Hmmm. They say curiosity kills the cat; in that case, after my meeting with Margaret, I was dead meat.

I hadn't been too sure how to approach her. It wasn't as if I needed to ingratiate myself with her, and rush up like some floppy puppy, hoping to be patted. Did I play it cool? Saunter up to her, stretch out my hand to shake hers, look her directly in the eye and say, 'Hi. I'm Paul. The guy who's been doing your daughter these past three months.' No, of course not. But nevertheless, the inference would be there.

In the event, it was a rather formal introduction, and I shook hands with a lady, somewhat shorter than my girlfriend and certainly broader, with a plumpness that was not soft and natural, but very solid and unwelcoming, encased as it was in a Crimplene, sky-blue trouser suit which hugged and rucked up between the many lumpy folds of her body, and exaggerated a stiff-legged gait, reminiscent of the pigeons in Trafalgar Square. As our palms touched, I felt and smelt the faint odour of perspiration overlaid with cheap talcum powder.

The day was not a success, in part due to Margaret's decision, conscious or otherwise, to play the lady dowager and make us feel how lucky we were to have her there; it was underlined with a certain cynicism and several cutting remarks about how she'd always been made to feel the underdog by her husband, from whom she was now thankfully divorced, and who had never respected her many virtues, which, during her visit to us, I had difficulty identifying.

So it was with relief I uttered my goodbyes to Margaret with the wish that I hoped to see her again soon – said with fingers crossed behind my back. I mused on whether the traits exhibited during her short time with us were those that could develop in Lucy; and indeed wondered whether I was already witness to the germination of that cutting cynicism in Lucy's behaviour of late. The events of that evening, when I came home with Foxy, suggested they had indeed developed.

I sat in the car, pondering my next move. The intention had been to leave the crate in the boot while I went in, asked after Lucy's day, and then request that she helped me carry the crate over the fields to the woods, and release the young fox there. But she'd been so grumpy these past few days, I wondered whether she'd be willing to help. 'You can but ask, Paul,' I said to myself, as I climbed out of the car. 'Can but ask …' I repeated, as I walked into the hall. 'Can but …' The words faded as I was greeted by a very, very long face. Obviously, the visit to Margaret's had not been one of the better ones.

'So how was your Mum?' I ventured to say, watching

Lucy noisily emptying the dish-washer I'd loaded and switched on before leaving for work that morning. Crash ... a pile of dinner plates slid into a cupboard. Side plates followed in equally noisy fashion. As did the knives and forks tossed into the cutlery drawer. She didn't have to speak to convey her mood. Oh, no. But when she did, it just verified it. Foul.

After Lucy's visits to her mother, I always asked out of politeness rather than actual interest, as the only concern I had for Margaret's wellbeing was the extent to which it affected Lucy's mood. I'd get a range of replies from a 'Not too bad' (Margaret was having one of her good spells) to 'Bloody awful' (no elaboration needed). But this evening there was a twist to her response, since, in answer to my enquiry, she retorted grimly, 'What's it to you?'

Ouch. Well ... it caught me on the hop. What, indeed, was it to me? I decided to ignore the remark and attempt a bit of sympathy – this was necessary, as it was Lucy's turn to cook supper. 'I guess Margaret's been having one of her off days. That's always difficult for you.'

She saw through that straight away and fired off another salvo: 'Don't be so bloody patronising, Paul.'

No. That approach certainly hadn't worked. Although, fortunately, it didn't stop her from starting supper. She yanked a ready-meal out of a carrier bag on the counter, slid off its sleeve, briefly glanced at the instructions, picked a knife out of the drawer and then proceeded to stab the plastic cover viciously more than the three to four times I knew was required – I wasn't a cordon bleu chef of ready-meal microwave cooking for nothing. I watched as she slid the tray into the microwave and slammed the door shut, picking up the sleeve to peer at the instructions again. 'Five minutes, peel back the plastic, stir, and reheat for a further minute,' I said quietly. The look she threw my way could have microwaved me to a frazzle in less than 30 seconds.

I wasn't sure how to steer the conversation from being a patronising sod to someone who had a young fox in the back of his car waiting to be released, especially as dinner was about to be served or thrown at me. It was clear whatever I said was going to be wrong, so I said, 'Actually, before we have supper, there's a young fox in the back of my car which I need your help with to release.' Besides being the wrong thing to say, this was the wrong time to say it, as Lucy screamed back at me, 'Why the hell didn't you say before I put the food in the oven?'

That's when I began to lose it. I'd been treading on eggshells since I'd got home, but I had now reached cracking point. 'I might have done if you'd bloody well let me,' I said, surprised at the vehemence in my voice. Was I really that screwed up?

Lucy stood in the middle of the kitchen, visibly trembling. 'Don't you dare be so RUDE.'

I slammed my fist down on the table. 'Hark who's talking,' I cried, my mouth opening wide – an action which caused a blob of spittle accidently to hurtle in Lucy's direction.

'That's great … bloody well start spitting at me.'

'Oh, for Christ's sake, don't be so petty.'

'There you go, putting me down again.'

'What the hell are you talking about?'

'As if you didn't know.'

'Oh for Christ's sake, Lucy. You're just in a foul mood.'

'Don't you DARE say what mood I'm in.'

'Oh, SORRY!' I couldn't help the sarcasm, but Lucy instantly picked up on it and proceeded to regale me with further accusations of how I always put myself first – 'Self ... self ... self,' is how she expressed it. I never considered her feelings ... always making her feel like the underdog.

Ping. The microwave went off. The food was now red hot.

Ping. So was my brain.

Underdog. Margaret had mentioned being an underdog. So there it was. The germination of similar feelings. But was I really to blame? Did I really make Lucy feel inferior? Surely she was a woman in her own right, albeit reflecting some of her mother's characteristics – perish the thought. If I was the cause of her feeling that way, then maybe it was best if we parted.

Ping. There it was. The solution. It had probably been there for some time, floating beneath the surface of our relationship; but neither of us had been aware of it. Or if we had, then we were reluctant to admit it.

Ping. Yes. Our time was up.

Only this wasn't the best time to say it. Foxy had to be released before we could think of releasing ourselves from each other. Or so I thought. But Lucy was having none of it. 'See to the bloody fox yourself,' she said when I mentioned his release again, hoping I could have appealed to her better nature. No way. I was kidding myself. Her better nature had disappeared under a volcanic eruption of ill-feeling. It had obviously been simmering deep down for some time and, now that the cracks in our relationship had been exposed, it had exploded with a vengeance, and was underscored by a final, savage, 'And don't expect me to be here when you get back,' and a storming out of the kitchen and a stomping up the stairs and a banging of drawers and wardrobe doors being opened and closed.

Ping. Ping. Ping. It was finished. Done for.

But there was still the young fox to deal with. The evening was drawing on, the sun slanting down behind Willow Wren, causing it to sink into shadows, rather like our relationship; and it would soon be dark on both accounts.

Back to Foxy. I slunk out of the cottage and round to the car, opening the boot, wondering whether it would be possible to cart the crate over to the woods myself. After all, it wasn't that heavy or awkward to carry, and, psychologically, I felt the need to take my mind off the trauma of the past 15 minutes. I levered the crate out of the boot, placed it on the ground and slammed the boot shut with more force than was necessary, but found it pleasingly satisfactory to do so. I dragged the crate along the path fronting Willow Wren, passing Mill Cottage, and wondered whether Eleanor Venables had been listening in to our row; but all seemed quiet and her car was missing, so I guessed she was probably over at her son's place. She usually went over on Fridays.

I switched my attention back to the crate, thinking that, when I reached the stile into the field, I'd have to lift the crate over, which could present difficulties. It was at that moment, out of the corner of my eye, I caught sight of the tall, stooped figure of Reverend James appearing from the gate to his garden; he hovered uncertainly on the spot, and then proceeded to glide in my direction. Could he have heard our altercation from over the way, and was now seeking to pour oil on troubled waters, or at least to offer some words – no doubt many, loquaciousness being his norm – of pastoral advice and reconciliation? God, they say, works in mysterious ways. Reverend James' ways were often a mystery, especially his verbose and convoluted sermons, which many times left even the hardiest of his stalwart parishioners perplexed and wondering what sort of path to righteousness they were being led up. The Reverend's path at that precise moment was leading to me.

'May I take this opportunity to wish you the benefits of a fine summer's evening, Paul,' he said, coming to halt by the side of my car, giving the crate a curious look and wrinkling his nose, his upper lip flaring as he did so.

'Oh, hello, James,' I said simply.

Reverend James clasped his hands together, while continuing to stare at the crate. With a big sniff, he queried, 'Would we have a creature that has had the benefit of your expert treatment within the confines of that container, I wonder?'

I shook my head. 'Not really.' A loud bang and a crash emanated from the upstairs window, causing Reverend James suddenly to look up. I quickly distracted him by adding, 'It's a young fox. I'm taking him over to the wood to release him.'

James beamed, his lips curling back to expose his prominent upper teeth in donkey fashion, and he nodded, sagely. 'Ah, I see. So one of nature's brethren is to have the chance to be unshackled from the confines of that box and be set free to return to the wildness of his familiar territory.'

'That's one way of putting it,' I replied, as another banging of drawers reverberated from upstairs.

If he'd heard it, the Reverend chose to ignore it and went on garrulously to say, 'If you desire some help in getting the young Reynard to the place where he is destined to find his way in the world again, I would be only too delighted to give you the means by which you can achieve your intention of doing that.'

'Thanks. It would be a great help.'

So with James supporting one end and me the other, the crate was shunted over the stile and carried across to the wood. Throughout, there was no movement inside, the only evidence that the crate contained a fox being the perpetual odour emanating from it, a fact that prompted the Reverend to say, as we bumped our way across the field, 'I trust the fox is of good health as there seems to be little to convey that he is still of this Earth as evidenced by the lack of movement within.'

'He's OK,' I said, praying I was correct.

Once we reached the edge of the woods, I took a winding track down through the yellowing leaves of the bluebells, the sun now sinking through a haze of yellow and pink cloud, suffusing the glade with an amber glow, throwing our shadows as long, black, distorted figures, which flickered and bounced between the tree trunks as we moved through them.

I was heading for a spot on the far side of the wood, a corner in which there was a sandy bank, partially obscured on its lower slope by a thicket of brambles and nettles, and in which there were several large holes dug in its side, yellow sand spilling out of their entrances. A warren. Or possibly a fox's earth. On top of the bank, above the tangle of briers, was a sward of grass, now silhouetted against the darkening sky. It seemed an ideal place to release the youngster.

'Here will do,' I murmured, putting my end of the crate down. Reverend James did likewise and, for a rare instance, remained quiet as I unhooked the lid of the crate and levered it back, stepping to one side once I had done it.

For a moment, nothing happened. Then the young fox's head appeared above the rim. He rapidly glanced in our direction before springing out and darting across into the brambles. The next minute he appeared on the top of the bank, paused sideways to look down on us, a dark-red outline haloed by the orange of the sky. Then he was gone.

'God be with you,' said Reverend James and, putting his fingers to his lips, blew a kiss in the fox's direction. I'm not too sure how Christian he felt when three days later his chicken coop was raided and three of his prize bantams were found with their heads bitten off.

My feelings were decidedly un-Christian when I returned to Willow Wren, now in darkness, Lucy's car gone, and, when switching on the kitchen light, found instructions for feeding her animals overnight, with a terse couple of lines to say she'd collect Queenie, Bugsie and the guinea pigs the next day, along with the rest of her belongings.

The ready-meal was still in the microwave. I reset it. As I did so, I realised my life, too, would have to be reset to get some warmth back into it.

Ping!

Done.

13
GORED
TO TEARS

Grappling with a young fox in the intimate confines of a small animal hospital's dispensary was certainly an unusual way of getting to know someone; uncomfortable, perhaps, that it was the Principals' daughter with whom I was getting up close and personal, but it was a pill I could happily swallow.

The next dose of medicine in my involvement with Jodie turned out to occur in a somewhat more exotic location, where my fertile imaginings of tight safari breeches, topees atop shimmering coppery curls and cracking whips were given even more free reign – alas, not striding across a parched, African veldt, a golden orb of sun sinking down in a tropical sky, but rather across a soggy stretch of municipal gardens in the centre of Westcott, a patina of grey, drizzly rain seeping down from a leaden one. Westcott Wildlife Park to be precise.

It was Beryl who set things in motion that Wednesday afternoon, an afternoon when Eric was off playing golf, as he did most Wednesdays, and Crystal was chock-a-block with appointments, leaving me to bear the brunt of any potential emergency that arose.

'Paul,' she called out, beckoning me over with one of her vermillion claws, as she spoke into the phone. 'Just a minute ...' She clamped her hand over the mouthpiece and looked up. 'It's Kevin over at the Wildlife Park,' she hissed. 'Wondering if you or Crystal could make a visit.'

'What ... now?' I queried.

Beryl nodded vigorously, causing her raven-winged hair almost to take off. 'It's Ollie. He's been gored by an antelope.'

Ollie? Ollie who? I wondered.

Beryl elaborated, 'It's Ollie, their ostrich. He's been attacked by a Thomson's gazelle and is apparently in quite a bad state. Kevin thinks he may need stitching up.' She gave me one of her glowering, hunch-shouldered looks, head cranked to one side, good eye tilted up. 'Well, I can hardly ask him to bring him in, can I?'

'No ... no, of course not.'

'And your appointments don't start until four o'clock. So you've a couple of hours spare.' Her glass eye glittered grimly.

'Yes ... I suppose ...'

'You don't sound too keen.' Beryl's neck sank even further into the hump of her black cardigan. She looked like a vulture about to tackle a lump of rotting meat. Me.

'Well ... it's just that I may need some help,' I explained, by way of my hesitancy. It was Mandy's half day off and Lucy was dealing with all the post-op cases and helping Crystal with her appointments, so how was I going to manage?

'I'll give Jodie a ring,' declared Beryl with a sudden ruffle of her feathers (shoulders). 'She said she'd be happy to lend a hand if ever required.' Her beak (lips) fell open as her claws (fingers) scrabbled for the phone. 'Just depends if she's at home,' she added with a rasping caw (her normal voice).

She was. And within ten minutes Jodie was standing in reception, a cycle helmet tucked under her arm, in denim jeans moulded to her long legs and a white T-shirt equally moulded to her pert breasts, the shirt just covering her midriff. It rode up as she leaned across to give Beryl a peck on the cheek and I caught a glimpse of the small of her back – tanned – and wondered if the neat set of buttocks below it had also been kissed by the sun. Mmm. I looked forward to finding out.

She handed her helmet over to Beryl for safe keeping, and turned to give me one of her ravishing smiles. 'Are you ready then, Paul?' she queried, tossing her head to shake out her curls.

Oh, yes, Jodie. Yes.

'You'll want these.' A dour voice cut through my fond imaginings.

'What?'

'These operating packs.' It was Lucy.

'Oh, yes, thanks,' I faltered, taking the sterilised instruments and drapes she thrust at me, her face set in a grimace. Her eyes briefly flickered across at Jodie – if looks could kill, then Jodie would have been dead meat and Beryl really would have had something to get her beak into.

It was only a few seconds, but it seemed an eternity such was the tension in the air. Or maybe it was just me being ultra-sensitive. Crystal snapped us back to reality when she swept into reception from her consulting room, enquired why her daughter was there and, on being told by Beryl about the ostrich, instructed me and Jodie, in no uncertain terms, to get our skates on before the bloody bird died.

'And you, Lucy,' she added, swinging round on her, 'please see that you're back in my consulting room pronto. There's a Great Dane coming in which I shall need help with.' As she spoke, the front door of reception opened, and through it padded an enormous, brindle-coated Great Dane, dragging behind him a diminutive lady, whose shoulders barely reached those of the dog leading her.

'Right, let's be off,' I whispered to Jodie, and the two of us edged past the dog and out to my car.

I'd first visited Westcott Wildlife Park back in November – on that occasion, as the assistant to Crystal – when we had to tackle Cleo, the camel with a septic toe. Apart from my big-game-hunter image of Crystal, any fantasy of the Wildlife Park as an environment for her to stride through had been quickly dashed by the reality of the place. Forget undulating paddocks teeming with giraffe, zebra and wildebeests. What we had was a mishmash of pens and paddocks awash with mud, in which there were two gazelles, a camel, some monkeys and an ostrich to head the list of the most exotic occupants. They were followed in decreasing rank by an aviary of budgerigars, some cockatiels, a moth-eaten mynah bird and finally a pen so overstocked with guinea pigs it meant that if one took fright and bolted, they all surged en masse through the puddles (Westcott's equivalent of the wildebeest migration across the Mara River).

That day in November, the park had been closed for the winter. Today, it was open to the public and, for the cost of a £2.50 ticket – I noticed the price had gone up since the previous year – you could experience the thrill of coming face to face with the residents; this often meant, besides the herd of rampaging guinea pigs, the odd, free-range rat glimpsed scuttling across from one shed to another.

The double gates to the park were wide open and there was a new billboard – barely readable due to the condensation inside the plastic cover – proclaiming the latest attraction: 'The Jungle Walkway'. It exhorted visitors to sample the delights of the park from the dizzy heights of the overhead jungle canopy. From what I could see, the jungle canopy being referred to was the sparse branches of two oak trees, one each side of the park, between which a slatted wooden footbridge with rope rails had been strung up. This enabled visitors who had sufficient courage to climb up a ladder and tentatively edge their way across the swaying bridge. The reward for all their efforts was to be able to peer directly down at the migratory habits of the guinea pigs below them (Westcott's equivalent of a balloon ride over the Serengeti). All the other inmates of the Wildlife Park were further away, their view obscured by the oaks' foliage. However, swaying around up there, having feasted on and digested the sight of panic-stricken guinea pigs squeaking and darting all over the place, there was a further opportunity to commune with and fend off some of the indigenous, crumb-hungry species found at that level – dive-bombing gulls, pestering pigeons and squirrels, curious to know why they weren't being fed from the safety and comfort of a park bench.

Having entered the park, I turned down the tarmac track marked 'Private' and drove through the tunnel of rhododendrons, now heavily laden with purple blossom, and out into the yard where Kevin Winters, the head keeper, lived in a vast, metallic mobile home that bristled with satellite dishes and aerials, like some intergalactic spaceship.

As Jodie and I jumped out of the car, the short, slim figure of Kevin bobbed into view from the adjacent prefabricated office block. He jogged over to us, accompanied by his two Alsatians, who bounded ahead of him, barking their heads off. Like they had done with Crystal the previous November, the dogs wrapped themselves around Jodie's thighs, clearly delighted to see her. She tickled their heads. Lucky dogs. Kevin threw his arms round her and gave her a hug, saying 'My, it's been a long time, Jodie. Great to see you.' She hugged him back and kissed his cheek. Mmm. Lucky man.

Jodie turned to me and grinned. 'As you can see, we know one another well.'

Oh, how I wished she'd be saying that about me.

'Since she was knee high to a grasshopper,' Kevin was saying.

'Don't know about a grasshopper, Kevin. More a young vixen perhaps?' Jodie turned and looked at me. That look was loaded ... Grrr. What a foxy lady she was.

'And how's Ben and Barnaby?' she asked Kevin, turning back to him. She was referring to his twin boys, dad lookalikes with their mops of black curls and coal-black eyes, who had helped out with the camel's operation last year.

'Yep. Fine thanks,' replied Kevin. 'They'll be sorry to have missed you.'

I knew what I was missing. Grrr.

Kevin extended his hand to me. 'Good to see you again, Paul. And thanks for coming out.' Having shaken my hand, he reached up and, in an apologetic gesture, tugged at a curl of his shaggy mane of grey and black hair, his lips parting in a rueful smile, revealing the gap between his front teeth. ''Fraid there's been a bit of an altercation between Ollie and one of the Tommies,' he said, his words whistling through his teeth like a singing kettle coming to

242

the boil. 'Ollie's come off worse and been gored. I think in the belly. But it's difficult to see.'

'See' in that context was a questionable word to use, as I wondered how Kevin could ever see in the clear sense of the word, since his eyes were obscured by pebble-opaque, round spectacles, the lenses of which were so thick and looked so murky it was a wonder he could see anything beyond the end of his nose, on which those spectacles were perched.

'Well, we've brought the emergency op set, just in case,' I said, as Kevin led the way down through the rhododendrons and out onto the gravel path that skirted the aviaries and the pen heaving with guinea pigs, and ran parallel to the high-fenced paddock, in which the two Thomson's gazelles were standing huddled together in one corner, their tails flicking from side to side, staring across at us like two errant schoolboys caught smoking, while in the other corner, under the sweep of an oak tree's branch, stood Ollie, the park's solitary ostrich.

Perhaps I'd been expecting a collapsed bird, legs sticking up in the air, or a paddock full of scattered black feathers, but there was no obvious evidence to suggest there had been any aggro. Kevin told us that he'd been alerted to the 'attack' when a member of the public had rung through to the office to report he'd seen one of the antelope repeatedly butt the ostrich, and at one point had lifted him right off the ground with his horn. There had been much flapping of wings, and much hissing and kicking by the ostrich, which had, at first, collapsed to the ground, but he then seemed to have rallied and got to his feet again.

'I just need you to check him over,' said Kevin as the three of us stopped at the small gate that led into the paddock and gazed across at the ostrich.

'Check him over ...' Hmm. It seemed such an innocuous statement. As if Ollie were a budgerigar that merely needed to be winkled from his cage, head held between two fingers, body resting in the palm of my hand, while I then proceeded to examine its undercarriage. If only. What we had here was 130 kilograms or so of solid, avian muscle, towering to well over 2.5 metres; and most of that muscle was located in a set of beefy thighs which, even at this distance, I could see were rippling with power. And those legs were designed not only for walking and running, but also for gouging one's stomach out should you get too near to a bad-tempered ostrich, or when a male was defending his females. Ollie lifted his right leg and stretched and clenched the long, curved claws of his two toes. He lowered that leg and repeated the same action with the other one. Boy, what power. An involuntary shiver ran down my spine.

'Guess that shows he's in a bit of pain, eh?' said Kevin, his observation ending with a soft whistle through his teeth and another tug at his hair.

Indeed it did, I thought, chewing my bottom lip. Pain ... bad temper ... a lunge at my belly. Great. What should I do? If I approached Ollie, his first move was most likely to be a rapid kick of his leg, aimed at disembowelling me with one savage swipe. The mere thought was gut-wrenching. My guts wrenched.

As if reading my mind, Kevin said, 'He is a big lad. But I think we could net him between us.'

'I'm game,' said Jodie, a comment which had both Kevin and I turn on our heels to her, Kevin's face full of thanks, mine full of lust.

'OK, let's give it a go then,' I murmured throatily, still looking at Jodie.

We retraced our steps back to the car and, while Kevin disappeared into the office to reappear moments later with a large roll of black netting tucked under his arm, Jodie and I pulled on some wellingtons and donned green overalls. She lifted the packs of surgical instruments and drapes from the boot, while I hauled out my black bag.

Back at the paddock gate, Kevin unlocked it and we slipped in. The two gazelles were still over in the one corner, still looking like naughty schoolboys, but now wondering what was afoot, both with their heads up, ears alert, tails busily flicking from side to side. Ollie, too, was not indifferent to our cautious approach. He shuffled on the spot, his neck arched, his head – bald save for a thin scattering of tiny feathers – turned in our direction, beady black eyes with their heavy lashes glowering suspiciously at us, while at the same time, his large wings were partially raised and outstretched, like heavy, droopy, black-feathered mantillas. If he was injured, then his injuries were not stopping him from being on his guard, ready to attack ... ready, no doubt, to put his claws to ripping good use should we dare get too close.

Kevin dropped the netting to the ground, and he and I unrolled it.

'OK,' he said. 'The idea is that two of us each hold one end up. The other brave soul stands in the middle behind the net to stop Ollie from charging straight through as we cast it over him. Does that seem feasible?'

Jodie and I looked at each other and shrugged.

'Whatever you say,' I muttered, turning back to Kevin. 'You're the boss.'

'OK, then,' he said. 'Let's give it a whirl.'

He and I held the two ends while Jodie did the honours as the 'brave soul' in the middle. Once in position, we tentatively advanced across the paddock towards the ostrich, the netting stretched between us like a tennis net, the lower edge trailing on the ground. Ollie became more and more agitated the nearer we got. He marched on the spot. He raised his claws higher and higher with each step he made. And with every step we made. His beak opened. He hissed. His wings flapped. They rattled. His quills quivered and quaked in much the same way my knees knocked and rasped against each other as we drew closer and closer.

I really didn't know what to expect. Would Ollie suddenly leap over the net? Or would he just charge it? He certainly wouldn't be able to fly over. His wings weren't strong enough for that. Only metres from Ollie, Kevin warned me and Jodie that we were about to cast the net as high and as far forward as possible.

He stopped. 'Right ... ready? One, two, three ... go!' he cried.

I threw my end of the net as high and as far forward as I could, while Kevin did the same. It soared into the air, fanning out over the bewildered Ollie. He looked up, startled. Then, as the netting slowly dropped and enfolded him, he collapsed to the ground, trapped.

The three of us ran in and stood on the edges of the netting in case Ollie attempted to kick his way out from under it. But he just gave a few feeble kicks, thus ensnaring his claws in the netting even more. He lay there, partially on his side, head stretched out on the ground, enmeshed, his breathing coming in wheezy gasps.

'Guess he's more shocked than we thought,' said Kevin, kneeling down alongside Ollie's flank, and pushing the bird's body more onto its side.

I tugged free the netting that was trapped under the bird.

'Hold on to this for me,' I instructed Jodie, cautiously lifting the netting up. That allowed me to worm my hand in and burrow down past the left wing with its mass of quilled, black feathers, now peppered with drops of rain, and slide it under Ollie's belly where I could feel the rough surface of his pimply skin. As I moved my fingers down and forward, I felt them suddenly become warm and sticky, like I'd just dipped them in a jar of warm syrup. The syrup was Ollie's blood. The jar, a hole in his side. I withdrew my hand, the fingers covered in bloody mucus.

'Not good,' I said, realising how obvious the statement sounded. 'We'd better get Ollie anaesthetised and see just how bad the injury is.'

Another problem here. How heavy was Ollie? 100 kilograms? 150 kilograms? How much anaesthetic should he have?

I drew up a dose from the bottle in my black bag, making a 'considered judgement' as to how much – in other words, a wild guess. Having injected it into Ollie's thigh through the netting, it was only a matter of minutes before all signs of life vanished and Ollie subsided into a heap of motionless feathers. Hell's bells. I'd overdosed the bird. My wild guess had really been wide of the mark. Shit. Then Ollie took a huge intake of air and resumed breathing again, albeit a bit erratically. Phew. Thank God.

Kevin quickly unravelled Ollie from the netting. Jodie stepped round to the bird's shoulder and, bunching a cluster of wet quills in her hand, pulled back his left wing. The quills – each the thickness of a pencil, the downy barbs dark and iridescent – rattled like bamboo canes. With the wing drawn out of the way, it allowed me to see the left side of the abdomen more clearly. And clearly visible was the wound. A gash about six centimetres or so long, the edges of the grey skin jagged and curled in on themselves, exposing a narrow band of yellow, subcutaneous tissue.

For a start, that skin was going to need stitching. But I had a feeling that there was going to be more to this wound than met the eye. I couldn't imagine the gazelle's horn would have just sliced through the skin and done no further damage. So it proved. I eased back the edges of the wound to discover a tear in the underlying tissues and a welt of torn, red muscle glistening beneath it. Damn.

'Seems the gazelle has punctured Ollie's abdomen,' I said, scrabbling to my feet, my heart thudding against my ribs. This was a far more serious problem. A penetrating wound. Internal organs could be damaged.

I guess Jodie must have sensed my concern, as, when she got to her feet, she said, 'It might not be as bad as it looks,' and gave me an encouraging smile.

Kevin chipped in, saying that I might be better doing the op over in the shelter, in the dry, and away from the public; and it was then that I became aware of the gaggle of people at the perimeter of the paddock, and several up on the footbridge above me, staring down through the drizzle with intense interest.

There was sufficient netting still trapped under Ollie to enable the three of us to drag him across the now sodden paddock and into the shelter, where, at least, there was some dry bedding to haul him onto; and it was away from prying eyes. With Ollie part levered onto his back by wedging a straw bale each side of him, Jodie set to work, without any prompting from me, first plucking the few small feathers that surrounded the wound and then cleaning the skin with antiseptic scrub she'd brought over with the surgical kit. Kevin, meanwhile, had dashed back to get a bucket of hot water and, having returned with it, I was able to give my hands a good scouring; that was the limit of our sterility. Not good. But then I reasoned if the gazelle's horn had sliced through into Ollie's abdomen as suspected, then infection would have already been introduced.

With drapes clipped round the edge of the gash, I used the finger and thumb of my right hand to retract the central section of the jagged, torn skin on each side. I eased my left forefinger through the exposed tissue beneath, gradually pushing it deeper and deeper with a sawing movement, feeling the knots of damaged muscle contract round it, feeling them resisting my probing. Suddenly, all resistance stopped. With a loud pop, my finger was inside Ollie's abdomen. Verification that the antelope had indeed ruptured the ostrich's abdominal wall. Now what? Did I just stitch up the torn muscles, so closing the abdominal wall? It was tempting. Oh, so tempting. But it would have been done without knowing whether any internal damage had been inflicted by the antelope's horn. Possibly it hadn't. In which case, with appropriate antibiotic cover, Ollie should pull through OK. But if there had been damage – say a rupture of part of the intestine – this was going to lead to peritonitis and Ollie would die a slow, lingering death.

I let out a deep sigh. Just what should I do? I started to panic, realising I was dithering. Come on, Paul. Make up your mind. What if I opened up Ollie's wound and rummaged round inside, checking his abdominal organs as best I could, and then found nothing wrong? He'd have been put through all that extra stress for no reason, especially as the extra time required to do it might necessitate topping up his anaesthetic – a risk in itself. Whatever I did, there were risks involved. Perhaps I should look inside. Oh, how I wished for Crystal to be here, giving me the wisdom of her advice.

Her voice – or rather the same sweet-sounding tones of her daughter – came to my rescue. Jodie tactfully said, 'I'm sure Mum would think the same as you and check inside.'

Right. That was it. Without further ado, I picked up a scalpel from the instruments that Jodie had tipped onto an outspread drape, and widened the wound until I could slide a hand in. I felt the warmth and feel of Ollie's internal organs: the smoothness of his spleen; the rounded outer lobes of his liver; the slippery lengths of his intestines, grey loops of which were coiling out from the wound and which I had to ease back in gently for fear that the whole gut might start tumbling out. As my hand swam through the peritoneal fluid the organs were immersed in, my movements made some of it slop over the edges of the wound and run down Ollie's pimply skin. Usually this fluid is clear, possibly slightly tinted yellow, but, with mounting concern, I noticed that Ollie's was streaked with thin ribbons of green.

'Uh, uh,' I said, grimly. 'Don't like the look of this.'

'What is it, Paul?' asked Jodie, picking up on my anxiety.

'This green staining. It means there's a leak from the gut. The gazelle must have punctured it.' There was a sharp intake of breath from Kevin and a simultaneous whistle through his teeth. 'We've got a battle on our hands,' I added, my voice full of foreboding.

The task in front of me seemed insurmountable. There were metres and metres of intestine within Ollie's abdominal cavity and, somewhere along that length, there was a tear in the gut wall. It only needed to be small – barely the size of a pin head – but that would be enough to cause faecal matter to seep out and contaminate the whole of the abdomen. I had to find and repair it.

'Well, here goes,' I muttered.

I cautiously hauled on one section of small intestine, pulling on it, hand over hand, as if I was reeling out a coil of hosepipe. It lay on the drape like the inner tube of a tyre. From it fanned a translucent, gleaming sheet of mesentery containing threads of pulsating dark red blood vessels. That section of gut seemed undamaged. I eased it back. The next loop of intestine I pulled out was stained green, growing greener the more of it I exposed; and as the final segment of it dropped out onto the drape, the damage was clear to see.

'Christ,' I swore, staring down at the mess in my hands. The tip of the gazelle's horn had sliced through the gut wall so that it was almost completely severed in two, only being held in place by its attachments to the surrounding mesenteric folds. Out of the two ends bubbled green faecal froth. Already tense from anaesthetising and opening up Ollie, the sight of the ripped gut sent my heart pounding even more, my hands shaking more, my breathing more rapid. The odds seemed stacked against saving the bird. And so it proved.

'Paul.' It was Kevin, speaking softly. 'Paul,' he repeated. 'I think Ollie's stopped breathing.'

I scrabbled across the straw on my knees to where Kevin was stooped over Ollie's head, cradling it in his hands. Ollie's pupils were dilated, the eyes wide open. I touched the corner of one. No blink reflex. His long neck was completely flaccid, draped down over Kevin's knees. I ran my hand quickly down to the bird's chest, hoping against hope that I could pick up a heartbeat. There wasn't one. His skin was cold. His chest devoid of movement. With a sound like a bottle of washing-up liquid being squeezed, Ollie's head dropped down and his beak slowly gaped open in the final throes of death.

'Damn,' I seethed, turning back to push the now blue loops of damaged bowel back in and roughly stitch the abdomen up, fighting back the tears threatening to well up, not daring to say any more for fear of choking on my words.

Both Kevin and Jodie were understanding, Kevin saying kindly that I'd done my best, a sentiment echoed by Jodie, who added that Ollie would have been unlikely to have survived such trauma. But I still felt that I could have done better. Maybe I'd overdosed the bird with anaesthetic? After all, I had been pretty gung-ho about the actual dose required. Perhaps I should have been quicker in tracking down the damaged gut? Maybe then the bird would have been less likely to have gone into shock. OK, if Ollie had survived the operation, there would still have been the peritonitis to deal with. That would have been a challenge. But at least the challenge would have been there. Now all I had was a dead bird lying in the straw in front of me. No challenge. I rose to my feet, disconsolate.

'Hey, Paul ...' It was Jodie, speaking gently. 'Stop it.' She had grasped my right wrist and was shaking it, her head slightly tilted, her eyes looking intently into mine. 'These things happen. Now you get washed and I'll clear this lot up.' She let go of my wrist and I did as I was told. Once I'd dried my hands on the towel Kevin had provided, he came over and took one hand in both of his.

'Thanks for trying, mate,' he said, blinking away the moisture behind his pebble glasses, while sniffing and whistling through his teeth. He then turned brusquely away to push a couple of straw bales round and over Ollie's corpse to hide it temporarily from public view.

On the way back to Prospect House, I drove in silence,

my thoughts going over the events of the past hour, wondering yet again if I could have managed the situation better. It was Jodie who broke the silence first, by reminding me again that I couldn't have done any more than I did.

'Really, Paul, you shouldn't berate yourself.'

'I know, I know,' I replied as we turned into the drive of the hospital. 'But I just can't help wondering ...' I braked and switched the engine off, turned to look at her and added, 'You know, despite the outcome, I really appreciated you coming along. Thanks.'

Jodie smiled, her Cupid's-bow lips parting, her cheeks dimpling. 'Paul,' she said firmly, 'you don't have to thank me, honest. Any time you need help just give me a ring. If I'm around ... well ...' She shrugged.

On impulse, I blurted out, 'Are you around tonight?'

Jodie's eyebrows rose, her eyes sparkled, full of mischief, and she purred, 'Would this be business or pleasure?'

I felt myself go red. 'Uhmm ... pleasure actually. You mentioned having a drink some time.'

'Yes. I did indeed. And yes ... that would be great.'

'Let's say, six o'clock, after I've finished evening surgery. Or is that too early for you?'

'No, six would be fine. In fact, why don't we have a bite to eat then as well? Unless you've got to get back.'

What was there to get back for? Lucy had left and I'd be heading back for a ready-meal for one. 'Sounds a good idea to me,' I replied, without a moment's hesitation, and arranged to meet Jodie in reception at the agreed time.

When I finished evening surgery, I skipped into reception feeling almost light-hearted despite the events of the day. Beryl was still behind the counter, tidying up, switching the computer off, stacking appointment cards. That surprised me. She'd usually gone by now. Then I realised why she was still there.

I was pierced by one of Beryl's odd-ball looks, akin to that of a ferret about to scare the wits out of an already witless rabbit. 'Jodie's waiting for you down in the office,' she said, in a manner which clearly meant 'What's going on here then?'

'Oh, is she?' I replied, trying to sound surprised, as if Jodie had been passing by on a whim.

Beryl wasn't fooled. 'Be careful, Paul. Be careful,' she warned. 'You could be playing with fire.' She hitched up the sleeves of the black cardigan, draped, as usual, over her hunched shoulders, and pulled the collar round her scrawny neck; and when I smiled at her, she gave a toss of her raven-winged hair and tutted. 'It's not a laughing matter.' She ferreted under the counter and dragged up her voluminous, black leather handbag, which she put on the counter in front of her; and then, placing both hands on it, she tapped her fingers against it like fluttering moths and said, 'I wouldn't want to see you get hurt.'

She clicked the bag open and withdrew a stick of crimson lipstick and a small mirror and proceeded to apply a further layer of red to her already layered lips, turning from the mirror once she'd finished, to look at me askew and add, 'Don't say I didn't warn you.' She smacked her lips together, dropped the items back in her bag and clicked it closed decisively. 'OK?'

I wasn't sure if she was seeking approval of her scarlet lips or referring to my association with what she apparently saw as a scarlet woman. So I simply nodded and half smiled, gestures I felt covered both possibilities.

Jodie, at that moment, bounded up from the office and greeted me with a cheery, 'Hi. How was surgery?'

Before I had a chance to reply, Beryl interjected. 'Busy as usual. Paul's quite in demand these days.' I saw her shoot Jodie a reproving look which she deflected with a 'Ready for a drink then, no doubt?' aimed at me. I bit the bullet and fired back with a 'Sounds good, Jodie,' and we both watched Beryl ricochet out of reception as a result. Bull's-eye.

We decided that a drink and a bite to eat round at the Woolpack would be the easiest option. Besides which, Jodie had promised to call in and say hello once she was back in the UK. Seems she knew Brenda and Bernie Adams, the proprietors. And yes, their Labrador, Peggy, she was equally familiar with. A bit on the fat side, she remembered. Still is, I said, despite the fact we attempted a slimming programme. Didn't work for the dog, but did the trick for Brenda. Lost quite a few kilos.

Jodie laughed at the idea that Brenda had followed Peggy's diet. Although that hadn't actually happened. It was the motivation that had done the trick. All jovially done – in keeping with the 'mein host' geniality of the Adams, which was reflected in Bernie's response to seeing Jodie walk into the bar, us having taken the footpath to the side of Prospect House down through the dimly-lit tunnel of rhododendrons – those vestiges of the house's Victorian gardens – and along the eastern edge of the Green to the pub.

'My, my … just look who it is,' bellowed Bernie, squeezing his way out from behind the bar to give Jodie a bear-hug embrace. 'So how's my girl then?' he added, stepping back, his hands still on her shoulders, his face beaming. Jodie assured him she'd never felt better. It was a sentiment I heartily agreed with. I thought she looked radiant with those sparkling, cornflower-blue eyes, with the merest touch of laughter lines to their corners, and the lightly tanned complexion of her cheeks, dimpling as she smiled. The sentiment was shared by Brenda, who had responded to Bernie's bellowing that 'their girl' was there by bustling out from the back, depositing the tray of glasses she'd been carrying, and hurrying round to greet Jodie in an equally effusive manner as her husband. It seemed hugs and kisses were the order of the day – and I hoped it could soon be my turn.

First, though, it was drinks on the house. Just the one glass of white for me, I insisted, although later I was persuaded that a second glass wouldn't do any harm. It didn't – it just loosened my tongue in more ways than one. Jodie also had two, the second with the shepherd's pie chosen from the blackboard menu – the pie homemade by their chef, said Brenda – while I was told the sea bass I'd gone for was freshly caught off Westcott pier.

Although the pub was quiet – only two other couples were eating in the restaurant area – such was the level of conversation, the animation, the ease with which Jodie and I communicated with each other, we could have been in the middle of an earthquake and not noticed (although I *was* conscious of a major tremor of seismic proportions developing deep within me). Only once, when Jodie asked how I found working at Prospect House, did I remind myself I was talking to the bosses' daughter here, and carefully worded my response, couching it in positive terms to the effect that it was giving me a good grounding in how a small animal hospital should be run. Sounded good. Jodie thought so, too, to judge from the smile she flashed me (more tremors).

I was asked what clients I'd seen. There was laughter at the mention of Miss McEwan and her mynah's 'dirty dick' (provoking a seismic surge on my Richter scale); encouraged, I told her about the church fête at which I'd been coerced into judging the pets. What a marvellous story, she said when I'd finished, and hoped I was keeping a note of all the anecdotes as they'd make the basis for a great novel. You know, a modern-day James Herriot sort of thing. I wish ...

Then it was my turn to learn more about her. How, having had an interest in animals, she had gone through the usual parade of pets as a child, including the hamster, the goldfish, the rabbit and a frisky young cat, too frisky for its own good and, as a result, it ended up under the wheels of some visiting friends' car. Despite tagging along to case visits made by her parents and helping out in the hospital on Saturday mornings, she found herself drawn more to the arts; so she did English, Spanish and Art at A-level, before going on to study English Literature at Exeter University.

After a further course to get the necessary teaching qualifications, she decided – a rather spur-of-the-moment decision – to undertake some VSO work and chose a project over in Costa Rica to put her newly-acquired teaching skills to the test. And now she was back, not quite sure where to go from here. Probably supply teaching until she decided.

With the second glass of wine – a large glass, I have to admit, which perhaps eased me more fluidly into what happened next – came the second phase of my tongue loosening, which constituted an act of a far more tactile nature than the mere exchange of words. It occurred on the walk back from the Woolpack in the middle of that tunnel of rhododendrons.

I'm not quite sure what got into me. Actually, that's not

true … I did know. Lust. Those groin-based tremors finally got the better of me. We were halfway along the path where the rhododendrons cast their deepest shadows – and where the Council had failed to ensure there was sufficient public lighting to illuminate, and so prevent, the goings-on of whoever stopped at that spot to partake in acts that would be certain to get other tongues wagging, if not those of the participants.

All had been above board when we left the Woolpack amidst cries of 'Come back and see us soon …' and I had a spring in my step, inasmuch as the word 'spring' evokes the thrust of nature and the arousal of sap in trunks – oh, yes, indeed. Our animated conversation on the pub's banquette had been punctuated by moments of flirtation; 'accidental' touching of each other's shoe, a hand brushed against a thigh, eye contact that said 'I fancy the pants off you …' which was reciprocated by the other, in a 'Yes please, how soon?' sort of way.

We walked side by side along the pavement, very virtuously, our arms swinging close to each other, occasionally touching. We turned from the Green at the lamp post on the corner, where the path up through the rhododendrons started. Still virtuous … still well mannered. Polite. In that vein, we managed to progress up the first third of the path, our arms touching more and more as we got deeper into the shade, the light getting weaker, my pulse getting stronger, our pace getting slower, until we began to see the light at the end of the tunnel ahead of us start to get stronger, where the floodlit porch of Prospect House glowed. Which meant the more we went on walking, the brighter the path would become.

It seemed we instinctively knew we had reached the exact spot equidistant from the two ends. The exact middle of the tunnel. The exact place where it was darkest. The exact place to indulge ourselves. We ground to a halt, turned and, without a word, ground into each other as if there were no tomorrow, as if we were 16-year-olds who didn't know better. But we were adults who chose not to know better, who knew exactly where we were, even if it was in the middle of a public footpath up from the Green. And so there we were, at it, in that tunnel of rhododendrons, and we continued at it by virtue of a quick hop over the railings and a plunge deep into the bushes. 'God I needed that …' was Jodie's panted response when we'd finished and I'd pulled my chinos back up.

'We must do this again sometime …' she murmured huskily as she climbed into her mum's car once we were back outside Prospect House, and had given me a parting peck on the cheek. I watched her rev and drive out before walking across to my own car. As I did so, I glanced up at the flat and saw a figure silhouetted in a window, looking down. Lucy. She must have seen me staring up as she quickly withdrew and the curtains were whipped across.

Driving over the Downs, Beryl's warning words reverberated faintly in my mind. 'Be careful, Paul. Be careful.'

I smiled to myself, shook my head and put my foot down. I knew exactly where I was going. At least, I thought I did. Oh, just how foolish could I possibly be?

Very.

14

HAVING THE QUILL TO LIVE

Everyone at Prospect House was sympathetic about my failing to save the ostrich; all, that is, except Lucy, who now unsurprisingly kept herself very much to herself and her contact with me was on a working basis only – the animals at Willow Wren had been sorted in her customarily efficient way, with Queenie, Bugsie and his two guinea-pig companions returning to Prospect House while Gertie remained at the cottage with the small flock of budgerigars.

'These things happen,' Beryl had remarked, reiterating the words spoken by Jodie, and, for a minute, I thought she meant my break-up with Lucy. But she was referring to Ollie.

Her comment reminded me of the other things that had happened that day – things that had happened deep in the rhododendrons. I felt my ears burn with embarrassment – and excitement – at the memory. Beryl was quick to spot them and, misinterpreting the cause of their reddening, uttered further sympathetic noises in an attempt to reassure me I'd done my best. If only she'd known I'd done exactly that in the bushes the previous evening.

Eric, in his ever bouncy, energetic style, whirled his arms around while he spouted off about the trials and tribulations of being a vet, the ups and downs of which he was simulating pretty well as he flapped up and down himself, declaring, 'You can winkle it out only to find it dies on you.'

'Sorry?' I said, startled. I hadn't really been paying much attention, rhododendrons still being uppermost in my mind, and wondered what he was referring to since I'd had no such problems in that department.

He gave me a funny look. 'Budgerigars, Paul,' he explained. 'They can curl up their toes even before you've got them out of their cages. Shock.'

I still didn't see how that related to the death of Ollie. But at least Eric had to be given credit for trying to be supportive. Bless him.

Crystal was more succinct. Naturally. 'From what Jodie tells me' – I shuddered for a moment, wondering what her daughter *had* told her – 'Ollie had a perforated gut, so the odds were stacked against him anyway. Just put it down to experience ...' – mmm, as experiences go, it was a good one – '... and get on with what you do best.' Mmm ... I'll certainly try ... ... and the sooner the better! 'Paul?'

'Sorry,' I said, pulling myself together with a shake of my head.

'No regrets for what happened then?'

'None,' I replied, looking her straight in the eye. 'None whatsoever.' Mmm ... it had, in fact, been a pleasure.

Even though Jodie had lifted my flagging spirits, despite all the later reassurances the episode with the ostrich left me feeling downhearted, very out of sorts; it wasn't helped by returning to Willow Wren each day to face coq au vin and fisherman's pie and chicken tikka masala ready-meals for one. The evening of the following Thursday saw me scrape out the last vestiges of a leek and potato bake from the bottom of its plastic tray, a little ashamed with myself for not having made the effort to turn the meal out onto a plate. My standards were beginning to slip. I had to be careful, otherwise, before I knew it, I'd be wearing my underpants for more than one day at a time without changing them. As it was, I'd already started sniffing at my socks, wondering whether I could get another day's wear out of them. But at least I hadn't stooped to applying the same test to the crotch of my Calvin Kleins. Well, not yet anyway.

I'd taken a mug of decaffeinated coffee out into the garden, wandering down the lawn, my mind only half taking in the border to one side with its banks of purple salvias, the blues of the delphiniums, the mounds of pink cranesbill, all now gradually blurring and darkening in the dusk of the evening, when the ring of the phone jolted me from my daydream. I wasn't on call, so the phone's clamour didn't set me off sweating, my pulse racing, quite so much as when on duty. I strode in and picked up the receiver and said, 'Hello?'

'Oh, hello, dear … it's only me.' It was my mother. Her customary patter followed. 'I'm not disturbing you, am I?'

'No.'

'Have you had your supper yet?'

'Yes, thanks.'

'You're keeping all right?'

I hesitated there. Didn't seem much point in burdening my mother with my woes. 'Fine,' I eventually said.

'You don't sound fine.' My mother was canny at

picking up on things, tuned into feelings. She could have given Madam Mountjoy a run for her money.

'No really, I'm OK. Just a bit tired, that's all.'

There was a sympathetic murmur down the line. 'You need to get yourself a good night's sleep.'

'Yes, Mum.'

There followed something that would ensure I didn't get that good night's kip. 'Sorry, dear, but I've got a bit of bad news, I'm afraid.'

'Oh?'

'It's Polly. She's not at all well. In fact ...' There was a pause, a break in my mother's voice. A sniff. 'I'm sorry, love. But she's dying.'

The receiver began trembling in my hand. 'Why? What's happened?'

Mum went on to explain. Our beloved African Grey parrot, a member of our family for over 20 years, had developed a growth on her neck. Dad had called in a local vet, a friend of his from Bournemouth's Conservative Club, as they hadn't wanted to bother me, knowing how busy I was. This vet had just peered through the bars of Polly's cage and declared she had cancer and that the growth was inoperable. That had been three days back, since when Polly had stopped eating and drinking and hadn't uttered a word.

'She is very sick,' croaked Mum, her voice breaking again. 'We don't think she'll last much longer and so we thought we'd better warn you. We know how much you love her.' There was another tearful pause. 'We all do, of course.'

I, too, felt weepy on hearing the news, my words catching in my throat as I tried to console Mum, while rapidly thinking what I could do to help. I decided that I'd have to get down to Bournemouth and see Polly for myself, if only to convince myself that nothing could be done to save her. I told Mum this. 'I can't promise, Mum,' I said, 'as I'm supposed to be on duty this weekend. But I'll see if I can swap round.'

I phoned through to Crystal's house and found myself speaking to Jodie – which provoked another raft of emotions – so, all in all, I felt pretty mixed up and must have sounded so as I gabbled on about Polly and could I have a word with Eric. Jodie said how sorry she was to hear about the parrot and if there was anything she could do to help then let her know, before Eric came on the phone and I explained the situation to him, asking if there was any possibility of him standing in for me the coming weekend and I'd do his rota the following one.

'That's no problem whatsoever, Paul,' he said, and he hoped I'd be able to do something to save Polly; he then added that Jodie would like another word.

She came on to say, 'Paul, if it means you might be operating on Polly, how about me coming down with you to lend a hand? I'd be happy to do so.'

I really didn't stop to think about the consequences, the sleeping arrangements, meeting my parents. I just said, 'Thanks, that would be a real help.' We agreed to meet up at Prospect House first thing Saturday morning and drive down in my car from there. I could hear the relief in my mother's voice when I phoned back to tell her I was coming down, but I warned her not to raise her hopes too much.

Friday was warm and sunny, a beautiful, early June day, but it did little to lift my spirits. Beryl, aware of my glum mood, suggested we got some Bert's baguettes for lunch and ate them on the Green. 'Get a bit of sun to the eyeballs …' she said or, in her case, eyeball. So at 12.30pm we left

265

the practice and trotted off down the rhododendron tunnel, sun streaming through the leaves, dappling the footpath ... that wonderful footpath! The memory was still fresh in my mind.

Beryl, her shoulders in their usual hunched-up position, swung her head from side to side, her handbag swinging in unison, as we passed through, staring suspiciously at a man who had been sauntering up the other way and had stopped roughly at the spot where Jodie and I had gone for each other. It being summer and a warm day, the man was dressed accordingly in light, cotton shirt and shorts, but I suspected Beryl thought he was a likely flasher and that, in more inclement weather, requiring the wearing of a mac, he would jerk open that garment to justify her suspicions.

'It's not safe along here after dark,' she whispered to me as we hurried on, past the loitering man. 'All sorts of things go on.'

Indeed they do, Beryl, indeed they do, I thought, my mood momentarily lifting.

'So,' said Beryl as we attacked our Bert's baguettes, having found a park bench to sit on, 'tell me a bit more about Polly.'

There was no encouragement needed for me to launch into how Polly and I first met. My father had been in Nigeria on a two-year contract with an oil company. One morning my parents were trailing through the local market, with me as an eight-year-old trailing behind them, when a trader in billowing, white robes sprang out of the crowd and danced round me, dangling a parrot cage from his hand. In the cage was a bundle of grey that growled and flapped as it was rocked to and fro.

'Young masa like dis bird?' queried the trader, his face splitting into a broad, toothy grin, the teeth stained red

266

with betal juice. My father grabbed me by the arm and attempted to propel me through the crowded market as I dragged my heels in the dust.

'Please, Dad, please,' I implored.

'Oh, go on, Jack, let him have the bird,' urged my mother.

'No,' said my father firmly.

'Masa ... *masa* ...' cried the trader, fearing the loss of a sale. 'To you, masa, special price ... 500 naira.'

Father continued to frogmarch me away. The trader darted after him. 'Dis bird, picin like much.' The cage was swung in front of me again and a pair of bewildered, frightened grey eyes stared out through the bars.

'Please, Dad,' I whined.

'Dis dum fine bird,' coaxed the wily old trader.

'300,' said father, stopping.

The trader laughed and shook his head.

Father took a step forward.

'Na ... na ...' cried the trader and stretched out a dusty palm. The cage exchanged hands. The African Grey parrot was ours.

'So how long ago was that?' asked Beryl, who had by now finished her baguette, and was surreptitiously glancing at her watch as she spoke.

'Oh, must be the best part of 20 years,' I replied, popping the last of mine into my mouth.

'Long time ago,' murmured Beryl, distractedly, fiddling with her watch, and glancing round her.

It was indeed. And it was quite a while before Polly and I became friends. For several months, Polly remained a frightened, nervous youngster. But her pale-grey eyes soon matured to a golden yellow. Her broken quills moulted out one by one and strong new flights burst through her wings.

267

Tiny, soft-grey feathers edged with white appeared over the sleek contours of her body and hid the scars of her capture round her neck; and her tail, a moth-eaten collection of six red feathers, erupted in a blaze of vermillion.

'Sounds as if she turned out to be a smart-looking parrot,' said Beryl, a little distractedly, looking down the path over my shoulder, adding in an excited gush, 'Why, look, there's Mr Entwhistle and Bess.'

I swivelled round on the bench to see Ernie hurrying towards us, his young Border collie trotting obediently by his side. As he drew level with us, he stopped and gave a little bow. 'Sorry I'm a little late,' he said, gazing fondly at Beryl before courteously turning to say, 'Good afternoon, Mr Mitchell,' with another polite nod of his head.

Ah, I thought. So much for Beryl's suggestion of having a tête-à-tête with me on the Green. There'd been an ulterior motive. I saw her blush as she got to her feet and exclaim that it was not a problem as Paul here had been entertaining her with reminiscences of his parrot.

'You will excuse us then,' she added, linking arms with Mr Entwhistle, who smiled at me, his blue eyes twinkling as he escorted her across the Green to pause before they crossed the road and headed into the rhododendron tunnel. That tunnel of love. Hmm. What next, I wondered? What next?

I settled back on the bench, my mood mellowed by the warmth of the sun on my face. There was still 20 minutes before I had to get back. Time enough for further memories to surface. And they did.

It was a long time before Polly could be coaxed out of her cage. 'Come on Polly,' I'd whisper, placing a piece of ripe banana just outside the open door. But she wasn't tempted. Father tried a more bravado approach and manoeuvred his hand into the cage in the rather optimistic hope that Polly might genteelly hop onto his finger. She did hop on, but only as a means to lash out and give him a savage bite. I didn't need convincing of the power in Polly's beak as I'd seen her splinter a block of teak as if it were a matchbox. Yet those black bone-crushers could perform acts of extreme delicacy – such as when she tackled a peanut still in its shell. She'd hold it horizontally and crack it open to display the row of nuts inside. She would then select one, carefully lifting it out, and balance it between the points of her beak and proceed to peel off the skin while rolling it around with her tongue. Fascinating to watch.

I continued to live in fear of Polly's beak until the day I smashed my aquarium. I was staggering through the lounge, the aquarium clutched between my arms, with the intention of changing the water in the kitchen. But as I swung round the lounge door, I caught the front panel of the aquarium on the door's handle. The glass cracked and exploded outwards. The contents – my snails, beetles and fish, lovingly collected from the local reservoir – cascaded onto the floor.

Howling with all the force an eight-year-old can muster, I ran out onto the veranda and stood sobbing in front of Polly's cage. She side-stepped across her perch and tucked her head down against the bars as if wanting me to scratch her head. Without thinking, too occupied with the loss of my underwater world, I stuck my fingers between the bars. Her head whipped up. Her beak caught my finger. But instead of biting it, she gave it a gentle kiss, her tongue running lightly up and down its tip. Then, she too burst out crying. From that moment on we were firm friends.

I felt my eyes prick with tears as I recalled the memory. Or maybe it was just the brightness of the June sun making my eyes water. Whatever, I jolted awake – had I really been dozing like one of Westcott's retirees? – saw that afternoon surgery was due to start soon and so shunted the memories to the back of my mind.

But they returned that evening, encouraged by my neighbour, Eleanor Venables, who had been privy to the terminal throes of my relationship with Lucy, on account of the thinness of the dividing walls, allowing her to hear every word of our many altercations. As a consequence, feeling sorry for my now solitary existence, she had invited me round for supper. I took some wine, which I, in part, blamed for the resurfacing of those memories. But then Eleanor did have a certain empathy with birds, as evidenced by the dealings the two of us had had with that cockatiel earlier in the year; and the fact that her son was a parrot fanatic, with four of his own.

'So tell me, Paul,' she asked, spooning out a second portion of sticky toffee pudding for me, 'was your Polly a good talker?'

I winced at the use of the past tense. Was? It brought me up sharp. Tomorrow I'd find out whether the use of that tense *was* appropriate. But up till now, Polly had been a wonderful mimic and also displayed intelligence in the choice of words she used. The range of her repertoire was astonishing. Having mastered 'Good morning', it was subsequently embellished with army slang so that at dawn we were woken, bleary-eyed, with a 'Wakey, wakey ... rise and shine, you shower ...' The Colonel's wife was amused when, on an occasion she was invited for tea, she swirled across to Polly's cage to be greeted with a 'Hello' in my mother's voice. 'Oh, what a charming bird,' remarked the Colonel's wife. Polly studied her intently, head cocked to one side, and then, in a very loud voice, still that of my mother, said, 'You've got droopy drawers.' The Colonel's wife's face went bright red. As did my mother's. There were no further invites for tea.

When I reached the age of 11, I had to return to the UK for schooling, although the holidays meant a welcome return to Nigeria and a reunion with my parrot. 'Watch'er, mate,' she'd say as if I'd only been gone a day instead of three months. Partings, though, were a wrench. Her cheery 'Bye-byes' would echo in my ears long after I'd boarded the plane back to London.

Then, all of a sudden, it seemed my father's contract was over and my parents were coming home for good. And so was Polly. They flew home; Polly went by sea as part of her quarantine and, in doing so, she picked up a few choice swear words and a 'Hello, sailor' in a Liverpool accent.

She was installed in the kitchen of our new home in Bournemouth and absorbed the sounds therein, only to throw them back at us magnified and distorted. Cutlery crashed into the drawer like scaffolding collapsing; filling the kettle was like Niagara Falls; melodies were snatched from the radio appallingly out of key. Her back-door bell imitation even had the effect of galvanising the Maltese we'd acquired to go rushing into the kitchen, barking at invisible visitors; this evoked a 'Go in your box, Yambo' from Polly, and when the little dog meekly obeyed, she followed it up with a 'Sit, Yambo' ... which he promptly did. He never learnt.

In the drive down to Bournemouth that Saturday morning, Jodie also seemed keen to hear about Polly, and I had no hesitation in complying; in particular, a tale which demonstrated Polly's intelligence.

As a titbit, Polly loved having a piece of buttered toast each morning and would say – very sweetly and in my tone of voice – 'Chop', that being the African word for 'food'. In time, she observed the sequences involved in producing the toast and, eventually, it reached the stage when, as soon as you opened the bread bin, she'd start to waddle up and down her perch saying 'Chop' in expectation of the titbit to come.

One morning, I decided to tease her. Having made and buttered my toast, I sat down with my back to Polly's cage and started to eat it, ignoring her repeated calls of 'Chop' made in my voice. Suddenly, the demands for her titbit stopped while I continued crunching and chewing. The demands then restarted, only this time they were very emphatic, stern and made in my father's tone of voice: 'Chop! Chop! Chop!' Clearly Polly was getting impatient. Yet I continued to ignore her. There was another pause, then Polly shouted out, again in my father's voice, a very angry, 'What's the ruddy matter with you?'

Jodie laughed out loud. 'Paul, that's amazing. I can see why she's so precious to you all,' adding in a gentler voice, 'and I realise how worried you must be.' She reached across the car and stroked my knee, giving it a gentle squeeze. Ooooh … eyes on the road, Paul!

My concerns for Polly overshadowed any embarrassment I might have felt about turning up at my parents' place with a girlfriend in tow. Likewise, it was the same for Mum and Dad when they were introduced to Jodie.

'Pleased to meet you,' said Mum, shaking hands as the two of us crowded into the narrow hallway, her welcoming smile belying the tiredness in her blue eyes, the shadows beneath them. But, as always, she was immaculately turned out: hair permed, a soft blue; smart, dark-blue 'slacks' – as she always called trousers; and over them, not tucked in, a cream blouse, frilled at cuffs and neck, with dainty blue-and-red flowers embroidered round its lower edge.

As we proceeded down the hall, Dad shuffled out of the lounge, in his usual baggy, brown cords and fawn cardigan. He murmured, 'Hello, Paul ... thanks for coming,' before acknowledging Jodie with a wan smile and weak handshake. He looked older than when I had seen him last – which must only have been a couple of months back. Yet his face had hollowed, his cheeks drawn in, the thin straggle of grey across the top of his head making him appear all the more gaunt. He ushered us into the kitchen, repeating what Mum had told me about Polly over the phone.

The reason for their concern was all too obvious. Polly was huddled low down over one end of her perch, next to her feed and water hoppers, both of which were full and looked untouched. Her wings were dropped and her feathers ruffled, standing out like a misshapen feather duster. Her head was partially tucked under her right wing, her eyes closed. Angled round in that manner, her neck was curved, stretched, exposing the left side in which, despite the feathering, a raised, pink lump could be seen poking through – the cancer. I wasn't going to say it must have been there for some time – that would only have added to my parents' anxiety – but no doubt it had been, it was just that the feathers would have obscured it in the early stages of its growth. But now it was big enough to be seen, and big enough to press on her windpipe and oesophagus and cause difficulties in breathing and swallowing.

I moved quietly up to her cage. 'Hello, Polly,' I whispered, hoping for a response. Polly did manage to pull her head from under her wing, blink and look at me; but then almost immediately tucked her beak back under again. It was heart-wrenching to see how poorly she looked and I had to fight hard against the bubble of anger I felt welling up that Mum and Dad hadn't called me in earlier. Although, in fairness to them, they had sought advice, but maybe even that had been too late in the day. Stop it, Paul, I reprimanded myself. No time for recriminations now; just let's see what can be done to save Polly.

I wasn't sure anything could be done. But no way could I let things be and see 20 years of friendship, with its provision of such marvellous entertainment, just slip away in an agonising and slow death.

'We'll set things up on the kitchen table here in case I operate once we've caught her up,' I said, a decision at last made. I didn't want to put Polly through the trauma of being caught up more than once – assuming that she had sufficient strength left in her to survive being handled in the first place. Jodie fetched my black bag and sterile op packs from my car while Mum cleared the kitchen table – blue Formica – the same table at which I'd teased Polly with the piece of toast many years back. With that memory, my eyes started to itch, my throat felt dry, as I fearfully contemplated what lay ahead and the most likely outcome – an echo of Ollie.

Dad led Mum quietly out of the kitchen, Mum with her arms folded, her hands at her elbows, clutching and unclutching them, while Jodie and I set to work preparing for a possible operation, laying drapes over the table, sliding the instruments and swabs onto them and drawing up the estimated dose of ketamine required to anaesthetise Polly. I worried that I'd miscalculate as I felt I may have done with Ollie. But it was a risk I'd have to take. I was aware my self-confidence was draining away. It was the firm grip of Jodie's hand on my arm, the look she gave me, and the words 'If anyone can save her, you can ...' that helped me to rally.

It was an easy task to extract Polly from the confines of the cage, wrapped in the towel Mum provided. She didn't struggle, not once. Lifting her up, I found she was as light as a feather, almost emaciated. She did squawk, though. A series of piercing, frightened shrieks which tore through me as I pulled one of her legs clear of the towel and injected the anaesthetic into her thigh.

'I'm sorry, Polly,' I wept, 'but it's got to be done.'

Her shrieks died away as, within minutes, she slipped into unconsciousness. I laid her out, on her back, on the table and Jodie taped down her outstretched wings as instructed. I then set to work plucking the feathers from Polly's neck to expose the tumour. I disinfected the area and covered it with a green drape that had a hole in its centre to allow me to tackle the growth's removal. It was large, a misshapen raspberry of tissue pressing on her windpipe; and it looked angry and swollen, tiny blood vessels pumping round its perimeter as I dissected it away from the incision I'd made in her skin. But it shelled out easier than I'd expected, with no damage to the underlying bed of nerves and blood vessels glistening beneath. Carefully, I sewed her neck up and she was placed on a wodge of cotton wool in the bottom of her cage to recover. Anxiously, we sat round, Mum and Dad joining us, cups of tea made and sipped while we waited.

As the anaesthetic wore off, Polly rolled onto her side, legs kicking out, until they made contact with the side of the cage, whereupon she clung to the bars, pulling herself over so as to be able to grip one of them with her beak. Then slowly ... oh, so slowly that it was painful to watch, she hauled herself up the bars, twice dropping back down until, on the third attempt, she reached the perch and levered herself onto it, where she swayed backwards and forwards but managed to stay on.

That evening she threw a fit. With a sickening rattle in her throat, she toppled off her perch and collapsed in a corner of her cage. Her shrieks of distress brought tears to my eyes but I didn't dare handle her for fear of killing her with the extra stress involved. So with a heavy heart, I switched off the light and prayed she'd survive the night.

My own survival that night was another matter. In my concern for Polly's welfare, I hadn't made it clear to Jodie as to whether we'd be staying at my parents' overnight. I'd thrown a few things together and I noticed she'd brought an overnight bag, so I guessed she was prepared for any eventuality – ready to bunk down wherever. In my bed, maybe?

However, there was a guest room. Once Mum realised we were going to stay and see how Polly was the next day, she tactfully said the bed in there was made up. Somehow, it didn't seem right to share a bed under my parents' roof, and even more inappropriate with Polly downstairs, fighting for her life. But I didn't object when, slipping into sleep, I heard my door creak open, the rustle of my bedclothes, and felt the warmth of Jodie's body as she curled herself round my buttocks and slid her hand over my thigh and murmured, 'Hello, big boy.'

I finally rose from an empty bed just after seven, hearing the agitated whispers of my parents down in the kitchen. I threw my clothes on, pounded down the stairs, wondering just what I was going to be confronted by. A dead parrot?

I pushed open the door and walked in. Mum and Dad

turned to me. 'She's still with us,' said Mum, the relief evident in her voice.

I looked over at Polly's cage and saw she was on her perch, a little shaky, but gripping it with grim determination. I walked over. As I drew near, she tottered across, and, putting her head down, pressed it against the bars for a scratch, and said in my voice, albeit a very croaky voice, 'Watch'er, mate.' I sensed then that she would pull through. I was ecstatic.

'I was so worried,' said Mum, filling the kettle. 'I could hardly sleep a wink all night. Heard you tossing and turning … and moaning quite a bit. So I guess you had a bad night as well.'

'But not that bad, eh, son?' said Dad with a wink and a thumbs up behind Mum's back.

'Well, it was a long day for all of us,' said Mum, pulling some teabags out of a caddie. 'So we don't mind if Jodie wants a lie in. But perhaps you'd like to take her up a mug of tea and see what she wants for breakfast.'

I saw the smirk on Dad's face when the tea was made and I took the two mugs Mum was proffering me. I knew what Jodie would like. So did my father. Really, as if I would, Dad. But I did.

Breakfast consisted of a full English; and it seemed a bit weird to be eating at the table where only a few hours earlier I'd been operating on Polly. She even participated in the meal, taking a small portion of toast liberally spread with butter; and she seemed to have no problem in eating it. I guessed, with the tumour removed, the pressure on her throat had been instantly relieved, so making it easier to swallow and breathe. She was certainly more perky by mid-morning, almost as perky as me, quite cocky, in fact. Mum noticed my buoyant mood and remarked on it, saying how pleased I must have felt to have done what I did. Dad caught my eye and just smirked again as he glanced across at Jodie. Honestly. Fathers!

Whatever the reason, be it the successful operation on Polly or the sex with Jodie, who, despite our intense couplings, had managed to maintain a demure innocence throughout breakfast, I had this tremendous sense of elation akin to the feelings I had when I'd graduated the previous summer. That suddenly jolted my memory.

'Hey,' I exclaimed, checking the date on my watch. Mum, Dad and Jodie froze. 'It's the sixth of June. A year to the day when I learnt I'd passed my Finals.'

'Yes, and you took yourself over to the Dorset coast for a celebratory walk if you remember,' said Mum.

'On your own?' queried Jodie.

'On his own,' answered Dad. 'Chapman's Pool, I think.'

'Oh, Hardy country,' exclaimed Jodie. 'One of my favourite parts of the world.'

Dad finished the dregs of his tea and said, 'Well, why don't you get Paul to take you over there today? Unless, that is, you have to get back.' He raised a hand to his eyebrow and made a pretence of scratching it with a finger to cover the wink he gave me.

'Would you?' Jodie turned eagerly to me.

'I'm sure she'll appreciate it,' chipped in Mum.

'I bet she will,' added Dad. 'It's a nice day for it.'

Oh boy ... he was at it again.

So that's how, an hour later, Jodie and I found ourselves clambering out of my car at the foot of the cliffs that stretched up from Chapman's Pool, first to breathe in the cool, salt-laden sea breeze that was blowing across the cove, then to pick our way down onto the boulder-strewn beach and along to the shale under-cliffs in search of fossils.

Undaunted by not finding any, we began the ascent of the steep cliff path, hand in hand, hauling our way up – the same path I'd scaled the previous summer on an equally gorgeous June day, the sun beating down from an azure sky, the waves crashing on the rocks below me, kittiwakes and guillemots winging across the surf and weaving in the eddies of breeze that buffeted the sheer cliffs and fanned up into my face. It had been heaven then. It was heaven now. Only this time, sharing it with Jodie made it all the more special.

In my solitary climb, my spirits had soared at the prospects ahead of me, prospects that materialised into the practice I was now in. A year of learning, a year of coping, a year of gaining confidence in the treatment of animals of all shapes and sizes. Those pets on parade, and their unforgettable owners: Madam Mountjoy; the Stockwell twins; Ernie Entwhistle and Bess; the Coles with their Boxer, Henry.

When Jodie and I reached the summit and lay stretched out on the cliff edge in a cocoon of soft, dry grass, a turf dotted with clumps of pink thrift and banks of gorse, their sweet, coconut scent drifting through the air, I was lulled by the muted drone of bees, the distant, raucous cries of gulls echoing up from the surf far below, and felt the warmth of Jodie's lips come down on mine. My spirits soared as they had done a year ago. I became a kite, swaying and dipping through the shimmering blue above me. High ... higher ... higher still.

Maybe Jodie *was* pulling my strings. But at that precise moment, suspended between heaven and earth, I was flying so high, I wished it would last forever.